rh

Praise for Rachel Cantor and *A Highly Unlikely Scenario*

"It's as if Kurt Vonnegut and Italo Calvino collaborated to write a comic book sci-fi adventure and persuaded Chagall to do the drawings. One of the freshest and mostly lively novels I have encountered for quite a while." —Jim Crace, author of *Harvest* and *The Pesthouse*

"*A Highly Unlikely Scenario* is a joyful book, full of the energy of undiluted invention and the thoughtful imagination of a writer to watch. It's a wild ride and much more—funny, intelligent and entirely pleasing." —A. L. Kennedy, author of *Day*

"Part Italo Calvino, part Ray Bradbury, in this extraordinary novel, Rachel Cantor explores questions of self-knowledge, true love and family, all while saving the world—and winning readers—in the past, present, and future." —Hannah Tinti, author of *The Good Thief*

"I didn't know I needed a mystical Jewish Douglas Adams in my life, but Rachel Cantor is it, and her Guide makes me *shep naches* every time I turn a page. Buy this book, *bubeleh*! It will surprise you in ways large and small, and it will fill you with delight." —Emily Barton, author of *Brookland*

"Cosmic and comic, full of philosophy, mysticism and celestial whimsy. A story of listening, of souls and bodies, that is at once both profoundly wild and wildly profound." —Charles Yu, author of *How to Live Safely in a Science Fictional Universe*

"A sharp, witty, and immensely entertaining debut . . . Cantor's skill in rendering complex and highly believable characters makes for an unexpectedly moving tale." —Emily St. John Mandel, author of *Station Eleven*

"A dystopian satire, a story about storytelling, believing and listening—*A Highly Unlikely Scenario* is ultimately a history of our own strange world."   —*The New York Times Book Review*

"[A] dizzying fabulist debut."   —*The Washington Post*

"Ultimately, more than incantations and codes, it's family Cantor cares about. *A Highly Unlikely Scenario* is about just that: Familial wisdom and love lost and found and shared anew, finally, conquering all."   —*The Daily Beast*

"[Cantor's] imagination is exhilarating—*A Highly Unlikely Scenario* will appeal to fans of sci-fi and people who just like to laugh."
—*Cosmopolitan*'s 10 Books by Women
You Have to Read This Spring

"A treat for those who like zippy sci-fi paced like the stories of Kurt Vonnegut."   —*Time Out New York*

"Rachel Cantor joins the ranks of authors who are able to turn philosophical concepts into whiz-bang plots, and make them funny as well. Throw in some family dysfunction, time travel, a librarian ingénue, and the possible destruction of the world, and you've got an adventure story replete with nerdy delights."   —*Tor*

"The book's plot, which concerns a future where fast food corporations run the world, is deliciously weird enough to work in its own warped way, walking the line between straight fantasy and fiction."
—*Flavorwire*

"A heroic tale unlike any other: a novel that is not about a quest but about learning that the world—our world—is full of extraordinary, mysterious wonders."   —*The Kenyon Review*

"This debut novel is a present to both sci-fi and humor fans alike."
—Barnes & Noble Book Blog, January indie books roundup

"In this roller-coaster debut, fast-food corporations rule the world and a peon customer-service worker has to save it . . . Cantor is in control of her material, and successful dystopian satire makes more sense while you're lost in it." —*Heeb*, Best Books of the Year

"Brooklyn-based writer Rachel Cantor has created a whole new world in her debut novel—a humorous and playful science fiction story." —*Brooklyn Eagle*

"Delightful . . . The sense of excitement in Cantor's prose, which propels this familiar story of a few silly, frightened people braving their way through a maddening, baffling world, is what compels us to keep reading." —*The Rumpus*

"An intrepid debut." —*Kirkus Reviews*

"Cantor suspends disbelief and creates a loony world entirely of her own, which is terrifically funny and effortlessly enjoyable . . . Highly entertaining and adventurous." —*Publishers Weekly*

"[A] rambunctiously smart, pun-spiked, and sweet dystopian romantic comedy . . . Cantor's funny and charming metaphysical adventure and love story is a wily inquiry into questions of perception, knowledge, mystery, legacy, and love." —*Booklist*

"Cantor's novel will be a great hit for fans of Douglas Adams's *Hitchhiker's Guide to the Universe*. There's a lot going on here, and all of it is amusing." —*Library Journal*

"The great pleasure of such novels is the world-building, in which the author invents a new universe while playfully commenting on our own. And what Cantor does of this is great, her impish prose and dry wit perfectly suited to the task." —*The Telegraph* (UK)

ALSO BY RACHEL CANTOR

A Highly Unlikely Scenario

GOOD
ON PAPER

GOOD
ON PAPER

A NOVEL

RACHEL
CANTOR

MELVILLE HOUSE
BROOKLYN · LONDON

GOOD ON PAPER

Copyright © 2016 by Rachel Cantor

First Melville House printing: January 2016

Melville House Publishing   8 Blackstock Mews
        46 John Street and Islington
        Brooklyn, NY 11201   London N4 2BT

mhpbooks.com facebook.com/mhpbooks @melvillehouse

Library of Congress Cataloging-in-Publication Data
Cantor, Rachel.
  Good on paper : a novel / Rachel Cantor. — First edition.
    pages ; cm
  ISBN 978-1-61219-470-7 (hardcover)
  ISBN 978-1-61219-471-4 (ebook)
  I. Title.
  PS3603.A5877G66 2016
  813'.6—dc23

                                        2015010161

Design by Adly Elewa

Printed in the United States of America
        10 9 8 7 6 5 4 3 2 1

For my parents, who taught me
most of what I know about new life

How many nights must it take
one such as me to learn
that we aren't, after all, made
from that bird which flies out of its ashes,
that for a man
as he goes up in flames, his one work
is
to open himself, to *be*
the flames?

—GALWAY KINNELL, from
   "Another Night in the Ruins" (*Body Rags*)

PART ONE

THE CALL

1

THE CALL

Twelve thousand envelopes wanted stuffing, there were twelve thousand labels to affix. Mr. Ferguson, Administrative Manager of Legs-R-Us, had particular ideas about *proportional* folding, and straight *affixion*.

Affliction? Durlene asked.

Affixion! I said.

Never heard of that, Durlene said.

Exactly! I said.

Why are you whispering? Durlene asked.

I was hiding in the supply closet, but Durlene didn't need to know that.

You need to airlift me out of here, I said.

You need to stick it out, Shira. I can't keep placing you if you keep quitting jobs.

I never managed to *stick*. I couldn't look at the walls of the schlock gallery, I couldn't bear the boss who kept telling me to *smile* or the funny smell in the church-office lunchroom.

I blamed Clyde. We'd gotten together last spring, as Good Scents prepared for Winter Wonderland. As a joke, the flavor techs threw a holiday party, complete with an inflatable Santa, and a menorah for me and the ancient receptionist. Clyde explained over imitation-raspberry-flavored eggnog that a woman's sense of smell is more acute than that of a man. Allowed to sniff a variety of sweaty T-shirts, a

3

woman will naturally be attracted to the one with the most compatible DNA. It was only when he dabbed soy sauce behind my ears that I realized I was being seduced. We French-kissed under the mistletoe: I guess I liked what I smelled.

But that was spring. By summer, Clyde's Gal Friday was back, and I was let go: a temp is a temp is a temp, after all; there'd been no talk of *us* or *tomorrow*.

Really? I'd asked while buttoning my top.

If the girl needs time off, I'll ask for you, he said.

I felt shabby, then, and out of sorts.

Since then, there'd been Falafel Dynasty, the Workers' Museum, the doll importer, and now the proportional-folding system.

I need something different, I told Durlene from the supply closet. Really different. A new start.

That's what you said before: I got you a *charity*!

I know, I said. Prosthetic legs, they're important.

Sticking is important, she said. Sticking means temp to perm. You do want something *permanent*, right? You're not one of these folks who thinks the world's going to end with Y2K, are you?

It was then that I got the call.

It was Ahmad. Friend of my youth, roommate, co-parent.

Gotta go, Durlene! Sorry!

Shira! I need you to stay! Do not quit this job!

Other line! I said. Gotta take it. Could be my kid!

Do not quit this job, Shira!

You shtupping your boss? Ahmad asked when I switched lines. Your voice has that breathless quality.

I'm not breathless, I'm whispering. Is Andi okay?

Of course Andi's okay, but you won't believe what I have in my hand.

Don't play with me, I said. You interrupted an important meeting.

Ahmad laughed. I couldn't help laughing, too.

You've got a telegram.

A what? I asked, even though I'd heard him perfectly well. (A *telegram*? Was there even such a thing anymore?)

A telegram, he said. Shall I open it for you?

4

I don't believe it, I said.

I assure you, Ahmad said. It is here in my hands. The young man who delivered it was quite delectable. We have a date—tonight. We're going *bowling*.

You sure it's not about Andi?

Andi is three blocks away. If something happened, science camp would call.

Wait, I said, and leaned back against a wall of copy paper, and told myself to breathe.

A telegram could mean only one thing. My mother, MIA since I was seven. She'd found me. Or she was dead and someone else had found me.

Don't open it, I said.

Ahmad didn't speak.

I mean it, Ahmad! Don't open it.

I heard a tearing sound.

Don't open it! I shrieked.

Oh! Ahmad said, and then silence. You won't believe this.

I hung up, then pleaded *Emergency* and left for the day, even though, as Mr. Ferguson reminded me, envelopes don't stuff themselves. I pulled Andi from science camp, whispering to her Enrichment Facilitator that Andi's aunt Emma had died, wishful thinking on my part.

Just in the nick of time, Andi muttered, dragging her Pretty Princess backpack behind her. We were learning about *tectonic shifts*. If the crust of the earth is moving, she said, shaking her braids, I don't want to know about it.

Indeed, I thought, and squeezed her, and suggested she take off her lab coat so we could be off to see the Wizard, which to Andi meant a trip to Kmart. Which earned me a hug.

I love you when you buy me things, she said.

2
NOT WHAT YOU THINK

Our apartment, lent to us by Ahmad's university, was a stately brick affair at the junction of Broadway and West End. By Manhattan and possibly other standards, it was enormous: come the revolution, it would be divided among three, if not four, proletariat families. We called it the Den of Propinquity—joking, because the place was large, also not joking, because some days it seemed hardly large enough.

The Den was decorated largely to Ahmad's taste: elegant and minimal. Large earth-toned kilims, comfortable leather couches, Chinese vases on sleek teak tables. My room, next to Andi's, was rather bare, though I'd lived in Ahmad's apartment since before Andi was born: a few posters tacked to the wall—Corot's *Isola Tiberina*, Caravaggio's *Calling of St. Matthew*. A single bed (natch), the obligatory rag rug. I've never invested much in things: any day—or so the theory went—we might move on.

Andi wanted to show Ahmad the satin clothes hangers I'd gotten her (her choice), but he wasn't in his room, and he wasn't in the kitchen. Which meant he was in his studio, where he painted when he wasn't teaching undergraduates about Depression Economics and the Economics of Change: fantasies that combined Indian gods, images iconic of the materialist West, and the Italian forms we grew up with—a haloed Ganesh squatting behind bars at the zoo, Ahmad, a donor in robes, kneeling before him. It was the one place neither Andi nor I could ever, ever go. I joked that Ahmad could keep the blue beards of his conquests there, if only his conquests were old enough to have beards, ha ha.

Put the hangers on the dining room table, I told her. He'll look at them later.

On the table, a note: *You won't be sorry.* Under it, a folded telegram.

Again that grinding in my belly. I turned toward Ahmad's studio.

Mom! Andi called out, horrified, but it couldn't wait.

Ahmad was in a far corner, drawing on an architect's table—so intently, he hadn't heard me enter.

Mom! Andi hissed at me from the door.

Ahmad looked up.

My hands were shaking.

Tell me, I said. Tell me what it is. Unless I shouldn't know. Unless it's something I don't want to know. Do I really want to know?

Sweetie! he said, and stood, noting Andi past my shoulder. You've got it all wrong! and he grabbed me. It's okay, he said, then whispered so Andi wouldn't hear: I promise it's not what you think. I promise!

My whole body was shaking.

Are you sure? I murmured into his ear.

I should have just told you. It's a job. Go! Look.

Why is Mommy crying? Andi asked, still standing at the doorway.

Because she's been offered the most amazing job in the world, Ahmad said. Anyone would cry. Go! he said, giving me a little shove. Look.

I got satin hangers for my dresses, I heard my daughter say. Look!

Let me guess, Ahmad said. They're pink?

They're pink! Andi exclaimed.

•

Damn it, I thought. Thirty-five years gone and still you do this to me?

I looked around for my mom-bag, where I kept the *MOM!* handkerchief Andi had embroidered, but couldn't find it. I settled for my sleeve.

Please, the telegram read, *you do to me the pleasure of translating my work. I am calling to you soon. Grazie. Romei.*

7

Romei? As in the poet, winner of last year's Nobel Prize for Literature, the only constellation in my sky for one sad moment in the eighties? Had Ahmad not said what he'd said, I'd have assumed the joke was his. (Last month, "Sonny Mehta" called, asking if I'd translate jet-engine specs for an anthology tentatively titled *Heaving on a Jet Plane.* I retaliated by having a barista leave messages from "Ollie North," asking if Ahmad could keep a secret.) Ahmad didn't approve of my underemployment, not when (according to him) the UN's Food and Agriculture Organization, located in Rome for reasons best known to history, would pay me good lire to translate reports on wheat varieties and integrated pest management: he knew someone who knew someone who definitely knew someone!

This joke wasn't Ahmad's, but I knew any number of translators, some of them exes, who were capable of such high humor.

I crumpled the telegram and threw it like a fast ball toward the kitchen.

You're littering, Mom.

Andi was at my side again, holding her satin hangers.

Your mom's a litterer, I said. You have homework?

Very funny.

I must have looked at her blankly.

Summer, Mom? Camp? Remember? I'm your only daughter, Andi?

Right, I said. Play till dinner. I've got to think about some things.

She didn't move.

Go on, sweetie. I'm fine. Okay, hug me first. That's good. Okay, hug me again.

•

We reconvened for tea. And cereal, because I hadn't had lunch. Ahmad tried to convince me the offer was serious. Why not? he asked.

It's not even an offer—it's a maybe offer. Besides, I know who did this, and it's not a Nobel Prize–winning poet. Pass the milk, please.

Who?

It doesn't matter, I said, looking pointedly at Andi. Just a person I used to know. A person who likes attention.

Ahmad waited.

A translator, I said. Someone I used to know but don't know anymore.

Did I know you once knew this person?

Maybe, maybe not.

After Ahmad and Roger broke up, we agreed never to bring men home again, not in thought, word, or deed. Out of consideration for Andi and, frankly, each other. An understanding we'd formalized one evening by spitting Armagnac out the window. Though usually we debriefed at the end of an off-site affair—debriefings Ahmad called *man-wakes*. Not this time.

You going to call him on it? Ahmad asked.

I'm going to give this telegram the attention it deserves.

Mommy littered with it, Andi explained.

I nodded, and the buzzer rang. It was a delivery guy. Holding a fax machine and a case of European A4-size paper. And a note thanking me for doing the *honore*. I must communicate with Romei only by fax, his work must *never* be interrupted by telephone. He would call to me; I would receive the first section "anon."

Expensive joke, Ahmad said.

The note had a fax number. It looked like a Roman telephone number. I brought my cereal to the study.

The study, just off the kitchen, was small but large enough for Ahmad's velveteen loveseat, a floor-to-ceiling bookcase, and an escritoire, on which rested my computer, slow but serviceable. It had once been an industrial-size walk-in pantry, back in the day when university professors "entertained"; since that ancient time, someone had removed the shelves and added track lighting, probably so it could serve exactly this purpose. Ahmad had his office at school, and that office had amenities like doors and windows, so this little room was mine. I'd rigged a door out of a drape and curtain rod, which offended Ahmad's aesthetic sensibility, but it was better, he said, than watching me hunt and peck at the keyboard while he was trying to cook.

I turned on my computer and visited the chat room of the Translators of Note. I was, nominally, a member, though largely on sufferance: I still went to meetings and organized our chapter's annual Bloomsday pub hop, but my translation oeuvre was not substantial. It consisted of what I'd managed to finish of Dante's *Vita Nuova* before I dropped out of grad school, plus a slim volume of stories by a writer who, like me, was said never to have reached her potential, and a few feuilletons—always the lesser-known works of lesser-known writers. It goes without saying that I never earned two dollars doing this good work. Except once: a suspect Italian-American society commissioned me to translate D'Annunzio, but they ran out of cash by chapter three.

I had a few projects going—a volume of Calabrian ghost tales, poems by a Trilussa contemporary—though by *going* I mean that I thought about them once in a while. They didn't capture my imagination, and always it seemed my spare time was better spent otherwise, like doing laundry or taking Andi to the park.

In the chat room, Josh, prime suspect, had been pronouncing just that afternoon. Using the handle "Chive Pancake," he'd shared his too-extensive opinions about an Ionesco opening he'd seen in Brooklyn the night before, performed by Kabuki actors—the lousy translation, the perfectly *awful* set design. He'd been comped by the lead actress, don't you know. He definitely was not in Rome.

If he hadn't sent the telegram, who had?

I had Ahmad hook up the fax machine on one of the shelves of my bookcase, then sent my own note:

I don't know who you are but your joke isn't funny. Go away.
P.S. I'm keeping the fax.

3

THE SINGULAR PILGRIM

Andi went upstairs to have dinner at Pammy's. Pammy's mother sometimes let them have cinnamon toast for dinner if Andi and Pammy said *please* and *thank you*. Andi didn't think we knew that, but we did.

Thanks, Mambo! she said. I love you when you let me do things!

She declined my offer to accompany her.

I never once met a bad person in the elevator, she said.

With Andi gone, the apartment was quiet. I lay down on my baby's bed, smelling her good Andi smell, and stared at the metamorphosis mural Ahmad had painted on her wall: on the upper reaches, escaping birds, Philomel, a shower of gold. Phaethon in his chariot of flame. On the ceiling, Orion, Castor and Pollux—heroes become stars the old-fashioned way: glow in the dark. In the corners, smiling like four happy evangelists, Andi and her *loco parenti*. Or rather, Andi, Ahmad, me, and a grinning giraffe, where Ahmad's ex-love Roger used to be.

Metamorphosis was overrated, I thought. Look at me: forty-four, and the thought of my mother turned me into a weeping seven-year-old. We don't change. We never change. If some deus ex machina turned me into a tree, I'd still be a tree on the verge of being a seven-year-old.

My father used to say, There's always door number two.

There's always another choice to be made. And that choice can change everything.

Maybe.

But I doubt it. He never made that choice, he never changed.

We don't change, but our lives do, sometimes. That would be enough, I thought—it would be a start, anyway. Because nothing about my life was as it was supposed to be. I'd veered off-track, as Ahmad was quick to point out. When he and I were young, it had seemed so clear. We knew we'd be famous: he as a painter, I as the world's first writing, dancing architect. Ahmad *had* become famous— for his theory of "freedom deficits" (when he was still a "Soviet expert," before coming out cost him his job at the think tank; they blamed the warming of the Cold War, but Ahmad knew). As for me, people often said I had a future, usually before I traded it in for another. My changes of heart had yielded "freedom surpluses," but little in the way of accomplishment: I'd written stories, translated this and that, contributed, temporarily, to the efficiency of marginal businesses throughout the city. Today I thought, *I don't need to be famous!* I don't even have to have a future! I'd gladly translate pest-management reports or poetry by a fake Romei if it meant I didn't have to go back to Mr. Ferguson and his proportional-folding system! But shouldn't I be able to imagine something more?

I couldn't imagine anything more.

I wrapped myself in Andi's quilt—a polyester extravaganza sewn by Ahmad's ex out of the disco shirts of a lover, long dead of AIDS (the *guilt quilt*, Ahmad called it)—and told life to wake me when it got interesting. I was just nodding off when the phone rang.

Pronto! Pronto! Hello!

A man with a Hollywood pizza-guy accent introduced himself.

It was Romei, or so he said in a passable imitation of Romei's voice, known to me and everyone in America from his cameo on *Seinfeld*, where he played a poet who may or may not have stolen Jerry's cigar (allowing Romei to say, *Sometimes a cigar is just a cigar*).

Do you know what time it is? I asked blearily, though in fact it was only seven.

You are Shira Greene, yes? The translator? This is Romei!

I swear he said it with a flourish.

Your joke isn't funny, whoever you are. Go away, I said, and hung up the phone.

He called again.

Shira Greene, this is only me, or do you say, this is I? Romei? The poet? Perhaps you have heard of me? I am writing *Romance Language*? Also *Bad Words* and *Baby Talk*.

Not to mention *Mother Tongue* and *Nonsense Syllables*, I said, yawning.

You are knowing my work! he said, and sounded pleased—too pleased for an actual Nobel Prize winner.

This isn't Josh, I said. But Josh put you up to it, right? Tell him I give you an A for persistence, but a C-minus for the lame accent.

I, too, am familiar with your work, the man said as if I hadn't spoken. I have read this translation of *Vita Nuova* . . .

I sat up. *Vita Nuova*? Not even Ahmad knew about this. I'd published it years ago as a grad student in a journal read only by dusty Dantisti. I later quit Dante when it became impossible for me to translate his noble love with a straight face. It wasn't something I talked about, *ever*.

It is for this reason, the man continued, that I am thinking you also translate my newest book, also entitle *Vita Nuova*, or maybe *Vita Quasi Nuova* . . .

Romei?

It couldn't be Romei.

I don't believe it's you—Romei, I mean.

You think I am something other? he asked, plainly amused.

Quote me something.

You wish me to speak something of my work?

The long poem "Perché Pascal," I said.

This is a short poem.

Appearing in which volume? I asked.

This *Nonsense Syllables* you are saying before.

Appearing where?

Is poem forty-seven, also it appear quoted in "Ormai Venerdì," this is poem fifty-seven.

Freak!

I am saying it to you. And he did—he recited "Perché Pascal," all two and a half lines of it.

Romei? Was calling me?

You are believing? And you are the translator? The translator from the Italiano?

Of course! It is I. She. It is she! Yes, it's me!

This is good! This is very good!

He had gotten my number, he said, from Signor Benny at *Gilgul*—a lit mag that had published some of my stories, may they rest in peace. It wasn't the first time Benny had acted as mediator: an agent had once "adored" a story he found in *Gilgul* and wanted to know if I was represented. (Though he wasn't looking for *stories*, it turned out, but novels, *big, juicy novels*, whatever those were.)

Romei's new work was important, he said. Like Dante in *La Vita Nuova*, he would use both prose and poetry to tell the tale of a woman—in his case, his wife. Whereas Dante embedded old poems in a narrative about the genesis of those poems, Romei, of course, would write *new* poems, only new poems. The book would be a gift to Esther.

He wasn't satisfied with his American publisher's choice of translator, a big-name poet with too large an ego to be faithful to his, i.e., Romei's, artistic conception. He'd dumped the publisher, said he'd pay for the translation himself. Now that he, like Dante, was *laureato*, he had money to burn, apparently.

One question, if you please, he said. You do not think the world is ending? No—how you say—*apocalypso*?

Do I think the world will end with Y2K? No, I do not.

This is good. I am speaking with one translator, he say all he do until January is—how you say—have intercourse. This is not for you?

I am available for work, I said

You are familiar with Roma, I think, he said. I am living in Piazza Santa Maria in Trastevere. You are knowing this place, yes?

I laughed. Yes, I was knowing this place. Ahmad and I had spent many an adolescent hour there—gossiping about upperclassmen,

plotting the revolution. While my father hunted Archaic Greek statues, and Ahmad's was a general in the UN's Green Revolution.

Excellent, he said. Also, you have much respect for the poet. I see
this from your story about Paul Celan, though you understand nothing of his work.

*Romei had read my story about Paul Celan? No one read my story
about Paul Celan!*

You read my story about Paul Celan? I said, a tiny tear forming
in one eye.

Of course! I must be knowing every thing of your work. I am
knowing Celan in Bucharest, yes? Quiet boy. You know, in Dante
celan means . . .

To conceal, I said, wiping the tear with Andi's guilt quilt. Third-
person plural.

You think he is meaning this when he choose this new name?

Names are consequent upon things. That's what Dante said, right?

You believe this?

I believe that when people change their names, they do so for a
reason.

And *romei*? he asked slyly. You know what this is mean?

Pilgrims whose destination is Rome, also in Dante. Is that your
real name?

What are you thinking?

I adjusted Andi's Pretty Princess pillow as I pretended to ponder
the question, though I knew very well it wasn't. I'd written a grad
school paper on the subject: "The Hystery-Mystery of Romei."

I think that when you left Romania at the end of the war, you also
chose a new name.

Why would I do that?

To announce that you were a traveler with purpose, not some
scruffy refugee?

Interesting theory, Miss Greene. And why the plural form?

Because you shared your journey with your entire generation?

He laughed.

Or maybe you preferred Romei to Roméo . . .

Ah, yes, the singular pilgrim! The name carry—how you say—baggage?

I smiled: at three hundred fifty pounds, Romei was no Romeo.

The whole world knows that Romei is not my given name. Only you know why I have chosen it. I am right for choosing you! This job, you are wanting?

He named an extravagant fee. Extravagant for a SuperTemp.

I don't know, I said, trying to keep from smiling.

You want more money, he said. This is natural.

Well, I said.

He offered another ten grand, half up front. But I must agree to finish by the end of the year. I must work on no other!

No other, I said.

I send, he said.

I know, I said. Anon.

Anon, he agreed.

I got off the phone and screamed.

Ahmad came running and I jumped on him and screamed.

Shira, my ears! They are delicate mechanisms!

Ahhh! I screamed.

The New Life, it was about to begin!

PART TWO

THRESHOLD

4

NEW LIFE

New Life! As when Dante, nearly nine, sees Beatrice for the first time and cries, *Incipit vita nova!* I, of course, had not come up with a *word*, much less a Latin exclamation—only a wild howling in my best friend's ear. But the New Life! It was suddenly so easy to imagine: exchanging insights and recipes for tiramisu with Romei at the Hungarian Pastry Shop, the translation published to mammoth acclaim, authors calling, begging for my help. I'm booked till 2020! I'd say. Twenty years? they'd reply. You expect us to wait twenty years? Montale would call, Dante himself would call: I am sorry I disappointed you, I can see how foolish I was to have believed love ordered the cosmos, to have allowed you to think your love was sanctioned by the Divine!

I could be magnanimous, finally: You ruined my life, Dantissimo, but I forgive you.

I'm proud of you, he'd add. In Latin.

Everyone would be proud! Ahmad would be proud! No more lectures about the UN. My father who art in heaven—his little girl! My mother who art who knows where? Who cared! My daughter? She'd be proudest of them all. I'd explain to her about *Vita Nuova*, Dante's place in the Western canon, Romei's place at the apex of the postmodern ridge of that canon, my place as a footnote at the apex of that ridge. Your mother, I'd say, has the mother of all opportunities. I love you when you're amazing, she'd say.

I *would* be amazing, the envy of grad students everywhere!

It had been the cool kids in grad school who'd read Romei. As I labored over Provençal precedents, they read his work during marathon sessions of sexual experimentation, they assembled on his birthday to chant his famed response to Derrida, who'd once called Romei's work seminal (*séminal*):

Who is this Derrida! What does he know!
Did he give up language! Did he learn to speak by reading!
He writes the language of lullabies! Fairy tales with happy endings!
This is the language of BETRAYAL!

Much as I longed to participate in that chanting, not to mention those marathon sessions, I resisted Romei, reading him only when forced to by my adviser. Once I did, I couldn't rid myself of him. He peered over my shoulder when I communed with Dante: *Reactionary!* he'd hiss. *Hunter after truth! Believer in cosmic order!* Ever stalwart, I shrugged him off and wrote not of his work but his life, his tendency to offer contradictory accounts of his past.

According to his book-jacket biography, Romei was the devoutly Catholic son of a Jewish convert mother, considering the priesthood when the war broke out. When his parents were killed by the Romanian Iron Guard, he hid in a grain silo, tended there by a nun whose wimpled beauty caused him to reconsider his vocation. Still, when he left Romania in 1945, he chose Rome, hoping for new life in the shadow of the Pope.

For two decades, he lived there in obscurity, interpreting for visiting journalists, appearing in a fantasy sequence in Fellini's *8½*, writing unremarkable verse until, in his forties, he "burst onto the scene," as they say, with *Mother Tongue*, a volume of iconoclastic poems so unprecedented, so bold in their treatment of language and meaning, so uncompromising in their conflation of loyalty and betrayal, they took Europe—or at least European poets—by storm.

He followed four years later with *Romance Language*, poems that extended his explorations into the constitution (or lack thereof) of meaning by language. More volumes appeared in the seventies and eighties, all celebrating his trickster persona, his inauthentic voice, his disconnection from language: *Bad Words, Baby Talk, Nonsense Syllables.*

There were other, less flattering versions of his life, of course, and this is what I wrote about. Some claimed that Romei had learned Italian not as a student of literature, but as a prisoner of war, or as a collaborator—making him both older and less innocent than we liked to believe. He was by one account a Red Brigades sympathizer, by another, an unrepentant monarchist. One Dutch historian claimed that he'd manufactured his Jewish heritage—though whether to create sympathy for himself or deflect attention from a fascist past, she couldn't say. A self-inflicted circumcision at the end of the war became septic, she said, leading to lifelong problems with erectile dysfunction.

What was true? The Great Man wouldn't say. And if he did, we couldn't believe him. We couldn't believe a word he said (he said), about anything.

When I gave up on T. in grad school, gave up on Dante, Romei taunted me: *Told you so, told you so.*

This has nothing to do with you! I shouted. Dante is a fake and a liar! I hate his stupid freakin' lyin' Dante guts!

He became my virtual companion, then, my only friend. I kept a copy of his latest in my back pocket as I wept in the stacks, or watched T.'s house, hidden by a stunted tree. Romei forgave me my failures. Why try, he seemed to say, when it was folly, all folly? We could count on nothing, certainly not the generosity of the gods. *There is no order,* he'd say, consoling me with tough love. *There is no beneficent judge! We are lonely nomads, monads all alone—get used to it!*

That made sense to me so I gave up on love, quit grad school, and married Ron, the accountant, because he asked. Romei quit, too— some said to care for his wife, who was sick, or maybe because he'd written himself into a corner.

Eleven years later, when the world had lost interest in Romei, when one could have been excused for thinking him dead, he won the Nobel.

It's about time, he grumbled on CNN. I'm broke and need to get my teeth fixed. He opened his mouth before 200 million viewers, and showed them a black tooth in back.

America was charmed. A half dozen celebrity dentists offered to do the work for free.

They rushed him onto *Larry King*, where he complained he couldn't find a suit to fit his, uh, portly posterior. Ralph Lauren asked for his measurements.

Maybe we were tired of hectoring laureates with their big words, their excess gravitas. Romei was a man of the people, or so he'd have us believe. We loved his curmudgeonly style, his malapropisms: he became our poet icon, though few of us read his work. But everyone saw him on *Letterman*, his goatee mostly white, his hair thick, his stomach carried high and tight like a late-term pregnancy. His wry humor, his outrageous insults made even Letterman laugh, a little.

Are you serious about anything? a starlet asked.

I'm serious about my spaghetti, he replied.

Journalists persisted, intent on solving the mystery of Romei. Barbara Walters inclined her head ten degrees to the left and said, Romei, may we get serious for a moment? You've said we mustn't talk about your wife. Why is that?

He walked off the set.

But now this very public, very private man was writing about that most off-limit topic: his wife. And it was I—*I*—who would bring that work to the (English-speaking) world.

Carramba! I shouted. It wasn't Latin, but it would do.

5

BEST INTERESTS OF
THE CHILD

I'd planned to do laundry that night, but Ahmad rescheduled *bowling* so we could celebrate. We sent Andi, newly returned from Pammy's with cinnamon on her lips, to get ready for bed, then Ahmad toasted me with what was left of the cabernet. At forty-five, he still looked like the boy I'd known thirty years before in Rome—fine skin, narrow frame, hair falling into his face. His soft-spoken demeanor caused some to think him harmless, but they were wrong: he was a sniper who flattened poseurs with a phrase and never felt remorse.

He wanted to know more.

I explained about *Vita Nuova* (Not that old chestnut! he exclaimed. I can't believe Luigi Pieranunzi made me read that in college. Why would you make students read that, when there's so much *good* Dante to read?). I didn't enlighten him about my translation, and I didn't have to tell him about Romei—Ahmad had read his work long before it had become fashionable—but I did explain about poetry and prose, the story of Romei's wife. And grad students everywhere, the footnote at the apex of the ridge of the postmodernist canon. Andi, I said, would have someone else to look up to. It wouldn't be just Ahmad doing Career Day! Nothing, I gushed, would ever be the same.

Let me adopt her, he said, sitting forward in his Eames chair. Let me adopt Andrea.

Oh, no, I thought. *Not this again.*

Ahmad, I said, we've been through this, like, a hundred times!

When I came home from India, pregnant and broke, I was desperate: how could I live in the City, an underemployed single mom? I considered returning to Suffern, where I'd lived for eight years as Ron's wife. Telling myself I *liked* being a wife, I *liked* Ron's jokes, his habit of counting socks and planning sex. Ron, who found the City dirty and, truth be told, me too. Where I'd thrown my life in the hot-water wash and watched it shrink. It would be less expensive in Suffern, I reasoned, but then I thought: living on the subway would be better than that.

Friends shrugged and looked embarrassed when I asked what I should do, as if I were asking something of them. Then I remembered Ahmad. He'd always been *logical*. Surely he'd have a better idea, one that didn't involve giving birth on the IRT.

I hadn't seen him for more than a year, not since Jonah, the unrequited love of his youth, had died in front of us, killed by a yellow cab on my thirty-fifth birthday. We'd been in high school together, the three of us (four if you count his sister Jeanette, though we weren't friends then); I didn't remember Jonah, but he remembered me. Actually, he more than remembered me: he tortured Ahmad for years with remembrances and besotted "what ifs." So that when the three of us were to get together for the first time in twenty years, it was me Jonah was watching, not the road.

Or so Ahmad said. He blamed me for Jonah's death, he *said things*, unforgivable things. He knew why my mother left us: It was obvious, look at me! What a slut I'd always been! All because I let Ahmad kiss me freshman year, though I was in love with T.—then I pushed him away, and was mean about it. He'd had choice words for me then, too, and our friendship, our beautiful friendship, melted away. When he called me twenty years later, I was about to divorce. I didn't worry about our falling out: I only thought *he knew me when*. When I'd been young, before my twelve-year detour with T., when I still believed my future was shiny and bright. If I could just see that Shira reflected in his eyes, I might know how to live again, but we were barely together five minutes when Jonah appeared across the road.

When I met him at the Palm Court of the Plaza, pregnant, a year later, I saw not the angry man who'd just seen his best friend die, but the dear, sweet, generous friend of my youth. We reminisced and laughed, and cut postage-stamp-size cucumber sandwiches into quarters just for fun. I told him about translation, how I'd just started writing stories; he told me about his transformation from conservative think-tank analyst to college professor and also-ran Nobelist. I'd intended to ask only for advice, but, giddy with how well we were getting on, I thought: He should be a part of my life, *our* life. I might not inspire my child, but he could. So I asked him to be my child's godfather. He shocked me by crying. Yes, he said, my God, yes!

It turned out he lost everything the night Jonah died. He came out, finally, losing not just his wife, which was no loss, but his sons as well.

We came to an understanding that day at the Plaza: I would be the child's one true parent, but Ahmad's name would appear on her birth certificate, his enlightened university would cover our insurance, her education. People would assume he was her (nominal) father, but we would know better: that her father was a Sikh I'd met in Delhi; when Andi was older, she'd know it too. We could even live at his place till we got on our feet. By some administrative fluke, his apartment was large enough for all of us, and then some.

We never left.

Ahmad turned out to be a great dad. He took on midnight feedings, and didn't mind changing nappies (as he called them). He sang lullabies in Urdu and watched our Andi sleep. Later, he shucked his Italian shoes to help her construct mega malls out of Legos, and had tea with her many dolls. He endeavored to explain conservative economics on Career Day and entertained Andi's friends by drawing pictures of them standing next to film stars. Still, I had to remind him: ours was an arrangement of convenience, in the best interests of the child. I was the mother: I made the decisions, I took the flak. Still, periodically, he asked about adoption. As it was, he'd say, his rights meant nothing. One blood test and they'd be gone.

Who's going to make you take a blood test? I'd ask.

Every time he brought it up, he had a new argument. This time he asked, what if something *happened*—to me, he meant.

You mean, if I decided to abandon my baby at the airport?

I wasn't comparing you to your mother, as you very well know.

If I *died*, then?

Or became incapacitated.

Or became incapacitated. Lovely, I said, holding out my glass for more wine.

We have to plan for contingencies, he said.

That's what the birth certificate's for! I said, or maybe I shouted.

He was concerned about our daughter's *development*, he said. She was reaching the age of rational discourse. It was time she knew who her real father was.

Rational discourse? The girl who insists she has a telepathic relationship with Tinky Winky? Who believes most Chinese words are made up?

Shh! he said. The look he gave me could have made raisins out of grapes.

If we don't tell her now, he said, she won't forgive us when she learns the truth.

You're such a drama queen! I said, and waited for him to say, *Better than a dairy queen*, which was his usual response. Instead he said, You're being selfish, Shira. You're thinking only about yourself.

You know that's not true! I said. She's way too young!

Whatever it is, I heard my baby say, I'm not too young.

We wheeled around in our chairs.

Andi was at the entrance of the living room, wearing her primrose flannel nightie, though it was August. I'm nearly eight, she said. In addition to which my Enrichment Facilitator says I have an old soul.

We're talking about Ahmad's secretary. She's way too young. Too young to water-ski.

Why would she think Ahmad was her father?

We were speaking metaphorically, I said.

I hate figurative language, my baby said. You know that.

I know that, I said, repressing a smile.

26

Tinky Winky was missing, it turned out. Andi distinctly remembered leaving him in the kitchen when she was building her Tupperware kingdom.

Searching ensued, till Ahmad found that bad boy grinning under Andi's bed.

6

COMFORT ZONE

The next morning I felt wonderfully well—the kind of *well* that comes from knowing *things are happening*, the New Life is upon us. I went to Cuppa Joe's, where I ordered a decaf-skinny-mocha-capp and two bear claws from Joe himself, a tall, bulky Iranian (né Ali) with whom I'd once been "intimate." I was still here often, though Joe had married a Persian maid half his age, siring black-haired twins.

I nodded at the regulars—it was too late for the silk-clad boutique lady, and the bespectacled Barnard student, but the latte-drinking actor who once starred in a sitcom about fat men was there, as was the black man with the deformed hand—then I stopped across Broadway to tithe Nate, our local panhandler who, over the years, had transformed himself from "down on his luck" to "Vietnam Vet" to "victim of Agent Orange" to "homeless man with AIDS (not homosexual)."

Can I offer you some change? I asked as I gave him his claw.

No, thanks, he said, I'm fine the way I am.

Our favorite joke.

I brought my breakfast to Straus Park, known in our Den of Propinquity as Slice of Park, because it's shaped like a piece of pie. Slice of Park commemorates Isidore and Ida Straus, who had a summer home nearby. Isidore immigrated to the U.S. in the 1850s and began his career in Macy's china department, eventually buying the store with his brother. He and his wife perished with the *Titanic*, but still, not bad for a new life!

The park had itself recently been revived. We'd watched out our window, bemoaning the Port-a-Potties, the loud equipment, the seemingly endless labor. But it was worth it, because, with minimal West Side fanfare, the park finally reopened. The rotting benches were gone, the statue of Memory was restored, her fountain no longer dry.

I sat often in Slice of Park when the weather was clement, feeling sun-blessed. From my bench I could see Joe's, People of the Book, the Dollar Store, the Love Drugstore. A few blocks away, beyond my sightline: larger parks, Cohn's Cones, the China Doll. Just north: Abdul's Papad Palace, the Eight Bar. Ten blocks south: Symphony Space, the express train. All my cultural, entertainment, transportation, snacking, and discount-shopping needs met within half a mile. I called it my Comfort Zone.

On this morning, I beamed out at the world—at the women checking themselves out in the drugstore window, the nannies pushing strollers, lapdogs bouncing in straw bags against matronly hips, *alte kockers* gesticulating in the Broadway island. The red-headed boy pushing a scooter as his brother reached desperately for it from his father's arms. At taxis, buses, kamikaze bike messengers, all honking, screeching, and converging *right here*, as if Slice of Park were the center of the universe—which to me it was.

New York was more than the places I loved, the people I cared about: it was the web that held us together, that made us all possible. It was the history of this park, of places that were no more—the Pomander Bookshop, the Ideal Restaurant, the Olympia Deli, the summer home of Isidore Straus—it was Memory! It was Iranian pastry chefs and Victims of Agent Orange, it was Old and New World ladies and men. I felt vast love for all who dared to make a life for themselves here.

It was in this exalted mood that I gave notice.

But you have a future in prosthetic legs! Mr. Ferguson said.

7

ODOROUS OBJECT

Once home, I thought I should dignify my New Life with a ritual—a sacrifice of some kind, a naked dance in the woods. The best I could come up with was to brew some Philosopher's Tea. The original PT, procured by Ahmad in Azerbaijan, was long gone, but I continued to refill the box with English breakfast. If the philosopher's stone could transmute base metal into gold, so too could PT transmute my oh-so-base thoughts into words; all that was inchoate would be graced with form. Hallelujah!

I drank it whenever I translated, which meant it had been a while. On the box, a reminder of the professional standard to which I aspired: *High-quality tea recalling odor and smack lemon. Store at a dry place away from odorous object.*

I brought my tea to the loveseat in the study. I didn't know when Romei would send his book, but I could prepare for that moment by rereading some of his work.

When I left grad school, I'd wedged my copies of his books under wobbly tables at the Hungarian Pastry Shop, my idea of a joke. I found Ahmad's copies and arranged them in chronological order against my chest, from *Mother Tongue* to *Nonsense Syllables*.

They emitted a mild electric charge: my body was buzzing, my arteries thrumming. I opened *Mother Tongue*, broke the binding, and began to read.

Maybe I fell asleep. There was the matter of the wine I'd drunk the night before and, well, the matter of Romei's poems. I put the books in my mom-bag and went back to Cuppa Joe's, where I ordered a mocha double-half-caff and, all virtue, said no to a chocolate bomb.

I read some more, then put the books away and stared out the window. If they had been my copies rather than Ahmad's, I might have slipped them under Joe's wobbly table and been done with it.

There was a time when I would have translated Romei for a latte and a package of peanuts. I felt close to him then; I could have gotten closer—I could have gotten very, very close. Translation requires, and generates, a rare kind of intimacy. Like sex done right, I've always thought. The translator makes a holy commitment to understand, to listen with all possible intensity, to step backward, ever backward, through the labyrinth of an author's ideas and devices, uncovering his decisions and triumphs, line by line, until she arrives, finally, at the moment of creation—*and before*, when words are merely phonemes and breath, and the author lies naked and drunk with his obsessions, visions, and agonizing aphasia. The translator, like one of Noah's sons, bears witness to this primal scene. It takes a strong stomach. And an attractive host. You had to *want* to get close.

When I translated Dante's *Vita Nuova*, I'd wanted to get close: Like Dante, I was in love, with T.; *Vita Nuova* seemed written just for me. Dante lived for his true love's greeting? So did I! His love was a paragon? So was mine! A glimpse of his love made him stupid? Me too! Beatrice was heaven-sent, Dante's love divinely sanctioned? T. and I were also meant to be. He was my Beatrice, the sum of all virtue, the reason I had been put on this earth.

I found my place comfortably between Dante's lines then, his nakedness didn't bother me.

Until it did. Romantic events shattered the pretty idea I had about God's plan for man, and with it, any interest I had in "getting close." I hated Dante then—Dante and his stupid *Vita Nuova*! The *libello*, his libelous little book, was nothing more than a reminder that I'd been abandoned not just by the love of my young life, but by every hope I'd had that the world was as Dante described—ordered, designed to manifest a greater Love.

Which was when I turned to Romei. He wrote about the impossibility of New Life, the groundlessness that lies between the lines. There was no sense in Romei that language could reach beyond its limitations, or the abuse done to it, to connect one self to another. Where Celan had written, *When only the nothingness stood between us, we found our way, all the way, to each other,* Romei instead would write, *There was only nothingness.* Not just the impossibility of meeting, but the impossibility of there being an Other there to meet.

There was no Other for Romei: just Romei and the failure of language to do its job. His mind was empty—not in a cozy Zen sort of way, but in a barren, all-there-is-is-void, no-point-in-even-trying sort of way.

This had appealed to me in my twenties; not so much now. I had a family, I had my Comfort Zone—what use did I have for the void?

I was staring, I realized, out the window at People of the Book. The bookstore Benny "Jellyroll" Jablonsky ran in addition to editing *Gilgul* and acting as part-time rabbi to his New Age congregation. A year ago, after helping me with German translations for "Rose No One," my story about Celan, Benny had made a pass at me, a clumsy offering between bookcases labeled *Trash Novels* and *Filthy Lucre.* I avoided the store now. But Benny had given Romei my number; maybe it was time I bought myself some books.

8

BILLBOARD ARTIST OF
THE HEART

Inside People of the Book, a green-haired girl wearing a child's tartan, a happy-face T-shirt (but not a happy face), and a Stop & Shop nametag that said "Hello, I'm Lila!" advised me that Benny was out. She wouldn't look me in the eye: she needed all her concentration, apparently, for the *Daily News* Jumble.

I wasn't surprised: Benny was probably at one of the rabbi gigs he took to support his literary habit (performer of interfaith marriages, virtual *mohel* for parents who want the celebration without the slice). Or he might be in his apartment two floors above the store, but I wasn't about to ring the bell.

I found Romei's books in Benny's Great Wall of Poetry. Handsome and pricey, they'd been reissued by Farrar, Straus and Giroux on the occasion of the Great Man's sojourn to Stockholm. His by-now-famous face, in different poses, filled the back covers: salt-and-pepper goatee, more salt than pepper. Straight brown hair, a centimeter too long. Pale, plump cheeks, pouchy eyes. Simple wire-rimmed glasses. Yankees baseball cap.

I brought the books to Benny's folding-table café (one table, reserved for Friends of Benny), drank the organic ginger beer Lila brought me grudgingly from out back.

The store hadn't changed in the year since I'd visited last: unpacked

33

boxes still blocked aisles and Marla, Benny's Persian, still held court in her book box. I went over to pay obeisance. She tolerated my head scritch, but withheld her purr, which she reserved for Benny.

How I'd missed this place! Over by the cash register, where best-sellers should have been stacked in attractive pyramids, stood that smallish bookcase holding issues of *Gilgul* and other literary magazines. What passed for impulse purchases among People of the Book.

I couldn't resist: I left my table to browse the bookcase, returned to find the table gone, my books gone. Irritated, I got new copies and asked Lila if I could leave Benny a message.

Sure, she said, opening *The Anxiety of Influence* and handing me a pen. Go for it.

Just then, Benny appeared, trotting down the steps from his mezzanine office, ritual *tzitzit* fringes flying from the four corners of his garment.

Benny was six and a half feet tall; before he became a roller-blading vegan he'd looked like a dark-haired Santa, with full beard and even fuller cheeks. At his poorest, he'd nearly sold himself to Macy's, but didn't—bad faith like that couldn't be atoned for in a single lifetime, he said. Also, he wouldn't tuck in his *tzitzit*, which Macy's thought might confuse the kiddies.

That was years ago. Now Benny was lean and suntanned: he said his morning prayers while gliding through the park in a cherry-red bodysuit—the only time he dressed without *tzitzit*.

Shir chadash! he sang out (his psalmic name for me: "new song").

Rabbi! I shouted.

Why didn't you tell Marie to come get me?

Marie?

Benny looked tired. More tired than usual. His owl eyes sagged, there was a softness to his patrician cheekbones, his eyebrows were turning a patchy gray.

Uh, I said, looking at Marie-cum-Lila, who looked me in the eye now, though blankly. I figured you were busy.

Don't mind her, he whispered, pecking at my cheek. She's brilliant but moody.

All Benny's protégées were brilliant but moody, which was why

34

his store was such a mess. The manic ones invented new shelving systems, the depressed ones watched as towers of dictionaries toppled onto not-so-politically-correct children's books. Given the state of the store, I guessed his latest beauty was of the latter affliction.

Benny led me to the back of the store, where he found the folding table and opened it in front of the section marked Victimization Manuals (books you and I might call Self-Help).

She's a graphic artist, he said, still whispering. Works exclusively on billboards.

Must not bring in a lot, I said, trying not to smile.

She's between grants, he said. The neck of his Rainbow Gathering T-shirt was frayed; he had a spot of dried tomato on his cheek, above his beard. So! Shira! he said. Nice to see you! What've you been up to?

Temping in Jersey. I'm too slow to type in Manhattan! I said, laughing.

Your parents must be proud!

I stared.

It's been a while. Sorry! Really! I forgot!

How long has it been? I asked, though I knew.

A year? he asked, as if astonished.

Did he resent being dumped? No, Benny wasn't a hider. Everything he thought, everything he felt was writ large on his face: he was a billboard artist of the heart.

He asked about Andi. She was about to start third grade, I said. Her current ambition: to be a White House intern, so she too could be on TV every night.

Benny looked at me blankly: he wasn't one for the evening news, apparently.

I see Ahmad now and then, he said. He single-handedly sustains my Nancy Drew section.

I laughed.

He's greatly interested in the mystery of things, I said.

I assume you're here because . . .

Yes! I said. He called!

•

Just a sec, he said, returning a kitten to Marla, who lay regal and sleepy-eyed in her Simon & Schuster box. She stood, and arched her back, and kissed Benny's hand, apparently uninterested in her prodigal chick, then followed him to his seat and leapt onto his lap. Her purr was prodigious.

Benny asked for the skinny. I gave it to him, *Reader's Digest*–style: *Vita Nuova*, Romei's strange requirement that I finish by the end of the year.

Shira, that's amazing! he said when I was done, looking at me in wonder, as if he thought this miracle somehow my doing. Which, given his belief in karma, he probably did. We must drink to your success! Ginger beer?

He put Marla gently on the ground. Offended, she returned to her box.

Libations! he exclaimed when he returned.

L'chaim, I added gamely.

I assume Romei is paying you?

A lot! I said.

Good! You can sponsor *Son of Gilgul*! It's reincarnating: next issue by Y2K.

I hadn't realized *Gilgul* was dead!

You'd know if you were still sending me stories, *ma cherie*.

I didn't bother explaining that I'd stopped writing. Ahmad had despised my last story ("Domino Effect," about Jonah); Jonah's sister Jeanette stopped talking to me because of it. I asked instead about the magazine. Benny clasped his hands behind his head and extended his long, jean-clad legs into the aisle.

I had a few lean years. My board forced me to close.

That's the fate of the gilgul, right? The soul eternally reincarnating?

Until we get it right. Some of us are going to be here a very long time.

I'm sure your gilgul's in great shape.

Humph, he said. So Romei's an interesting guy, huh?

I accepted the change of subject.

Imagine, I said, giving up your homeland and language to write *terza rima* in Roma!

Exactly! Benny said. Prose writers change languages all the time—Nabokov, Conrad . . .

Ionesco, Tristan Tzara, if we stick to his countrymen. But poets? It isn't done!

Except by Romei.

I assume he was fleeing censorship and communism, I said.

Or the country that killed his parents, Benny said pensively, staring into the middle distance, which at People of the Book meant the shelf for Games People Play.

Of course, I said, remembering. Benny's father had been a Russian POW who'd ended up hunting down Nazis after the war. He wasn't a nice man, may he rest in peace. Benny's mother had escaped to the U.S. in 1939 after the murder of her first husband, whom she hadn't particularly liked. She'd been a dancer; in America she kept books for her brother-in-law's *schmatta* business. The family she left behind died, like most families left behind.

It makes sense he doesn't write in Romanian, I said. He would have been an imperialist poet *non grata* in Romania. No one would have published his books there. Who's going to read poetry in Romanian, if Romanians in Romania can't?

Paul Celan wrote in German, Benny added, but German was his mother tongue.

Right! I said.

But still, he said, imagine!

We sipped our drinks, imagining.

So what do you know about his project? This would be his first since, what?

Nonsense Syllables.

And his first "story."

Yes, I said.

What is this *Vita Nuova* business?

Early work of Dante, I said. Written in 1294, before the *Comedy*, before his exile from Florence. Really, you don't know it?

Benny laughed. Not my cup of tea, exactly.

Vita Nuova traces the evolution of Dante's love for Beatrice and his poetic response to that love. He includes relevant poems, which he explicates ad nauseum.

For example?

For example: I was thinking of the blessed Beatrice when I swooned and had a vision of the blessed Beatrice and out popped a sonnet about the blessed Beatrice, this one here, in which I swoon, have a vision, and write a sonnet about the blessed Beatrice. Story, poem, explication.

Benny laughed again.

My case is resting, he said. But it's not just poems and explication—you said it's a story?

After a fashion, I said. Not quite as gripping as the *Divine Comedy*, but it has something of a "hero's journey" structure.

I described to Benny what I considered to be *Vita Nuova's* mythic structure (but refrained from offering a copy of the essay in which I elaborated this theory): Call, Threshold, Deception, Muse, Death, Test, and Return. The call identifies Dante as the ur-hero of all story: Adam called by Eve to taste; Sam Spade called by the blonde to solve a mystery. Sometimes the hero is reluctant: happy in his easy chair, he tries to avoid the call, he hides out or runs away. Odysseus feigns madness to avoid the draft; Rick tells Ilsa he's a sideliner.

The hero eventually has to come around, though, or there can be no story. He makes his commitment, crosses the threshold, and thrusts himself into story, where, aided by mentors, inspired by beauties, deceived by tricksters, challenged by opponents, he makes allies, surmounts obstacles, faces death, and is reborn to face his final test. Victorious, he returns to Kansas bringing exactly what his people need—the elixir, the golden crown. Sometimes he also gets the girl. Not something I made up, I added.

But eccentric when applied to Dante, Benny said.

Not commonplace, I agreed. Especially when you consider that Dante's hero battles sin, not dragons.

What kind of sin? Something juicy?

Just your garden variety, live-your-life-you're-bound-to-sin kind of thing.

So young Mr. Dante is a hero in this book about poetry. Can a book about poetry have a hero?

He *is* a hero, in his own mind! He's called by love to be a poet, though of course he loves from afar. He writes poems, which of course come up short because nothing is good enough for Beatrice. He tries to contemplate her perfections, can't always manage it, gets advice, the advice changes—then Beatrice dies, and he's thrown off course—maybe he even despairs. He finally has a vision of Beatrice in heaven—an ineffable vision—that sets him up for life—aesthetically and, we assume, spiritually. That's enough to make him a hero, right? A man on a lonely journey toward the good, trying to live his life right? A pilgrim hero!

Coming soon to a theater near you!

Hah! Though his victory is just as inevitable as that of any dragon slayer. Redemption is always the light at the end of the tunnel, isn't it? Even when Dante strays, you know his narrative will keep him on the straight and narrow . . .

Sadly, we no longer believe in such a thing, Benny replied.

The straight-line narrative to salvation has been discredited, yes.

By Romei, among others. So what's Romei want with it? He doesn't go in much for story.

Or tradition. And now he's taking on the Big Guy.

If you take on a Big Guy, you take on his Big Work, no?

Right, I said, the *Divine Comedy*. You admit you've reached the middle of your life's journey, and you survey the terrain.

Romei's hardly at the middle of his life's journey! What is he, seventy by now?

At least seventy-five! I said.

So he's reached the end of his life's journey, Benny said. You say *Vita Nuova* was written by a young man about recent events, but Romei, being old, writes about *temps perdus*.

Yes! I said. Dante writes with pre-exilic promise, Romei from the perspective of been-there-done-that. Another thing: Dante is nothing if not certain—life has meaning and he knows what it is.

Lucky man! Benny said.

But Romei's made a career out of ridiculing nostalgia for meaning. What will he do now? Stick to his guns, reject Dante's straight-line narrative to salvation? Or has age placed him in the trenches, where all sinners cry out to be saved?

Silence.

Benny?

Do you believe in forgiveness? he asked. What do you think it is?

Forgiveness? I said. No idea!

Not your favorite subject.

You could say that.

We sipped our ginger beer.

Why do you think Romei's going public? Benny asked. He's always been so private.

We talked about this for a while. Okay, more than a while. We wondered about the same things, then found additional things to wonder about.

At one point, Benny sent Marie to get vegan donuts from Cuppa Joe's; she came back empty-handed: all out, she said, lacking the resources, apparently, to find an alternative.

We didn't come to a satisfactory conclusion about the mysteries of Romei, but our discussion had been more than satisfactory. When I left, I promised to stay in touch. Benny bowed low to kiss me good-bye, his long beard tickling my neck.

I must be a freak, I thought as I started crossing the street: I'd found our conversation arousing. Had Benny felt it too, the bodily effect of two minds meeting?

Wait! he cried, and waved me back to the store. I blushed as he had Marie credit my card thirty percent. *Gilgul* alumna, he explained to Marie, whose fingernails, I noticed, were speckled green to match her hair and her eyes, which were empty and flat. She was not as young as I'd thought—in her mid-thirties, at least. I found myself wondering if Benny was seeing her, much as I'd wondered about Gilda, the tapestry artist who'd stolen his stock of erotica and the contents of his

40

cash register when she'd left, or Yasmeen, the daughter of a sheikh, who wore a veil, though she hoped for a career on the stage.

I decided no, he couldn't be involved with a sullen, drugged-out fraud of an artist. Who dressed like a child. And was willing to deface books. Could he?

9

Y2K POETRY

We always dressed for Friday Night Dinner: on this evening, Ahmad wore the smoking jacket I'd gotten him at Goodwill, while Andi wore her Pretty Princess backpack and tutu. For my part, I'd brushed my hair and put on some Docksiders. Tonight, because we were celebrating, we went out. Andi requested the China Doll: she enjoyed practicing the Chinese she'd learned at Chinese-Spanish-French quadrilingual preschool. She also knew she could make an entire meal there out of pancakes.

You're looking radiant, my dear, Ahmad said, as we walked over. I think the absence of Aurora-driving, gold-toothpick-toting flavor salesmen agrees with you.

That was six jobs ago, I said.

Still, he said.

It's the glow of clean living, I said.

It's a shtupping glow, he replied. Who is it?

Andi was a few steps ahead of us, skipping and singing a science song.

No one! I said. I'm not shtupping anyone!

Shira Greene, it is not acceptable to keep things from your oldest friend. You know I live vicariously through your adventures.

Ahmad sometimes said outrageous things, and sometimes he believed them: I had few adventures these days and rarely discussed them, whereas he had adventures galore.

42

No adventure, I said, but I did see Benny today—and I told him with increasing animation about the Great Wall of Poetry, the numb-nut salesgirl who couldn't buy donuts, Benny's incisive commentary, how fun it was to talk about books, and didn't he think Benny cute in his own rabbinical way, for a guy with long legs and gray, patchy eyebrows?

Benny? he asked. Bookstore Benny? Careful!—and he grabbed my arm to stop me walking into traffic.

Oops, I said. Andi, of course, had crossed safely and was staring into the window of Cohn's Cones.

When we arrived at the China Doll, Andi insisted on a toast, and a Shirley Temple.

Topeka! she cried, after we'd ordered and I'd explained why we were celebrating and answered Andi's several questions (what's a Dante, what's a postmodernist canon)—Topeka being Andi's version of Eureka, a term that referred not just to *aha!* moments but to any experience of fulfillment, wonder, gratitude, surprise. *I get it! I've got it! Waffles for breakfast! Topeka!* Then she sang a version of "For She's a Jolly Good Translator," which sounded very much like "A Hundred Bottles of Beer on the Wall."

Ahmad sang that I was jolly good, but he didn't look so sure.

What is it? I said, moving my mom-bag off the table to make room for Peking duck and mooshu pork.

We don't know much about this chap, do we?

What's to know? I said, peeling off pancakes for Andi. Nobel Prize, college fund, braces, Barbie Dream Palace.

He gave me a look. For one thing, his university would cover Andi's tuition; for another, Andi's teeth were coming in and they were beautiful.

You hate literary translation! he said. You said it's the last refuge of logical positivism!

I never! I don't even know what that means! Pass the *hoisin*, please.

At our Halloween party you dressed as the *traduttore/traditore* and ranted about the untranslatability of all texts.

The what? my baby said.

The traitorous translator, Ahmad said.

43

That sounds like a dumb costume, she said.

Maybe I've seen the light, I said. What's this about? Last night you said this was the most amazing job in the world.

I've been thinking—I do that sometimes. Why does he want to publish the translation before the original? I've never heard of that. Is he giving up on his traditional European audience?

The U.S. is a helluva market.

It doesn't make sense, Shira.

Didn't we have another dish?

Red bean paste, said Andi, for dessert. *No!* she said, pushing my hand away. I make my own pancakes, remember?

Why does he want a draft by the end of the year? Ahmad asked. Did he explain that?

You can't ruin this for me, I said.

Who's ruining anything? I'm asking questions!

No fighting, Andi said. I hereby forbid it.

Y2K poetry, I said. He wants a draft by the end of the year because he's a millenarian. He wants his work to defend him come Judgment Day.

And Jesus the Judge reads only English? Ahmad asked, half smiling.

Stands to reason if God is an American, I said.

God is an American? Andi asked.

From that sublime height I managed to shift the conversation to millenarian madness (which Ahmad told Andi had something to do with hats): our favorite babysitter's twelve-step program for Y2K readiness; Yeats' "rough beast" slouching, even as we speak, toward Bethlehem; Dante's mysterious messenger, identified by the number five-fifteen, ready to announce the end of days.

Andi had been playing with Mr. Fork and Mrs. Knife, putting them to bed between two chopsticks.

You know, she said, this isn't the most fascinating conversation we've ever had.

Andi, I said, before she could elaborate, let the grown-ups finish their conversation, then we can find something you can talk about, okay?

It's late, Ahmad said. I think it's time.

He was right. Andi was tired, so Ahmad flew her home like a 767 jet.

10

A FAIRY TALE

It was a typical weekend. Ahmad took Andi to Coney Island to satisfy her ambition to ride the Cyclone six times without throwing up. The outcome of this venture was an Andi-Ahmad secret, but the stain on the front of her jumpsuit told all. Sunday, Andi and I went to the Natural History Museum to look at lizards, then had ice cream at Cohn's Cones (my Cohn's Cones koan: *Does a hot dog have a Buddha nature?* Hers: *What is the sound of one cone dripping?*). Sunday night, Ahmad went for sushi with a clutch of conservatives, remnants of a once-powerful cabal of Republican advisers, displaced by the warming of the Cold War. They still got together to drink sake and make jokes about Nancy Reagan's astrologer.

Andi was starting school in a week, so she and I were at her closet going through her clothes. When my phone rang, she ran to my room, wearing only her tights, Mary Janes, and day-of-the-week underwear. To retrieve my phone, I thought; in fact, to answer it.

Hello, she said, before I could take the phone from her. She must have thought it was Ahmad. I shook my head. *No!* She listened a moment, then handed me the phone, disappointed.

Who is this? Romei asked.

Hello? I said. It's Shira.

Who is this child who answer the phone?

My daughter, I said.

Not that it's any of your business, I thought.

You have a daughter? I know nothing about a daughter. How old is this daughter? What is this daughter name?

Andrea, she's seven, almost eight.

Silence.

The name of your husband?

I am happily single, I said.

Silence.

She is healthy, this Andrea? (He pronounced it in the Italian style: Ahn-*drey*-ah.)

Very.

Long silence.

I may speak to her?

Weirdo.

I looked at her, my sweet, beautiful thing with her straggly braids and impatient expression.

Mo-om, she said. I'm tired! It's time for bed!

It was an hour before Andi's bedtime. I put up a finger—one moment.

Maybe some day she tell her friends she talk to Nobel laureate.

Make it quick, I said.

Andi accepted the phone with a quizzical look.

Who is this? she said.

I tried to move my ear toward the phone, but Andi turned away and started nodding seriously, as if Romei could see her. Okay, she said finally and handed me the phone.

What did you say to her? I asked.

Andi put her hands on her hips.

Mo-om! she said.

She is very intelligent, this Andrey-a.

I wasn't sure if this was a statement or a question. I assumed the former, though she hadn't said a word. Maybe when dealing with Romei this was a sign of intelligence.

Of course, I said, and looked at her proudly. Very intelligent.

She rolled her eyes again, and plopped onto the bed with a *humph*.

So you may tell me about *Vita Nuova*, please.

Vita Nuova? What do you want to know? and gave Andi a look that said, *Patience, my precious.*

Whatever seem relevant, he said.

Deep breath. Was he testing me? Would I really have to sing for my supper?

Vita Nuova . . . , I said. I'd discoursed on the topic just a few days before, but now, talking with the Great Man, my mind was a blank.

College fund, braces, Barbie Dream Palace.

Vita Nuova poses a number of problems for the conscientious translator . . .

Bah! Romei said. I am caring nothing for this! What is making you feel, this book?

Andi was holding a dress up to her front, a frilly one she knew I hated.

Feel? I asked stupidly. I don't feel anything when I translate.

This I think is not true. I think you are not liking this work.

Devil!

I like it okay.

Miss Greene, if we are to work together we must be making one agreement.

Yes?

Andi was swirling pirouettes, dancing with her frilly dress. I smiled.

Just one minute, I whispered to her.

Full disclosure!

Full disclosure?

Yes! Full disclosure. You don't like this *libello*, is okay! We are friends now, you tell me.

I don't know . . .

You do not like. I know this.

Okay. You're right: I don't like *Vita Nuova*. Dante says his book is about love, but as far as I'm concerned, he knows nothing about love! He never gets close to Beatrice! He stares at her, he worships her, when he's very lucky, she says hello. He's in love with an idea, not a person! Love is something he experiences only in his imagination.

You think love is not something we experience in the imagination?

You know what it reminds me of? I said, ignoring his question. It reminds me of poets who translate other poets, not because they're interested in the original, but because they want to turn it into something that looks like *them*. Dante says his world revolves around Beatrice, but in fact, it revolves around him—his longing, his words, his precious emotions. You can't be faithful if you think only of yourself.

You think fidelity is possible? he asked.

In a translator or a man? I said before I realized what I was saying.

Either, he replied. Both.

Andi was making a show now of picking up her good school dresses one by one with two fingers and letting them drop, like smelly garbage, into the give-away pile.

I shook my head at her and crossed the living room to the study.

You mean absolute fidelity? I asked, as I sat on the loveseat. Pure translation, pure unwavering love? Of course not. There's always a rupture, always an abandonment. The translated one is always betrayed.

Yes, he said. I am reading this essay—how you put it—of the *traduttore/traditore*.

I blushed. He was referring to the essay, published when I quit grad school, in which I railed about the impossibility of translation, the age-old notion that she who translates is both translator and traitor. I waited for the obvious: If you hate Dante and you don't believe in translation, why did I hire you? Instead, he said, And why you think he do this, Miss Greene?

This?

Why you think he not get close to Beatrice?

Is it important?

To me, yes it is.

I think he cares more about his Beatrice poems than he does about Beatrice. He cares about art, not love. *Vita Nuova* is not a romance, it's a manifesto explaining Dante's shift from *lyric* to *narrative*.

I think is not this. He not get close to Beatrice because he is fearful, as you say. Of rupture, abandonment, betrayal. Is simple.

Maybe, I said, though I'd never found psychological analysis all

49

that compelling. And thought: *Fancy words for a guy who speaks only pizza-man English.*

And the new life, Miss Greene? What are you thinking? What is this?

Andi had arrived in the study and was doing jumping jacks in front of the loveseat.

The new life? I asked, trying not to laugh. *Grad students everywhere, footnote on the apex of the ridge of the postmodernist canon.*

Yes, what are you thinking?

It's not clear what Dante means by *new life*, is it? I said. As you know, the Italian words *vita nuova* don't appear anywhere in the text, just the Latin *vita nova*. You remember the first lines: "In that part of the book of my memory before which little can be read, one finds a heading that says, *Incipit vita nova.* Under that heading I find written the words that I intend to transcribe in this little book—if not all, then at least those that are significant."

I recited the lines in Italian, to show him I could.

Some say this new life refers to a sexual or moral awakening in boyhood. Others say it refers to a shift of poetics occurring in mid-life.

Yes, Miss Greene, he said impatiently, but what is your feeling?

My feeling? I asked.

This is what I am asking.

I think we have to credit Dante with his new life precisely when the text announces it, which is to say, when he first encounters Beatrice. But a new life at eight and three-quarters can hardly be new to an author of thirty. Or can it? Can a "new" life span an entire lifetime? What kind of "new life" is that? The new life, we realize, coincides with the onset of memory. Before it, little can be recalled; after, much is remembered. Memory equals awareness of self in time—self plunged into narrative, if you will, self become both object and observing subject. For Dante, then, the new life is nothing less than the life of consciousness—activated by love, empowered by imagination, moderated by reason. Understood this way, a new life experienced in childhood can still be new at mid-life.

Andi stopped jumping and stood over me.

Very interesting, Miss Greene. And what do you think?

I was still congratulating myself on a well-delivered monologue and impressive punchline.

I just told you what I think. What do you mean?

Precisely what I say: What do you think?

What do I personally think about the new life?

This is what I ask.

I think Dante's new life is a fairy tale, something for children to believe in.

I love fairy tales, Andi said, but I don't believe in them.

What do you mean by this? Romei asked.

Dante believes we choose new life: if we're ready to walk the straight and narrow, we can leave our old life behind and achieve salvation. I don't think so. Stuff happens. People get sick, they win the lottery. But they don't change.

You think Dante believe that people change?

Of course! Why else would he switch to story-telling? Lyric poems are about the moment, but stories are about change. Dante changes as a result of his encounters with Beatrice, he becomes a better man, a *salvageable* man, or so he would have us believe.

Look, Mambo, my baby said, bringing her face to mine. I think a tooth is loose. A molar!

GO! I whisper-shouted. *Back to your room!*

Beatrice isn't real, I added, so she doesn't have to change. An idea can be perfect forever.

Andi stomped out of the room.

Very good, Romei said. Thank you. I send tomorrow.

11

SLEEPING WITH
NANCY DREW

I had been talking rather a lot about *Vita Nuova*, but it had been
sixteen years since I'd read it. My copies were all in Ahmad's storage
locker, together with other reminders of times past. It wasn't a place
I liked to visit.

I returned to Andi's room. She was lying on top of her bed, reading Nancy Drew.

We'll finish this later, I said, gesturing at the pile of clothes on the
floor. In the meantime, pajamas.

Mmm, she replied.

I'm going to the basement, I said. Ahmad's home from dinner;
he's in his studio. When I get back, bedtime.

Mmm, my daughter said, so I took a deep breath and the elevator
down to the basement, where I found *Vita Nuova* and my translation together with three binders of notes from a box underneath six
others. Which meant I had to open the other boxes and leaf through
them—college papers so full of critical jargon I couldn't understand
them, mementos from a trip to Greece, matchbooks from my wedding. Divorce decree, receipt from the Delhi hotel where Andi had
been conceived, baby clothes too precious to part with, early drafts of
stories, a topographical map of northern India, the latter a reminder

52

of the road not taken: Dharamsala, my destination *interruptus* when I found myself with child.

In another box: mementos from my freshman year of high school, which I spent in Rome, during my father's second sabbatical. My yearbook, for example, which contained the only photos I had left of T. In his senior picture, he sits, smugly, in a rattan chair, his girlfriend of four years on his lap, even though she didn't go to our school—that's how inseparable they were considered to be. In Lavinia's ears, glinting in the black and white sun, fat diamond earrings, gift of her movie producer papa. In the second shot, candid this time, T. leans against a Roman column smoking a cigarette. You can't see what he looks at through his Ray-Bans—it's off-camera, and away from the ruin that entrances the rest of the class. For years, I hoped it was me he looked at so possessively; I was in that art history class, I was on that field trip, wherever it was. I'll never know, nor will I ever be sure that the boy in the semi-distance, with the floodwater pants and Indian mirrored manbag, is Ahmad, giving T. the evil eye. Ahmad knew about us, somehow; I never knew how.

Also, photos of Ahmad and me that same year. The dynamic duo doing all the great poses: cross-dressing American Gothic, Shira pursing her lips, Ahmad holding a devil's trident. Sistine Chapel redux—our fingers almost touching, Ahmad wearing rubber gloves, Shira's nails painted dark against a bright white sky. Impossibly young, and happy. We didn't know yet how it would be: fighting that spring over T., reconciling after my divorce, words spoken when he blamed me for Jonah's death, reconciling again over Andi. And there she was, our red-faced baby, sleeping in my exhausted arms. Dribbling carrot in her high chair, smiling a demented orange smile, Ahmad behind her, brandishing a spoon. Aunt Emma trying to smile over Andi's stroller, managing only to look disapproving, Andi raising her hands and face to the sky as if blessing the host.

Also, photos I discovered when my father died, too small, their edges white and scalloped, from our first sabbatical—of my father, complacent, Eleanor, my mother, laughing, Shira, seven, wearing an orange Danskin shirt-and-shorts set, distracted always by something outside the frame. My mother, her eyes shaded by cat glasses, wearing a broad-brimmed hat, pointing at the Pantheon; I, crouching at her feet, conversing with pigeons, in the background reading a book, smiling fiercely above a decapitated statue. My father, the photographer, Eleanor his object, I there only incidentally: because her arm encircles me (I seem uncomfortable, suspicious), because I squat in her shadow, privately playing.

There were no photos after that year, no photos after she left us.

Feeling too tender, I carted the volumes, notes, and binders to my study, where I found Tinky Winky sitting on a stack of Italian dictionaries.

Had he been there before?

Are you in exile again? Just like Dante! Look! and I showed him an Italian edition of *Vita Nuova*, a rumpled Garzanti with its outdated bibliography and puzzling snippet of Giotto's *Life of Maria and Life of Christ* on the cover. Inside, an engraving of the Poet in Profile, his arrogant, heavy-lidded expression, his laurel wreath, his ever-present snood.

I know! I said. He's insufferable!

I doodled on Dante's face, gave him bloodshot eyes and pimples. Then tucked him under some secondary sources.

Tink looked at me funny. Not a word from you, I said, and chose a photocopied article, settled back onto the loveseat, a tape recorder balanced on my chest like a kitten. "Dante and the Schoolmen," I dictated. *Domenico da Firenze sees the influence of the Scholastics in Dante's use of . . .* etc.

I read prefaces, afterwords, footnotes, marginalia. I reacquainted myself with debates that raged in the '70s. I read about Dante's politics, his theology and fondness for numbers; I lost myself in criticism structural, post-structural, post-non-denominational. I read everything, in short, but *Vita Nuova* itself.

When I finally thought to look at the time, it was after midnight.

Andi! Oh, no! Was she still awake? I tiptoed into her room, found her sleeping with Nancy Drew. I carefully removed the book from her hand, found her Brooklyn Zoo crocodile bookmark, put the book under her pillow next to her flashlight, in case she woke up and had to read some more.

My dear, my dearest, my sweetest sweetest heart! How could I have forgotten you? Next morning I'd have to pretend I'd done it on purpose, so she could feel her late night was a gift and not evidence of maternal neglect. Gently, I maneuvered her under the covers.

Why is that man my uncle? she said, slipping her thumb into her mouth.

I stifled a laugh, unable to imagine what she must be dreaming.

You have no uncles, I whispered. Good night, precious pumpkin.

I hate pumpkin, my beautiful baby said. I kissed her angel cheek. The bad man did it.

What? Had someone hurt my baby? Then I remembered Nancy Drew.

The perils of late-night reading.

12

SLUMBER PARTY

I returned to the study. Maybe I was ready to try again. I retrieved the book from my pile, this time the English version with the simpering figures on the cover, a Renaissance vision of the supplicant Dante, the celestial Beatrice. My response was visceral: a trembling of the veins, a heaviness of the head.

Life had offered little recompense for the love I'd lost. I was twenty-seven when I learned that T., thief of my heart, had married.

We were in the Village—my father's apartment, I don't remember why. I still imagined new life with that old love—a fairy tale that began in Rome when I was fifteen and danced for him in the chem lab, imagining myself his Salomé. It didn't matter that in high school he was all but engaged to Lavinia, just as, twelve years later, it didn't matter that he lived in D. C. with Diana: I still believed in happily ever after. It was only with me he could *be himself*, he said. Washington was so full of phonies, and Diana—well, there was a limit to what she could understand. It would happen, I still believed. Feelings as strong as ours didn't come out of nowhere.

We made love on the couch that day breathlessly: we didn't make it to a bedroom, we rarely did. After, unclothed, I danced for him, because he asked, because I felt no shame. I was turning a dreamy circle, when I caught a glint of gold.

I stopped short; my hair, which was long then, and innocent, fell into my face.

What's that? I said.

My *love tool!* he laughed, because he thought I was pointing at his thing (as he called it). But no, I was pointing at something far more potent—that *thing* on his finger. His gaze darted guiltily. I saw that he'd meant to take it off, that he'd always taken it off.

Dante was no help: if I'd had a gun, I'd have shot his *thing*—for all those years of subtext, for making me believe what I wanted to believe, which was that we were meant to be. I didn't have a gun, so I attacked him: punching his chest and pulling his long Nordic hair, pounding his ribs and scratching his arms. I even bit his cheek—for all the times I'd been careful to never leave a mark, to never ever leave a mark.

Take *that* to your Princess Di!

He used his tennis arms and elbows to hold me off. I realized he had an erection—my anger was turning him on! Defeated, I let him go, found my father's bathrobe, told him he had to leave.

I didn't want to hurt you, is what he said as I pushed him out the door.

After, something made me look in the White Pages: if he could lie about his marriage, he could lie about anything, and there it was, his name, his address, not in D. C. but New York, the Village, just blocks from my father's apartment.

Every few weeks that dreadful season, I pulled my hair back and walked. I told myself I needed to think and I walked—from the Upper West Side to his tawny, tony townhouse, with its black iron banister, its box of geraniums, its garden the size of three loaves of bread. I stood across the street, under a stunted tree, partially hidden by its piebald leaves, looking for T. through the blinds, trying to understand where I'd gone wrong. I imagined Diana, his virgin hunter, wearing gardening gloves and Land's End chinos, kneeling over that paltry bit of earth; *she,* I knew, could make something grow—why not me?

I was unmoored. The universe, which had seemed benign, ordered, concerned with my future, revealed its indifference. I stopped going to classes, I disconnected my phone, took up smoking, cut my hair with garden shears, stuffed everything that reminded me of him into a garbage bag and, exhausted, allowed it to sit, gaping, on the living room floor. My dissertation, which included the translation and introductory essay, devolved into a disquisition on the impossibility of love, the impossibility of translation, our shameful, *sham-ful* enterprise. I published the essay, what there was of the translation, and married. And never loved again.

Fifteen years later, the lines of Dante's little book still wrapped like ivy around my inability to finish my degree, the collapse of my belief in a life made new by love. How could I return to Dante, how could I entwine myself in his lines, his lies, his lying arms?

I put Dante back in his rightful place at the bottom of the pile and went online. A happy voice advised me that *I Had Mail*. From Benny.

Thanks for coming by!

I'd barely replied when I got an instant message from "Jellyroll_ Baruch": *Bartleby?*

Ahab! I typed back.

Late, isn't it? Don't mommies get up at the crack of dawn?

Sometimes we worry till the crack of dawn.

Andi okay?

She's fine. Why're you up?

Got any flags? he wrote. We could semaphore out the window. Then he "laughed out loud." I enjoyed your visit, he added. Let's not wait another year.

You could call my cell, you know. You wouldn't wake anyone.

There was a pause.

I like writing you, he typed back.

Oh, I said.

Don't think I didn't notice you didn't answer my question before. Do you believe in forgiveness? What do you think it is?

Forgiveness? I wrote. Whence your interest in forgiveness?

It's the month of Elul, he wrote. Our time of reckoning. I tend not to do such a good job—asking for forgiveness, forgiving others. You know the drill. Help a poor Jew out.

Why did Benny think I knew anything about forgiveness? He knew my history, he knew my mother's original sin. Couldn't he let it lie?

My reply: I don't know the drill: I'm an unbeliever. I don't see the point of ritualizing our expiation of guilt. Does fasting make our anger go away? Does saying I'm sorry make anything better? We hurt people, people hurt us—we get over it or we don't. No matter what, we feel bad.

I sent the message, then waited. Benny was thinking, or I'd put him off with my reply.

More, he said.

More?

Yes, please.

If that's true, I wrote, what can forgiveness possibly mean? You pretend a thing didn't happen? You acknowledge that it happened but pretend it doesn't matter? If it matters, then by definition forgiveness isn't possible. If it doesn't matter, what's to forgive?

Silence.

More, he said.

Really?

More. I'm listening.

I thought a moment, then typed:

Dante suggests a three-part technology for penance: Confession (admit your sin), Contrition (feel sorry for what you've done and say so), Satisfaction (make reparation and change your evil ways). This makes sense to me. But I don't think he tells us how to forgive.

More silence. I checked my horoscope. *Change is afoot*, it read, which made me laugh. Was it really a foot? What were its preferences in footwear?

As you point out, Benny eventually replied, there's a lot in our traditions about how to atone, less on how to forgive. Apologies help, but what if the offender isn't sorry, what if the damage is very great?

My point exactly! I wrote. Are you worried about forgiving or being forgiven? Knowing your good sweet nature, I assume it's the former.

You've too high an opinion of your old friend. Or maybe you expect too much of 'persons of the cloth.' We all do things we wish we could undo, no?

I suppose, I typed. My interest in this topic, never strong, was exhausted. Whatever it is, I wrote, I can't believe it's enough to keep you awake.

Did I say it was keeping me awake?

Isn't it?

Maybe.

What is it?

Silence.

Subject for another day, he wrote.

Okay, I replied, wondering why we were "talking" at all.

Sorry, he said. I want you to like me. I can't tell you my faults all at once.

Okay.

There was a pause.

Can I call you?

I thought you liked writing me.

Now I want to hear your voice.

When the phone rang, I was slipping into bed.

You wanna know what I think forgiveness is? Benny asked.

Sure, I said. Not really, I thought.

I think forgiveness is a movement of the heart from our own hurt to that of another.

Meaning?

I can't say it any better than that. Remember the Celan quote from that story you wrote? "When only the nothingness stood between us, we found our way, all the way, to each other?"

Of course, I said, smiling because in just a few days, two people had brought up that story, which I'd thought everyone had forgotten.

That's what my head says, Benny continued, but how to make that leap? Even as I urge my flock to make peace over the High Holidays, I'm stuck. Every year it's the same.

I've been thinking about that quote, too. Weird, huh?

No coincidences. So what do you think?

About forgiveness? Celan talks about meeting halfway across the void of subjectivity, misunderstanding, and depleted language. But he assumes a 'we' who want to meet. Not everyone's willing to make that leap—I don't think I am.

Hmm, Benny said. I didn't know if he was agreeing, disagreeing, or had even heard me.

I yawned into my pillow, turned and stretched my limbs.

You in bed?

I froze.

Kitchen table, why?

He laughed.

I'm not coming on to you! I heard the "rustle of bedclothes," I thought maybe you were tired.

I'm in bed, but I'm okay.

Liar! he said. Fiction writer! What're you wearing?

Benny!

Just kidding! What's keeping *you* up? What're you worried about?

Stuff.

Oh, c'mon! You're not worried that I won't like you! Tell Uncle Benny what's wrong.

The whole Romei thing, I said, thinking, *Simple is good.*

I wish I were there. Then I could tell if you were serious.

Of course I'm serious. But you can't come over.

Benny laughed.

Look, I've got some baggage, I said. *Vita Nuova.* Some not-so-great memories.

A bad reading experience?

Don't make fun of me, I said.

I'm not.

Oh.

Mm, Benny said.

You sound like my shrink, I said.

You have a shrink?

No.

Oh, Benny said, confused.

There was a pause.

You know, he said, I've never experienced New Life. What's it like?

I laughed.

Not what it's cracked up to be!

Would you care to say more?

The New Life takes no prisoners!

What does that mean?

No idea.

This is fun! Benny said. Like a slumber party!

I didn't know guys had slumber parties.

We didn't. But we always wondered what you did at yours.

I'll tell you sometime. It isn't interesting.

Don't tell me then. I like my fantasies intact.

Perhaps because I was tired, I found myself wondering what Benny might fantasize about. Waify would-be artists in torn fishnet stockings, unbuttoning their tie-dyed halter tops, Benny in his skullcap saying whatever blessing one says before a striptease . . .

But really, Benny said. You can't be worried about the translation, right?

I was just talking to Tinky Winky about it, if that's any indication.

Pinkle winkle, Tinky Winky, pinkle winkle, Tinky Winky.

I beg your pardon?

That's what Tinky Winky sings. Don't you watch the show?

You do?

Sure. They live in a chromedome and eat Tubby custard.

You're kidding, right?

I wish I were.

Benny?

I used to be a Big Brother. It was my little brother's favorite show. All he wanted was to watch TV. He said he felt safe on my couch, holding my hand and watching TV.

You're sweet, I said.

I thought you knew, Benny said. So what did Tink say?

If this is the New Life, I want my money back! This is nothing like happily ever after!

Hah! Speaking of which, I read your *Vita Nuova* today. What an odd little book! Probably the most non-Jewish book I've ever read.

Eh?

Well, exile is our defining metaphor, as I'm sure you know. We do small acts of repair, we try to fix the brokenness, but our exile never ends, not until we are collectively redeemed at the End of Days. But for Dante—for all Christians, I suppose—individual pilgrimage is the defining metaphor explaining our life's journey. What did you call it the other day, the straight-line narrative to salvation?

Life as intentional journey toward a redemptive end. The hero-as-pilgrim's journey. Pilgrims' progress, as it were. Backbone of all story.

Maybe that's why I hardly read stories these days, Benny said. Anyway, *Vita Nuova* is chock-a-block with pilgrims, isn't it? The figure of Love dresses in pilgrims' gear, Dante meets different types of pilgrims, pilgrims are everywhere—as if we wouldn't get the point.

You know what *romei* means, right? Pilgrims whose destination is Rome?

He hadn't read his footnotes, apparently. I explained.

Romei sees himself as one of Dante's pilgrims? Benny asked. That most nihilistic of writers thinks he has a journey to make toward a redemptive end?

That's what he thought when he moved to Rome and named himself.

Whoa, Benny said. I had no idea. What was my point?

Least Jewish book you'd ever read.

Right! We don't have that straight line.

We? I asked.

We Jews, Benny said. Or is it us Jews?

It's *you* Jews, remember? I don't count.

I Jews, then. *I* Jews got the spiral. Moses never made it to the Promised Land.

You're not making sense, I said. What's the spiral?

I'm getting sleepy.

Oh, no! Tell me about the spiral!

Benny pretended to snore, honking into the receiver like a cartoon pig.

You're thinking of Yeats' gyre? I asked. His spiral staircase? Nietzsche's theory of eternal return? They weren't Jewish. Freud's return of the repressed?

I want *you* to tell *me* a spiral story, Benny said. Otherwise I'm going to bed.

Oh, no! I said. Stay up with me and talk about narrative line!

What good are you? Benny mumbled.

G'night then, I said.

Don't let the bedbugs bite.

You're not going to make me get off first, are you? I said, and we agreed to hang up on the count of three. I smiled into my pillow. But sleep? No. I was thinking about straight lines and spirals, exiles and pilgrims, redemption within reach and ever deferred. Were there any pilgrims left, I wondered, journeying with confidence toward a happily ever after? Weren't we all homebodies now, couch potatoes eschewing narrative? I had been, till I heard Romei's irresistible call. Or maybe we were exiles, as Benny said, running from chapter to chapter, chasing an endless spiral (which went where, exactly?). Or refugees pushed by plot points out of our comfy chairs, no noble destination except away-from-here?

What would that narrative look like, I wondered—the narrative of the passive, the buffeted, the confused? Not heroic. I thought of the irony of Dante-the-homebody writing about a pilgrimage of the soul in *Vita Nuova*, then Dante-the-exile a few years later, pushed out of Florence, writing about Dante-the-pilgrim in the *Comedy*. The irony, too, of Romei the exile turning to heroic narrative.

There would be no sleep tonight. I put my father's bathrobe on and set some water to boil. Then returned to the study with some PT. It was three in the morning and I was sipping tea, my hair a fright about my head, taking notes about Dante's straight line to salvation, his meaningful march toward The End, that great resolution in the sky—and checking lines, first one, then another—and why not begin at the beginning? Next thing I knew, I was reading the thing. The dreaded *Vita Nuova*.

You know what? I didn't collapse. Dante's *libello* didn't reach its razor edges into my soft, my throbbing heart. I wasn't overcome by memories—of T., of romantic failure, the loss of love. I didn't think of the past at all. I thought about Romei's work, excited to get to it.

Go figure.

Tink, balanced on my pyramid of books, just stared at me.

I told you so, he seemed to say.

13

TECHNICAL DIFFICULTIES

On Monday, I was putting away laundry and explaining to Super-Temps that an opportunity had arisen that required me to suspend relations with their fine establishment—temporarily, that is, till Y2K—when I heard the low hum-whir of the fax across the apartment. Anon! It had arrived! I did a little dance, right there in front of the linen cabinet, something between a *hora* and the pogo.

You sure the aliens aren't making you queen of Venus? Durlene asked.

They haven't been in touch, I said.

If so, I'll have to leave you to it.

No need to leave me to it, I said.

My best bookkeeper is waiting for the Second Coming in a potato field, she said.

Silence from the study. Paper jam? I dropped a stack of tea towels back into the laundry basket and brought the phone to the fax.

You sign with someone else? Durlene asked. What did they offer? We'll match their rate, more or less.

I lifted the pages from the tray. Ten pages, numbered in fine European lettering. The A4 size, slightly longer, more narrow than our standard letter. Strange in my hand, that unfamiliar shape.

Ten pages, there were no more.

I got a job through a friend, I said, jerking open the paper tray and checking for jams.

A friend, Durlene said. Is that a euphemism for competitor?

I'd never sign with anyone else, I said. Now as to the question of my hourly rate . . .

Ten pages? Maybe Romei was having technical difficulties. Maybe I was having technical difficulties. I unplugged the fax, plugged it in again.

Shira? Are you there? Mr. Ferguson was quite upset.

Why?

You quit without notice! Durlene said. Look, I'm authorized to offer you an additional twenty-five cents an hour.

The fax whirred and hummed but there were no more pages. I plopped onto the velveteen loveseat, pages on my lap.

Fifty cents, Durlene said. That's my final offer.

•

Ten pages. I didn't know what to make of that.

I put a Pop Tart in the toaster, then went to visit the Flying Girl.

The Flying Girl was Ahmad's most treasured possession, drawn by Jonah the day he died. I often snuck into the studio to see her. She flew above a light-soaked table, in a drawing of Jonah's mother pointing (with a chicken bone) at a childlike me, floating over his mother's head like an angel: fourteen-year-old Shira leaping for a volleyball.

I'd immortalized Jonah's drawing of the flying girl in "Tibet, New York," a story I wrote about Jonah's last weekend.

I don't understand, I said, sitting cross-legged before her like a devotee. Is Romei testing me? He's in an almighty hurry, but he only sends ten pages? Am I translating on spec?

Sometimes the Flying Girl spoke cryptically; today she just said, You're dropping crumbs! Ahmad won't like that!

Oops.

Have you looked at the pages? she asked.

Not exactly, I said.

You're fearful, she said.

Never!

You know I'm right.

I knew she was right.

I needed courage. Because now that the pages were here, it was obvious: I would fail. I'd be revealed as the dilettante, the fraud I knew myself to be—an unworthy, pretending to be People of the Book. Romei would find someone else—a poet, someone with a track record. His former translators—a dashing Poet Laureate, a fashionable translator of literary theory—were dead, but surely they'd been survived by folks more qualified than I!

Normally I could turn to Ahmad for a pick-me-up. He'd understand. But he was cranky, for some reason, on the subject of Romei: I wasn't in the mood for another lecture about the UN. My best girlfriend Jeanette should have been good for a pep talk, but she wasn't talking to me.

Look out the window, the Flying Girl said. Your answer's right there.

Benny? I whispered.

Silly rabbit! she said. Go!

14

SECOND COMING

It had been two and a half decades since I was lyricist for the proto-punk band Gory Days (*What's behind Door Number Two? It had better not be you, you, you!*). In our Den of Propinquity, we listened to *qawwali* and Raffi, but sometimes when I was alone I played the band's one cassette—the relentlessly pornographic *Second and Third Coming*—tapping my tambourine ironically against my thigh. When I entered People of the Book, and heard that Benny's raga had been replaced by a grunge band I didn't recognize, I felt old. I also felt like pulling my ear drums out with my fingernails.

And there she was, our sleepy connoisseur of noise, head resting on a pile of lit mags. Snoring, her hair no longer green but red, white, and blue. Dreaming up her next billboard, I was sure.

Hello! I shouted in her ear. When she didn't respond, I went behind the counter and switched CDs: out with the Bloody Monkeys, in with Nikhil Banerjee.

Hey! Marie said, lifting her head. Who said you could do that?

I'm looking for Benny. He around?

No, she said, and put her head back down.

Yo! Girlie! Look at me!

Marie looked up, confused. I could see her T-shirt now: cotton-candy pink with glittered words: All-American Girl—which I guess explained the star-spangled hair.

Where is he? It's important.

Out, she said, blinking.

I took out my cell phone and called Benny. I could hear the phone ringing in the Annex, then I heard Benny—in stereo, as it were.

Sleeping Beauty says you're out, I said, glaring at Marie, who was upright now and pinching her cheeks. Benny laughed and walked down the stairs.

Wanna share the joke with the rest of the class? I said, putting my phone away.

Benny introduced us. I was a "talented writer," Marie an "innovative artist."

Grab a table, he said. I'll be with you in a sec.

As I started toward Benny's ad hoc café, I heard him say: You okay, pumpkin?

To borrow my daughter's language: it made me want to puke.

Then, heaven help me, the girl began to cry.

•

It was ten long minutes before Benny made his way to the table.

You didn't say anything, did you? he asked.

What could I have said? She said you were out.

She's on some new meds. They're making her sensitive.

Whatever, I thought, unsure why she should stir such emotions—in either of us, for I hadn't mistaken the look in his eye.

Two visits in two days! he said. To what do I owe the pleasure? That it? he asked, and walked two fingers toward my folder. I pulled it away.

You can't, can you? he asked.

Not really.

But maybe you can tell me what you think? Broad impressions?

I, uh, haven't read it yet.

Benny raised his shaggy eyebrows.

I was on my way to Joe's, I said. I was going to read it there.

And somehow you ended up here?

To buy presents, I said. For Andi, and Ahmad.

Presents?

Books.

I guessed that. You have Romei's first work in I don't know how many years and you're buying presents?

Something like that.

Hmm, Benny said, grinning.

What's so funny?

What are you getting them?

I was hoping you'd suggest something.

I have a new *Selected Poems* by Pessoa that Ahmad would like and, uh, three dozen Nancy Drews to pick from for Andi. Ahmad's been buying them in alphabetical order, so if you start with the last book you should be safe . . .

The last book being?

The Witch Tree Symbol . . .

You don't know that!

I do, he said.

I laughed.

But what a cad I am! he said, rising. Would you like some ginger beer?

Sure, sweetie, that would be nice.

Benny raised his eyebrows again. *Sweetie?* he seemed to ask. I gave him a look that said, *Term of endearment, goofball.* And blushed, damn my susceptible cheeks.

•

While Benny got the ginger beer, I got the books, and congratulated myself on a win-win excuse. Andi and Ahmad deserved to share in my good fortune. I threw in a Pessoa bio and *The Wild Cat Crime* for good measure.

Benny returned with bottles and bendable straws, Marla following.

You can't tell me about the work, he said, but you can tell me how you'll go about it, right? I've translated a few poems here and there, but I can't say I have a method. I'll bet you do.

Marla had jumped onto Benny's lap and was now batting his beard lazily with her paw.

You want to know my method? he said.

Is that weird?

I laughed.

I use a Buber-Rosenzweig *leitwort* approach, I said. Not as fancy as it sounds. When Buber and Rosenzweig translated the Bible into German, they always translated the same word the same way. They didn't look for "pleasant-sounding" variations; they didn't translate "according to context." "White" didn't become "cream" so it could rhyme with . . .

Bream.

Exactly. Words echoed the way words are supposed to, like leitmotifs in music.

Benny was smiling.

What? I asked.

I know Buber, he said. I know Rosenzweig.

Sorry, I said, blushing again. Of course you do.

Marla by now was curled into herself and sleeping, a purring ouroboros.

You used this approach for Dante? he asked.

I caught flak for it in grad school, I said. You get stuck with certain words, which means sometimes you sacrifice sound or rhythm. Everyone's all into Dante's "sweet style," so they had a problem with this. I thought it was worth it: words repeat in *Vita Nuova*, and when they do, they become more meaningful. Take the word "pilgrim," like you mentioned last night—*peregrino*. *Vita Nuova* is full of pilgrims, right?

The *romei*, among others.

Exactly. There's even a pilgrimming spirit! These images concentrate toward the end of the book, leading Dante to his final vision, which points him toward the path he must take—as a sort of pilgrim himself. But remember that earlier, when Love offers dubious advice about which path Dante should take, he does so in the guise of a pilgrim, forcing us, if we remember that image, to compare encounters and decide which path is best. We can't do this if the earlier pilgrim is translated as "traveler," as often he is.

Benny was smiling again.

I haven't seen you so *intent* since that first time I heard you read! At Trixie's! I said.

The reading had been part of a short-lived series at a macrobiotic café, organized by my former writers' group (The Purple People Eaters). It had to be Trixie's because my first reading had also been my last. Before I went to India, before Andi.

A banner day, Benny said, presumably because that's when we met. But it's getting late, he said, standing. Fascinating as this is, I gotta go.

Or you'll turn into a pumpkin? I thought, then remembered: there was only one pumpkin in this room.

Maybe you'll come in again tomorrow, and the day after? he said, leaning down to kiss my cheek. My heart lurched just a tiny bit, silly thing. I looked past Benny at Marie who, fully awake now, gave me the finger.

Shall I tell you what I did behind my friend's back?

I shan't.

15

THRESHOLD

I sat down in Slice of Park to look over Romei's pages for the first time. Prose and poems in more or less expected proportion. The pages clean, double-spaced, no typos or handwritten insertions. A subheading on page one: "The Call."

Odd.

"The Call"? As in my essay, which Romei had read—he'd said so. Was he borrowing my idea? No one else I knew of had compared *Vita Nuova* to the hero's journey, or maybe it was coincidence.

The first pages of *Vita Nuova* recount Dante's call to love. His first vision of the eight-year-old Beatrice (in delicate crimson) causes his spirits—vital, sensual, natural—to exclaim (again in Latin): *Ecce deus fortior me, qui veniens dominabitur mihi!* "Here is a god, more powerful than I, who comes to rule me." This god being Love, the not-always-reliable mentor who accompanies Dante through much of his journey.

Nine years later, Dante again encounters Beatrice. This time she greets him, which so overwhelms him, he has to retire to his room. Thinking of her, he falls asleep and has a vision: Love—a terrifying figure!—force-feeds Dante's burning heart to a semi-comatose Beatrice, then carries her off to heaven. This time Dante's call to love prompts him to write; he crosses that threshold by writing a sonnet

74

(about Beatrice eating his burning heart) and sending it ("anonymously") to poets of note. His response, in other words, is to become A Poet. What would be Romei's "call," I wondered, and what his response?

I went to Joe's to find out.

PART THREE

DECEPTION

16

A MOST SPIRITUAL COMMUNION

Joe made me a double, offered it to me with a wink. I stepped over his infant twins, who were crawling among the regulars like puppies, begging sweets. I smiled at the Old Jewish Couple, the corpulent actor, removed the *Reserved* card from a front window table, and nodded at the boutique lady, who looked smashing in her painted silk blouse, and the Barnard student, absorbed in her Gramsci.

I looked at Romei's pages more carefully. They seemed to correspond with the first four "chapters" of *Vita Nuova*, chapters that comprise a mere six pages in my Italian edition. In these opening pages, Dante promises to transcribe events from his "book of memory"; Romei instead says he'll rely on the "book of the mirror." I guess this meant he'd look at his past *subjectively*. Not a radical or even an interesting claim.

But he also said he'd "write of her that which has never been written of any other." Now that was interesting, for it is with these words that Dante *ends* his tale. By making this promise up front, Romei says: Sorry, Dante, the superior poetic has arrived and it is mine. In saying so, he challenges Dante to a duel, naming me, of all people, as his second—to watch his back, tend his wounds, and bear witness to his victory.

I considered getting a chocolate bomb, decided against it. Instead

I left my belongings on the table, and ran across to the Love Drugstore to get a hard-backed notebook.

Door Number Two: Notes for a New Life, is what I wrote on its
cover. And on page one: "The Call." Then I shut the notebook and
began to read.

•

The first thing we learn about Romei in "The Call" is that he's blocked:
he can't write. He's wandering through Rome, regretting the emptiness of his mind, the impermanence of his income, when he sees,
is struck out of his self-absorption by, Esther in the park. She sucks
delicately on a finger, is absorbed in a notebook, the sun streams down
onto her bobbed brown hair.

Romei suffers often from unrequited love: there are women all
over Rome with whom he cannot bring himself to speak. In Esther,
however, he senses a weakness (*una debolezza*) that makes it possible
for him to approach, a helpless carnality, a vulnerability that finds
expression in tentative gestures, a tendency to put hands to face. He
stands over her, blocking the sun (rather as, in my story, Paul Celan
stood over my young protagonist Rose). Gold shines from her bright
brown eyes.

What are you writing? he asks, in English.

A translation, she replies. *Song of Songs*, in her spare time, something in rather short supply (she gestures toward a child flying circles
in the grass). Her expressions are particular, unforgettable. She has few
perfections, yet somehow her parts—her fleshy nose and thick ankles,
her sweater set (a Beatrice-inflected crimson), her chewed fingernails
and readiness to satisfy his curiosity—add up to a compelling whole.
Modest, yet direct; anxious, yet eager to please; decorous, yet wanton.

Why does she do this? Romei wants to know.

It's the only thing she knows how to do, she says, as if apologizing.

Why the *Song of Songs*?

Because it's the greatest love poem ever written, she says. Mutual,
mysterious. Embodied and erotic, suggestive of a most spiritual com-
munion (*comunione*, with all its religious undertones).

80

I don't remember that, he says. In fact, he's never read the *Song*. The priests of his childhood forgot to mention it, and as an adult he finds himself drawn to classical and medieval verse. Esther intuits his ignorance, "reminding" him that the *Song* concerns the innocent, impassioned love of a man and a woman.

Here, she says, placing pages on her knee, I'll show you. You read the part of the boy. I'll read the part of the girl.

He stands there stupidly.

I have not guarded my vineyard, she says.

He sits down quickly, close enough to read, approaching her "threshold," or so he says.

My dove, hiding in the shadow of the rock, he replies. *Let me see the sight of you, for your voice entices me. You are lovely to behold.*

They continue, "the lover, the king" and his "sister-bride," sitting ever closer on their bench, becoming drunk on poetry, seduced, the narrator says, much as Paolo and Francesca, swirling in the winds of Dante's *Inferno*, were seduced by tales of adultery.

Pretty story, the child murmurs, falling asleep at their feet.

One imagines one knows what will happen next: Romei will *cross* Esther's threshold—but in fact, we don't know: this was all he'd sent.

•

I returned home, presents in hand, to find Ahmad reading a fat Indian novel on the couch, Andi leaning into him, reading a Nancy Drew. I was reminded, not for the first time, of their resemblance—not just their brown skin and shiny black hair, but their bright, smart eyes, their quick features and watchful expressions. I smiled, remembering how Aunt Emma, my father's sister, had listened to the story of how I'd met Andi's father in Delhi, looked back and forth between Andi and Ahmad, as if to say, You can't kid a kidder.

My family, my beautiful family!

Ahmad's sons thought him a monster, or so he'd been told—he wasn't allowed to see them, not that he went back to Pakistan much. When the youngest is eighteen, he said vaguely, he'd get in touch. They'd understand: a parent never stops loving his child.

Until that time, I thought, he has us. He'll always have us.

You saved me, he said more than once. You saved *me*, was my standard reply, taking us in when I was pregnant—but it was more than that.

My father and I had waited for my mother at the airport, ready to return home after our first sabbatical in Rome. She must have been delayed, he said, white-faced. We'll get on the plane, she'll be on the next one for sure. At Kennedy, a light snow falling, we met the next flight, and the next.

I'd thought all losses permanent till Ahmad came back into my life.

I walked up behind him and kissed the top of his head.

Thank you, I whispered. Thank you.

17

TRADUTTORE/TRADITORE

It was raining the next morning when I took Romei's pages back to Cuppa Joe's and read them again, this time as a translator.

I'd once loved translation, before I got all complicated about it. Weighing poetic elements, deciding which to highlight, which to sacrifice—because not everything can survive translation. The eleven-syllable Italian line doesn't transfer easily to our English pentameter: you'd think it would exceed the capacity of our ten-syllable line but, being syllable rich, Italian condenses at the rate of four English feet per line. What's a translator to do? Preserve the length of the original line by padding the translation? Sacrifice meter for concision, semantic accuracy, the original line breaks? It's something of a lose-lose situation. Hence the age-old notion that she who translates is both translator and traitor: *traduttore e traditore*.

Over my computer I've taped a quote from Nabokov, who knew something of the chasm between languages, and strongly preferred the "literal" to the "literary": "I want translations with copious footnotes," he wrote, "footnotes reaching up like skyscrapers to the top of this or that page so as to leave only the gleam of one textual line between commentary and eternity. I want such footnotes and the absolutely literal sense, with no emasculation and no padding—I want such sense and such notes for all the poetry in other tongues that still languishes in 'poetical' versions, begrimed and beslimed by rhyme."

Indeed!

At Joe's, I identified two questions I'd need to think about. First, Romei's *Song of Songs* fragments: had he played with the original? I had no idea. I'd have to consult some English Bible translations. Then there was the matter of Romei's first poem. If Dante's first poem describes a dream (in which Love feeds Dante's heart to Beatrice), Romei's describes a wet dream: his inkless pen, refilled by Esther, explodes onto the page in the form of a self-fulfilling prophecy (a sonnet about an inkless pen refilled, exploding). I'd have to check, but I was sure it had been fashioned out of fragments of Romei's earlier work, recast here out of context as something new.

His "pen," for example (his *penna*, or *quill*) was free-floating in the earlier poems, never associated with anything other than itself (*penna qua penna*); now it resonated: it meant pen, but also *wing*, the poet's words, the *uomo di penna* (the man of letters), even the poet himself, as in Italian, *penna* can be a figure for *writer*. *Penna, penna, penna*. Dante's birds fly with plural wings (*penne*), but in Romei, one might well ask: What is the sound of one *penna* flying—maybe the sound of Icarus *spennar* (defeathered) and falling?

How I wanted Benny's opinion! I looked out of Joe's window, hoping to see Benny on the street. Then I could "run into him," let something slip.

Bad girl.

But I *would* need Benny, wouldn't I? He could tell me about the *Song*! He knew everything there was to know about the Bible. His rates would be reasonable: a single vegan donut oughta do it.

It had stopped raining. I gathered my books and papers, waved goodbye to Joe, and rushed to the Den, where I emailed Benny and faxed Romei: I need a Bible consultant, Benny's a Hebrew scholar, could I possibly show him Romei's work?

Did I specify that I only wanted to discuss a few lines? Why split hairs?

18

REAL PEOPLE

After dinner, Andi staged a Miss America pageant for her dolls. Ahmad played Bob Barker (in the left corner, weighing in at a sturdy seven ounces, is . . . *Julie*? Julie is a corn husk doll from the Indian Plains. She likes to water-ski and . . . *what*? Make brownies! Please welcome *Julie*!). As judge of this solemn entertainment, I tried not to laugh as Tink and her teddies strutted their stuff down a Wheaties-box catwalk.

When my phone rang, I didn't want to answer.

Romei didn't say hello: He just wanted to know, did I get the first pages? What did I think? He was calling from Rome, there was a strange delay in his responses.

Why would the Great Man care about my opinion?

Time for a station identification, I whispered.

What do you mean what do I think? I asked, buying time as I slipped into Andi's room. I only got ten pages. What happened to the rest?

I send you the first part; the rest is not finish.

Not finished? How could he know the beginning if he hadn't written the ending? He'd hired a translator before he'd even finished the work? I didn't believe him. He was testing me, just as I thought, prepared to cut his losses!

So what are you thinking? he asked.

As it happened, I'd scribbled my "thinking" in my Door Number Two notebook just that afternoon.

As best I can tell, I said, your object is to write a mature, post-exilic love story, an inversion of Dante's youthful, *pre*-exilic fantasy. Undoubtedly, you hope to define an ultimate poetic, a poetic perhaps related to love, or perhaps to eros, more broadly defined. Indeed, the tension between Dante's *narcissistic* form, concerned with the solitary writing subject and the inaccessible love object, and Esther's interest in a mutual, embodied passion, where the beloved co-authors the text, as it were, is established early and suggests a competing poetics, a dialectic which I assume will be resolved by the end of the book.

I looked up. Ahmad had poked his head into the room.

Real people don't talk like that, he whispered, then left the room. Silence.

I took a breath and sat down on Andi's bed.

And the story? he asked. What are you thinking?

What do you mean?

Are you interesting in this?

Was I interested in his story? As it happened, I wasn't. I suspected the author's purpose to be self-serving: the world should forgive him for breaking up a marriage. Assuming the world cared—and I didn't think it did. I certainly didn't.

I'm reserving judgment, I said. The characters don't seem quite real.

He made a sound like a snort. I tried to explain: Why would a lovely stranger initiate erotic play-acting in a park? Was the narrator that irresistible? By his own admission he wasn't. Would she turn out to be something other than a projection of the narrator's erotic fantasies?

I knew I was talking about his wife, but I couldn't help myself: "Esther" and the narrator were characters in a work of art. It wasn't my job to "like" them, or pretend they were real!

This is the response of a spinster, Miss Greene. You think I give one fig for poetics? You are not the reader you think you are. I call again in one week.

And he was gone.

Fuck him! I thought, and pounded Andi's guilt quilt with my fist. *Where does he get off talking to me like that!*

He called me a bad reader! *Me?!* A bad reader!

What had I missed? I hadn't missed anything. Had I?

No! I thought. Real people don't talk like that! Real people have it out, they say what they mean! If he thinks I've missed something, he should say so!

Spinster! He called me a spinster?

I'd had my share of affairs, but I didn't bring them home, I didn't allow them to become Andi's concern. Andi came first for me, always, which was maybe why I disliked Esther: her happy ending was decided, but what would happen to the child as Esther played out her mutual, her embodied, her co-authored passion?

Spinster? I *was* a spinster. What of it?

19

MORNING PEOPLE

I slept too few hours, got up to see Andi off to camp, then fell back asleep. I woke up again some time later, found Ahmad still in his bathrobe.

When I became a mother, I'd had no choice but to become a morning person; Ahmad never quite made the transition. His mornings with Andi, he was usually silent (hair on end, pajama bottoms inside out), no doubt to spare us his ill humor.

Late night? he asked.

Romei had called me a bad reader. I'd stayed up half the night trying to prove him wrong. I reread his pages and *Vita Nuova*, then read them again. My opinion hadn't changed. No need to explain this to Ahmad, no need to tell him he might be right about Romei.

Besides, he looked barely awake. I lifted his wrist and looked at his watch.

Ten? Don't you have a department meeting?

I called in sick.

Ahmad never called in sick, not even when he was sick. I waited.

Mirabella's been in touch.

Mirabella? I asked, leaning over to put a hand on his shoulder. It had been ten years since his ex-wife, forced by her brothers, had taken their sons from the U.S. to Karachi.

He explained.

Though in *purdah*, Mirabella had gained access to the Internet

88

through her cousin Shamseh, who'd finagled a laptop from her parents, saying she wanted to write *ghazals* for her fiancé, Jamal. Her younger brother had hooked her up to the Internet—her parents had no idea. Shamseh now had pen pals all around the world, she visited chat rooms disguised as Fork, the nongendered performance artist; Geraldine, the day trader; Lola, the Lesbian Leather Girl—all genres she'd become familiar with on the Net. A disciplined woman, she downloaded Shakespearian sonnets, spent one hour each day translating them into passable Urdu, then presented them to her parents, who planned to have them printed on vellum as a gift for Jamal.

No one seemed to recognize that they weren't, strictly speaking, *ghazals*.

Young Shamseh, aware that Mirabella had experience of the world, confided her several secrets—the existence of the Internet portal, her increasing conviction that she was not exactly *normal*. Mirabella, intoxicated with the thought of escaping *purdah*, however briefly, told Shamseh she thought her desires entirely normal, aligned with Allah's plan for the world, there were plenty of girls like her in the West, yes, it was true what they said about Ahmad, but he was a good man, God-fearing in his own way. Though of course she thought Shamseh an abomination.

In time, as Shamseh shared her correspondence with a certain Glenda, who didn't know that "Lola" was a Pakistani in *purdah*, promised to a man twice her age, Mirabella even came to wish her well. I think I love her, Shamseh said, referring to Glenda, black kohl tears slipping down her cheeks. What's wrong with me?

Mirabella found Ahmad on the Web. She was surprised to learn that he was no longer at the think tank: he'd become an academic! And here was Hassan, their oldest, about to finish secondary school! Not even her family's connections could get him into university. But in the U.S., *insh'Allah*, he could go to college, maybe the university at which Ahmad taught. She would appeal to her brothers: Hassan *had* to continue his education, how else could he make a name for himself? Ahmad would pay for it—it was his obligation as a father, the least he could do after the shame he'd brought them. The boy was a good Muslim: he wouldn't be swayed by his father's perversions.

Her plan: Hassan would go to the U.S. first, then the others. They would stay, Mirabella could visit and eventually stay on herself. Her sons would be of age, no one could make them go back. Maybe she could even send for Shamseh. Would Ahmad help? Would he pay for the boy's college?

It took Mirabella all night to work up to this request. First, she wrote about the boys—Ahmad's first news of them in a decade (the youngest was a squash player, the middle favored Ahmad's father, and so on). She said her brothers had intercepted her letters; Ahmad didn't believe her, but said he'd do what she asked—*if* Hassan lived with him during school vacations.

You're kidding! I said.

Ahmad shook his head.

The bitch is using me, of course. I'll let her, because my ends justify her means. But she's desperate—she'll pursue this plan . . .

Even if it means breaking your heart all over again, I said.

Well put. I have no way of knowing if a reunion with Hassan is likely or impossible. And this was three days ago!

I'm sure it'll work out, I said. Why wouldn't it? I put my arms around my best friend's neck and kissed his hair, silky like that of a child. He clasped my hands in his cold, dry fingers and kissed them back.

Do you ever think our decisions too costly? he asked.

Don't you ever think that! I said, moving around so he could see my face. Ever! You are the bravest person I know! You did exactly what you needed to do.

I'm a role model, I know.

Look at me, I said. You *are* a role model! Your sons would be proud to know you! They *will* be proud to know you!

Ahmad just shook his head and left the room.

20

WITHOUT YOU, WHO KNOWS

The next afternoon I received another fax from Romei: I attach the next section. You may share with Mr. Benny but I pay him no fee. Please fax the first. Also photo of your little daughter.

Fax the first? I'd just gotten it three days before! Was he mad? He wanted Andi's photo? How strange was that? But I had permission to work with Benny, so I gathered my King James, Romei's pages, my *Door Number Two: Notes for a New Life* notebook, and went to Joe's, where I bought a half dozen vegan donuts, tithing one to Nate, who bowed.

Before going into the bookstore, I stopped at Benny's side display. Customers who guessed its organizing principle (talking animals, revisionist gothic) got free stuff, usually a book from the display. Today? Millennial madness.

Marie's hair was a cornflower blue, to match her corduroy overalls, and braided in two tight braids that stuck out over her shoulders. On her nose she'd penciled blue freckles; from her ears dangled blue-tinted condom earrings—handy in an emergency, I guessed.

He in?

Who? she replied. I controlled the urge to slap her.

Benny.

No, she said, and returned to her word find.

I smiled and walked toward the steps, looking over my shoulder to catch the defeat in her eyes, but she was immersed, scratching her forehead with sky-blue fingernails.

Benny wasn't in his annex. Too embarrassed to return directly downstairs, I entered the office, thinking to leave him a note, taking care not to trip on the boxes that surrounded his desk. On the walls, photos of *Gilgul* alumni, many famous now, no longer in need of Benny's tender mercies. Also a few like me who'd missed the posterity bus.

The desk took up most of the room. Benny had found it in the Garment District—it had a built-in ruler along its front for measuring bolts of cloth, and was covered with invoices and order forms and oversize Hebrew books, their titles stamped in gold on leather bindings. Also a newish-looking copy of *Vita Nuova*, an industrial stapler and, in the back, an ancient computer with a scrolling screensaver that read, *Breathe! Breathe!* On top of the keyboard, my email, printed out, with the words *Shir haShirim* written on top.

Benny was doodling my name?

I was saved the embarrassment of searching for other evidence of interest by the plaintive mewling of a kitten. One of Marla's brood, hidden by Marla for reasons of her own, and forgotten. For a cat with so much practice, Marla was one lousy mother. I put the donuts down and searched between boxes, in boxes, and finally under Benny's desk . . . where amid the dust bunnies and crumpled bits of paper, a decaying cherry pit and something that might have been mouse droppings, I saw a photo propped against the wall, of two fat men laughing, their arms around each other. I reached for it, looked at it in the light.

Topeka.

Benny was wearing the black beret he'd favored during his Santa Claus phase; Romei was holding a book in the air as if it were a trophy. In purple ink in the right-hand corner, an inscription:

To Jellyroll,
Without you, who knows?
Yours, Romei

I didn't notice if Marie watched me as I left.

92

21

GHOST IN THE ANNEX

Benny called. Strange, he said. I seem to have a ghost in my annex.

Why didn't you tell me you knew Romei? I asked. On my way home I'd slammed his millennial madness window with my hand, which earned me jeers from the boom box–bearing boys in Slice of Park.

It *was* you! Benny said. Donuts are a novel calling card, but you might have left a note.

Why didn't you tell me you knew Romei?

I published his first English translations in *Gilgul*—I thought you knew.

Why would he think I knew that?

Why would you think I knew that?

Didn't I say?

Never mind, I said. For some reason, Benny wasn't telling me the truth.

Isn't that why you asked me about him?

Never mind, I said.

Where did you find the photo?

I didn't answer. It had been so plainly hidden under the desk. And recently: the photo was clean despite the dust bunny convention. I thought about this a moment and hung up. Fuck him.

When the phone rang again, I let it go to voicemail.

We seem to have been cut off, Benny said in his message. Or

maybe not. Listen, I published Romei long before he was famous. We can talk about *Shir haShirim* whenever you want—I've put together some commentaries and . . . Oh, shit, he said, and hung up.

Shir haShirim—it wasn't a play on my name! I should have known. *Shir* was *song*—I knew that: Benny's name for me was *shir chadash*, new song. *Shir haShirim* was the *Song of Songs*. I'd thought Benny had been doodling my name, when in fact he'd been lying— about what I couldn't guess.

He knew Romei. No wonder Romei had asked him for my number. He wasn't just an editor who'd published my stories, he was Romei's dear friend, without whom who knows!

I have a problem with duplicity. If I'd been Dante's wife, I'd have kicked him out the minute I got wind of Beatrice. What's a second chance but license to repeat the offense?

I splashed water on my face, grabbed my purse, and slammed out the door. Real people have it out, they say what they mean! I'd give Benny what-for. I'd been happy to have him in my life again, but I couldn't imagine what he might say to convince me to stick around.

He didn't have to: through his window I could see the back of his cherry-red bodysuit, his arms wrapped around Lila-cum-Marie, who sat facing me on the counter like a child, her short legs entwined around Benny's waist, her flat eyes looking at me over his shoulder. Her expression didn't change, or maybe she smiled.

What was I to do? Interrupt them? Pretend I didn't see? Would Marie tell him I'd been there? I didn't think so. I'd never mention it—what would I say? I chose not to enter your store because I realized you were boffing your salesgirl? So I moved on, in the direction of Cohn's Cones, as if that had been my destination all along.

So what if Benny wanted the narcoleptic Marie, with her tragically torn fishnet stockings and her Pop Tart art, what concern was that of mine? So what if he wanted to be with someone whose firm, young body helped him forget he was hurtling like a locomotive toward death, what did I care?

Idiot.

22

THE ALL-IMPORTANT
COUPLET

I woke up Friday to find more pages from Romei and an email from
Benny:

*I have the feeling I've angered you. I'd like to apologize, but I don't
know what I've done. This happens rather a lot: please give me another
chance. I've enjoyed having you around. Call before sundown if you can.*

Yeah right, I thought, and shut off my computer.

That afternoon, we witnessed Andi's camp graduation. Ahmad
gave her a Nancy Drew, wrapped in silver paper, which made me angry—we'd joked about the silliness of *camp graduations*. He also said
he'd cook a special Friday Night Dinner.

To recapture ground, I offered to take Andi to the park. She asked
if she could get ice cream, and pointed east across Broadway, between
the Love Drugstore and the Dollar Store.

Huh? I said, since Cohn's Cones was north. This place was new:
Nice Cream. Damned if I could remember what had been there before.

Can we, Mom? Can we? Andi tugged my arm.

It was a stinky, sticky end-of-summer day, the kind that insults
you with its heat, so Andi may have had a point, had she not had cake
and cookies and stevia-sweetened brownies at camp. Knowing that
the you-don't-want-to-spoil-your-dinner argument didn't cut it with

Andi, who always wanted to spoil her dinner, I said, You can't swing and hold ice cream at the same time, right?

She considered this, then nodded in sage agreement. Then, as I tried to remember whether that particular play on words, *Nice Cream*, had a name—or *Cohn's Cones*, for that matter—she told me about someone named Ovidio. A boy nobody wanted, not his father, not his mother. He lived with an auntie who wouldn't let him watch TV.

You know, I said, walking her across Riverside Drive, Ovidio is the name of a famous poet, though he's usually known by his Latin name, Ovid. His full name was Ovidio Nasone, I guess because he was nosy.

Ovidio isn't nosy, she said. He may have a broken nose, though.

That's sad! I said. She nodded. You'll need to be a good friend to him, then, won't you?

Andi looked at me funny, as if to say, Why do you say such weird things?

When we arrived at the park, I covered her with sunscreen. Then we Eskimo-kissed and she scampered off in her pink Marimekko to join two girls from science camp.

Have fun! I shouted, as if she needed my blessing to enjoy herself, and marveled that she could run in this heat, when I felt brave just for breathing. I sat on my usual bench in the shade in front of the fountain, took off my Birkenstocks, and buried my toes in the sand that drifted from the sandbox. Then rummaged for my *MOM!* hankie and used it to mop my brow. Andi was already leading the girls in an intricate game that involved running in concentric circles: they could dizzy themselves while tagging each other out—a twofer where everyone got to be "it."

I picked up the section that had arrived that morning: "*Lo Schermo.*" Usually translated as *screen*, *schermo* in *Vita Nuova* also means *protection* or *defense*. It refers to the practice of using a "pretend," or "screen," love to distract attention from a "real" love.

So, "The Call," followed by a threshold of sorts, and now "Deception." Romei could only be following the structure I'd proposed in my paper. I ought to have been flattered, but instead I found it odd—troubling, even.

At this point in the book, Dante, smitten, stares at the now-married Beatrice in church. Another lady, standing between them, believes that Dante stares at her. What an opportunity! He decides to use this second lady as a "screen love," to deflect attention from Beatrice. For years—*years!*—he pretends to love this blameless girl; people talk, he writes her poems, a brilliant stratagem! Then she leaves town. What's a poet to do? Love, disguised as a grubby pilgrim, suggests another who might serve as a substitute "defense." But when gossip about this new lady reaches Beatrice, Beatrice snubs him.

Dante is devastated—poor Dante! He retires to lament and is again visited by Love, who this time suggests that Dante address Beatrice directly—through the mediation of poetry. Art will thenceforth be his only "screen."

Critics remind us that screen loves were a convention of the time. Some question the innocence of these affairs, but no one—*no one!*—asks if Dante's screen loves (or his wife) are ill-used as a result. No one asks if he was right to make one lady the object of gossip to save the reputation of another.

In what follows, Romei, to his credit, makes explicit the cruelty and deceit glossed over by Dante. The narrator's courtship depends on an ever-escalating series of deceptions, practiced with increasingly less concern for consequences. The narrator invites himself to parties where Esther is likely to appear, polyglot affairs evoked through cascades of jumbled language: *The Wasteland* meets *La Dolce Vita*. Esther drifts toward Romei, a bit high, highball in hand. He grabs the attention of the crowd, tells raucous stories of an invented past—aristocratic loves, artistic coups, meetings with remarkable men—discovers a garrulousness, a facility for fakery, he hadn't known he'd had. Esther affects indifference but neglects to introduce him to her husband.

His first poem in this section concerns one of these "performances." An English sonnet, inverted so the all-important couplet, the *rima bacciata* (the "kissing rhyme"), appears on top, where all couplets secretly feel they belong. Three quatrains follow, subordinate now, a Babel-ing Greek chorus.

I scanned my memory of Romei's books and concluded that the sonnet was neither an old poem nor a patchwork of old poems. It was a pastiche, a Romei poem playing at being a Romei poem, a parody of the work Stockholm called the "strangulate cry of a remaindered generation."

Romei, enchanted by his new life, realizes he's been in hiding, a prisoner still of his grain silo. He liberates clothes from the closets of drunken friends, takes any opportunity to practice his new persona. He watches Esther read and write in the park. Sometimes—a limber man, apparently—he watches her from a tree. Sometimes he comes upon her "by chance," takes her to the Catacombs, the church of skulls, places where she trembles and must touch his sleeve. Over cappuccino, using half sentences, broken words, she confides a certain unhappiness: her husband is kind but . . . One doesn't . . . He can't, which is to say he won't . . . not really. Her gabbling is captured in an Italian sonnet replete, of course, with weak feminine rhymes.

One day, in front of Masaccio's *Expulsion*, in a scene brimming with elevated language, elegant artifice, Romei kisses the back of Esther's neck. She doesn't stop him—in fact, she kisses him back. The scene's artificiality, its nonliterality, is made plain by the fact that the painting in question, a fresco depicting the ejection of Adam and Eve from Eden, is not (in "real life") in Rome, but attached—firmly, we hope—to the walls of a Florentine chapel.

Esther seeks him out. She waits in Piazza Santa Maria, umbrella in hand, as if they had a date, she calls asking about Italian authors. They meet on weekdays when her husband is away, which is often. When the narrator thinks a man has touched Esther in a tram, he punches him, pulls her out at the next stop, presses her against a building—he can't stop kissing her face, her neck, her shoulders till poked by a grandma in black: *Vergogna!* she cries. Shame on you!

Indeed.

Some nights, crazed by the thought of her, the narrator calls, her husband answers, the poet babbles in Romanian, *as if that were a disguise.* Poem number three, written, appropriately, in twisted *terza rima*, concerns the language of these calls: three voices, uncomprehending, frantic, hurt, propelled then stalled by rhymes that never quite arrive at their destination.

Then one day in the Vatican, Esther whispers in Romei's ear:

Come to me tonight, I'll be alone. They stand before Raphael's *Parnassus*, the triumph of Poetry, the great ones bearing witness to his victory: Homer, Dante, the muses. Romei is no longer an exile, no longer an isolated poet rejecting tradition. He has slithered his way into the very home of the Pope, he has claimed his place in the confraternity of art. That night, Romei takes Esther by candlelight. Her face is lit by fire, her post-coital languor enflames him to unprecedented acts of virility.

Despite his hyperbole, Romei is reticent about their lovemaking, preferring to dwell on their stratagems and lack of remorse. Art becomes a screen for them both. He's brought to Esther's home, is introduced as an expert in the Bible, Hebrew literature—everything he knows exactly nothing about. He's agreed to help Esther with her translation, she says, not bothering to temper her excitement. Romei acts the fool, tells self-effacing stories, unfunny jokes; he tries to downplay the threat, which must have been as palpable to the husband as the chicken on his plate.

Sonnet number four recounts this dinner conversation.

Later, while washing his back, Esther reminds her husband what she's given up for him—her studies, her youth, her ambition. She plays on his soft spots: his need to indulge her, to see her as someone who needs indulging. Despite her attention, his "spots" remain soft, described in language that can only be called flaccid. It's unclear what the husband suspects: they don't care. Romei tosses stones at her window, misses, shouts apologies to shopkeepers who open their shutters in response, he takes her to restaurants *where they might be seen.*

The section is honest and peculiar: their passion is plain but there is little evidence of love, certainly not the kind which (I'm told) sustains a couple for forty years. What Esther seems to desire is not Romei so much as escape from marriage: she is stifled, he is free! Romei's motivation is more complex: he enjoys his new self, it pleases him to see her take risks for him—he has nothing to lose, or so he thinks; also, he likes to see her flush under the pressure of his hand, and when she says, *Yes, yes!* he begins to feel he's found a place in this world.

The fifth poem concerns the pleasure the narrator takes in artifice and orifice (*artifizio e orifizio*), and his concern, the perennial concern of the male lover, over his lady's pleasure: Is it real or is it Memorex?

Charming. This was what Romei wanted to share about his wife? I couldn't imagine why.

But I was troubled by something else. I went through the pages again—slowly—and counted seven images and ideas familiar from my stories: stone hitting bedroom window, woman helped off a bench, a first kiss to the back of the neck, roast chicken on a plate . . . They weren't extraordinary, I held no patent. But still: coincidence?

Disgusted, I stuffed the pages into my folder and reached for last week's puzzle. There was still the betrayal of the husband to look forward to.

I couldn't wait.

•

My crossword was a patchy mess when I realized it was time to go home. I looked over at the playground to call Andi.

She wasn't there.

She wasn't running in circles, I couldn't see her on the swings or on a seesaw. I couldn't see her anywhere.

Andi! I shouted, grabbing my mom-bag, but leaving Romei's pages, Andi's shovel and pail on the bench. Andi! I screamed, and ran barefoot from the fountain. Andi! I screamed as I ran around the jungle gym.

And saw there, behind a tree, the edge of a Marimekko dress. And there, by the whirligig, a science girl, face hidden in her hands, counting to one hundred.

23

OH HAPPY DAY!

I was surprised on returning home to detect the unmistakable scent of an Oh Happy Day Cake. An upside-down macaroon concoction Joe made us on special occasions, as when Ahmad published another book or Andi found a dollar on the street. I guessed that this was yet more camp-graduation nonsense, but resolved to be chipper.

Tradition mandated that the cake be eaten *before* dinner, because that's the way God intended it, and served with as many candles as the frosting could support, so that Andi, acting as proxy for the celebrant, could blow them out as a way of sharing the joy. Which she did tonight, in just four tries.

Hooray! we cried, and passed around slices, admiring the cake's macaroon lightness, its admirable upside-downness. Then Ahmad stood and clinked his glass with a fork.

Friends, Romans, and country girls. I have an announcement.

Announcement? He must have heard from Mirabella. He must be about to tell Andi she has a brother—or rather, a half-brother half of the time.

A pause as he allowed suspense to build. Andi didn't care: she was eating her cake.

I have decided, he said, . . . to buy a house!

A house?

You're kidding! Where? I asked, thinking, let it not be Brooklyn! The Village would be a drag, but Brooklyn—impossible!

Connecticut! he said, and named a town, a hamlet known for its green lawns and polite Republicans. It was on the commuter line, but only barely.

Oh, an investment! I said. I was confused for a minute! Good thinking!

We'll need a bigger place, he said, and looked at me meaningfully. Have you . . . ?

He shook his head one degree: he hadn't heard from Mirabella.

But wait, I said, you want to move there? To *Connecticut*?

I'm hoping, *assuming*, that you'll join us . . . me there. There will be lots of room.

You're assuming *what*? I asked. We'll move to *Connecticut*?

What's Connecticut? Andi asked, having finished her cake.

A stupid place very far from here, I said. Nowhere you'd ever want to live.

A wonderful place very close to here, Ahmad said, looking at me in disbelief. With lots of kids, plenty of room in which to ride your bike . . .

I don't have a bike.

We'll get you a bike.

You're not getting her a bike! Ahmad, that's enough!

I want a bike! Andi cried.

Jesus, Ahmad! I understand that you might need . . . space, but Connecticut? We are not moving to Connecticut. You can find a bigger place here. What about the university?

They've already given me three bedrooms. If the number of my, uh, dependents goes up, technically we'd still only need three bedrooms. Given that you and I are . . .

I get it! We'll figure something out.

I can't buy an apartment big enough for us all, not even on my enormous professor's salary. And last I knew, you weren't able . . .

I *get* it! I said. We'll rent. I'll contribute.

In Forest Hills, maybe. If we have to go that far, I'd rather buy. Something nice. With space out back for a studio. And a pool, he added, looking at Andi.

A pool! Andi said.

Ahmad, we can't just pick up and go!

I don't think you're trying to understand my situation.

I understand your situation but aren't you acting a bit rashly, considering . . .

Ahmad's face went hard.

Say it.

Nothing, Ahmad. Sorry. I didn't mean it.

Considering I don't know the outcome of *current events*?

I hope it works out, really I do! Why doesn't he take my study?

Why doesn't who take your study? Andi asked.

Ahmad shot me a warning look.

We're just talking options, sweetie. Ahmad, we have a life here.

You have a life here. If you can call it that.

If you can call it that? What's that supposed to mean?

SuperTemps has a branch in Fairfield County, Ahmad said. I checked.

I stood, glaring. To Ahmad, I would always be underachieving Shira, Shira-going-nowhere, never-realizing-her-potential Shira. When I published stories, Ahmad didn't like how I portrayed his precious Jonah. When I temped, he said I'd earn more translating for the UN. Nothing was good enough for his high-achieving highness, not even translator to the stars.

When do I get my bike? Andi asked.

We'll talk about this later, I said, and began bringing dishes to the kitchen. No seconds for anyone—I was too angry.

Ahmad followed me to the kitchen.

That was snide of me, he said. I'm sorry. But you can't actually expect Hassan to live in a pantry.

You're not sorry, I said, slopping Tibetan takeout into bowls and bringing it to the table.

Andi, Ahmad said after we'd passed the food in silence, tell us a story from school.

So Andi talked about Pammy, who'd insisted that if Andi didn't start wearing a bra *very* soon, her *bosoms* wouldn't grow. Andi concluded that Pammy wasn't quite "right in the head," but she'd put up with her "for the moment."

Ahmad laughed in all the right places.

Mo' momos? he asked. Andi giggled.

Dump me momo dumplings! she exclaimed.

I got up with my plate; I'd had enough. Celebrating with an Oh Happy Day cake, as if it were a done deal! Did he no longer even feel the need to *consult* with me? Apparently not, because he knew what I'd say: Connecticut? It was unthinkable!

Moving was easy for Ahmad: he was attached to people, not places. Well, bully for him! With the exception of a few sad years in Suffern and some sadder years in Rome, I'd lived my whole life in Manhattan; it was the only home I'd ever known. I had no family left to speak of, other than what I'd managed to create for myself; I had only this city: New York was witness to most of my past, and the only place I could imagine myself—packing Andi's lunch for Bronx Science, organizing Bloomsday pub crawls for the Translators of Note, bringing grandchildren to the planetarium, watching the lively world from Slice of Park, eventually joining the *alte kockers* on the Broadway island. When I tried to imagine going back to the 'burbs, I felt panic, as if the world had run out of air. As if I were still married, still oppressed by my husband's unimaginative good intentions, anxiously comparing lawncare products at Herb Groh's UGrohIt, saying silent prayers over stunted shrubbery. What could life offer me there, what could life offer us? A place where each day, if we played our cards right, would be just like the day before. I could never let Andi live like that, her horizon no farther than the next picket fence. Could I afford to support her here on my own? Of course not. Is that what Ahmad was counting on? Undoubtedly.

What were you thinking! I said, when he arrived in the kitchen with more dishes. Making a decision like that without consulting me! I am not a child—I have a life here!

We'd be better off there; Andrea would be better off there.

Why would you say that? Why would we be better off there?

Why wouldn't we? he said, opening the dishwasher.

I started counting reasons on rubber-gloved fingers: museums, the Film Forum, the Balalaika. What's in Connecticut? Lyme disease, off-road vehicles that never leave the road . . .

Good schools, Ahmad said, counting on his fingers. Parks not overrun by rats . . .

Connecticut? Connecticut isn't ready for the likes of us!

That's bollocks, and you know it. I'd think you'd be willing to do this one thing for me. After all I've done for you.

All you've done for me? You did me a favor by letting me give you a family?

It's time for a change, Shira. You're in a rut! We both are. Andi needs role models who can show her how to change, take risks.

You think living in Connecticut is a good example of risk-taking? I shouted.

Ahmad was maddeningly calm. This was how he worked his opponents into a lather. I was no exception. As if on cue, Andi arrived in the kitchen wearing her Supergirl pajamas and clutching Tamika, her African American Orthodontist Barbie. Ahmad growled and chased her around the kitchen. She squealed as he picked her up and held her upside down by the ankles.

Six points if you don't laugh, he shouted, and she tried, with Supergirl resolution.

Good night, Angel, I said, kissing her feet, then turned half upside down to kiss her nose. Who's going to give you your story tonight? I asked, thinking, *Pick me! Pick me!*

Ahmad! she shouted. Get me down from here!

Ahmad flew her out of the room like a 320 Airbus, my little flying girl, and I stayed behind and cried: big tears, plop, plop into the Palmolive.

24

MYSTIC CLAM SHACK

Over oatmeal the next morning, Ahmad explained Andi's options: she could hang out all day doing nothing or she could have extremely good fun with him *on an outing*.

This is what's known in the kid business as a no-brainer.

What should she bring? Andi wanted to know. Bag lunch? Shovel and pail? Should she wear play clothes or dress up, should Mommy curl her hair or braid it?

Ahmad put down his cup, appeared to concentrate. Wear the Gap Kids overalls I bought you, and that green and pink flowered T-shirt. Sneakers. Braids, no curls. Ritz Bits in a baggie. One Ho Ho, pre-wrapped. Two dolls, your choice. And books for the car.

Topeka! Andi cried, jumping up. We're going on an excursion!

Ahmad had a 1986 Mercedes SLE, with leather seats and a faux-wood dashboard, which he stored at great expense and rarely drove. Andi hopped in circles and shouted again, We're going on an excursion! We're going on an excursion! Then ran out of the room to get dressed.

You can come, too, Ahmad said, in what sounded like an afterthought.

I didn't think so. Ahmad's excursions usually involved traveling to outer boroughs to find curry ingredients he could just as easily find in Manhattan or driving along Riverside Drive so Andi could count boats on the Hudson. Then they'd find themselves in a park so Ahmad could read economics journals and Andi could play. Not my idea of a good time. Besides, I had work to do.

I spent that morning considering Romei's first poem, looking for antecedents in his early books. I'd been right: every line was a fragment of an earlier poem. He'd employed his earlier "anti-narrative" poems to tell a story—of how Esther refilled his inkless pen, allowing him to write "anti-narrative" poems. Twisted!

I had already read all the pages Romei had sent me, I'd read them carefully more than once. It was time to "trot" the work: I'd retype the original, leaving five or six spaces between each line, then handwrite a quick "literal" translation above each line, adding towers of alternative translations above problem words, which is to say most words. I'd use different colored highlighters to note difficult phrases or lines I didn't fully understand. If its rhythm was complex, I might scan the work, or I might note its rhyme pattern. On the back, I'd make notes about possible approaches, which elements seemed most important, what the author was getting at; I'd also start a *leitwort* lexicon, for key words that appeared several times. I'd end up with an indecipherable page, full of color, ornament, and scrawl, which I'd then throw away so I could get down to the real business of translation, trusting that everything I'd noted had sunk into my cells, available when I needed it.

And if it hadn't, there it was, in the wastebasket, where it would remain till I was done.

I left the house just three times: to get a mocha frappe from Joe, a dunedog from Cohn's Cones (Cohn's served all manner of beach food—wieners, pretzels, slush), and another frappe from Joe. After the latter, I snuck over to Benny's side display, which now featured books about motherhood and Jimmy Hoffa. Labor? Going into Labor? Labor Day!

But thinking about Benny made me angry, so I returned to Joe's for a cookie and ate it in Slice of Park. Benny and Marie were probably on an excursion, too, it being Saturday, when Benny always closed his store—everyone excursioning but me!

I'd just finished my cookie when Andi called.

I made a friend, she shouted. Her name is Lisa. She has a hamster, but she thinks it's dead. She doesn't mind being my best friend if I don't make her play Chutes and Ladders. She's nicer than Pammy. Now that Pammy's got chicken pox she thinks she's so cool, but she's not!

I couldn't remember the last time my daughter had strung together so many sentences.

That's nice, I said. Where did you meet her?

But Andi had passed the phone to Ahmad, who promised fried clams, then said, What? What? You're breaking up!

•

I was setting the table for dinner. I thought fried clams was a joke, but was bringing out the Bounty just in case. And rehearsing what I *should* have said to Benny three days before, what I'd definitely say next time I saw him, which would be never.

Ahmad was first in the door.

Don't be alarmed, he said as Andi burst in behind him, her arm in a cast up to her elbow, shouting, Look, Mommy! Look! Look!

Andi! I cried, dropping the Bounty. What happened?

Look what I got! she shouted, raising her cast in the air. Her name was already written in sixteen colors along the ulna, and along the other side, Ahmad had drawn her, making a comical face and falling out of an apple tree.

Which was when I saw the cardboard tub: *Mystic Clam Shack.*
Mystic?

You took Andi to Connecticut and she fell out of a tree?

Look, Mambo! Everyone can sign! Ahmad got me magic markers that smell like fruit!

How wonderful for you, I said, glaring at Ahmad, who shrugged. Do you want to tell me how you fell out of a tree?

Headfirst, she said, chasing a squirrel at our new house.

Into the kitchen! You, Ahmad! Into the kitchen!

•

Ahmad claimed not to understand. Kids hurt themselves all the time. It's just a fracture, and besides, he wasn't buying, just looking.

Just a fracture? I shouted. Just looking?

There were too many things for me to be angry about to know where to begin. He let Andi go up a tree? He'd taken her to Connecticut? To see a house? If he'd thought it was okay to take her to Connecticut, why hadn't he told me?

It's not like you asked, he said. You could have asked.

Why should I ask! You know how I feel about Connecticut!

You were happy to be rid of her, Ahmad said softly.

How dare you! I shouted, then lowered my voice. How dare you say I was happy to be rid of her! That's a terrible thing to say!

That's why you didn't ask. Because you didn't care. You wanted to work.

I didn't ask, I said, my voice rising again, because I trusted you!

A small voice behind me said: Ahmad, would you draw my bath? Tink already burned himself.

Ahmad shot me a look that sent a cliché of shivers down my spine.

We ate our clams cold and in silence, in front of the TV.

25

STUNNING VICTORY

After the *Friends* rerun, Andi wanted Ahmad to tuck her in, but I insisted.

C'mon, kiddo, I said, and she led me, reluctantly, to her room. Her pajama tops were on backwards. How many days had she worn them? Another night wouldn't hurt. Her room was more or less in order: on the floor, a Barbie at the Beach coloring book, Monica Lewinsky paper dolls (Monica was Andi's idea of a superhero: on TV every night, everyone talking about her clothes. Monica's job may have lasted a minute, but she was no temp!). On her child-size desk, a children's dictionary, a half-empty box of crayons. In the floor-to-ceiling bookshelves, dozens of Nancy Drews, also a four-poster bed for Tamika.

Where's Tink? I asked.

In exile, she said.

Again? I asked.

He wouldn't do as he was told so I put him in the bathtub.

You didn't drown him, did you?

How could I drown him if he's not real?

Okay. Into bed.

She hesitated.

I want to say my prayers, she said, and got into position.

You kneel beside your bed?

That's the way Pammy does it.

I knew she'd started doing this, but I didn't know she kneeled—like a cherub in some Jerry Falwell newsletter. I called on my father's ancestors for assistance.

You know, Jewish girls don't kneel when they pray.

Really? she asked, interested. What do they do?

I didn't know. I tried to remember scenes of synagogue prayer from movies.

They sit, I said. Sometimes they stand.

Pammy kneels.

Well, she's not Jewish, is she? I said, beginning to despair.

I want to do it like Pammy.

Okay. I'm just telling you. So you know.

Now I lay me down to sleep . . . , my daughter from another planet said, then scrambled into bed.

Do you say that because you're afraid? I asked, aware too late that the question was leading.

Of what? she asked, and I was caught. I couldn't say, *afraid of dying*.

I don't know. School beginning?

She looked at me blankly. School was three days away, an eternity in child time.

Why would I be afraid of that?

What about nightmares? You know what my mother told me to do if I had nightmares?

You have a mother?

Of course I have a mother—what did you think?

Andi shrugged. When she shrugged, her whole torso got involved, one shoulder higher than the other, head cocked, the very picture of puzzlement. I had to laugh.

If you have a mother why don't we see her?

I stopped laughing.

Because she's not a nice person, Andi.

Then I don't want to know what she said about nightmares, she replied reasonably.

I don't know why I persisted, acting the part of Cora, a character from one of my short stories, who invents tales about a grandmother her daughter never knew.

My mother said you had to tell yourself you were in a nightmare. Then you could either make the dream better or you could wake yourself up.

I tried that, Andi said. It doesn't work.

I stared at my daughter, that miraculous mix of spirit and flesh.

Maybe you need practice, I said, still wanting to give her something, something she could use. Were you afraid when you fell from the tree?

If I fell again I wouldn't be afraid!

Oh?

I'd pretend I was flying, she said, and spread out her arms.

I sat down on her bed, trying to take that in.

You're supposed to tuck me in now.

I pulled the guilt quilt up to her chin, making sure her cast was outside the blankets.

Ahmad tucks me in tighter.

I want to talk to you about Connecticut, I said.

She looked at me solemnly.

I know you had a good time there.

She didn't reply, expecting to have to wait out a lecture.

You did, didn't you?

She nodded.

Just because you have fun there doesn't mean it's a good place to live. Think of the things you'd miss in New York. Your playgroup, friends at school, musicals . . .

Ahmad says we can go to matinees on weekends.

What about Pammy and Martina? You'd miss them, wouldn't you?

Pammy's stuck up, and Martina doesn't like me anymore.

Really? Why?

I don't know, Andi said, shrugging.

You had a fight with your friends? I asked, stunned. They'd been inseparable since Chinese-Spanish-French quadrilingual preschool.

Andi nodded.

Ahmad says these things happen.

Why didn't you tell me?

I don't know, Andi said, shrugging again. You were busy.

I always have time for you.

You said I mustn't disturb you when you're working.

I couldn't argue with that—I had.

There's always time. I always have time for you.

Oh, Andi said.

Really!

Okay, I heard you.

There are lots of things about New York you'd miss if you left. You don't realize it now because Connecticut is so new.

I'd miss Ahmad more.

What makes you think Ahmad would be there without us?

It's obvious. Besides, he told me.

That's not certain, I said, as if that made a difference.

Plus, Andi said, the house is near a mall. There are no malls in New York City. Just stupid stores one after the other. No malls, no indoor waterfalls.

We'll talk about this more later, I said, leaning over to kiss her cheek, having no arguments to offer now except that of my own need.

I'd have a bike, she added, and a pool. Does your mother live in Connecticut, is that why you don't want to live there?

My mother has nothing to do with this.

It's two against one, Andi said.

Moms have veto power, even in a democracy. Ask anyone.

You never want me to have any fun!

That's silly. Of course I want you to have fun!

I'm staying up all night.

Fine. As long as you turn out the light.

You don't think I can do it.

Good night, Andi.

You don't think I can do it! she shouted as I shut her door. You don't think I can do it!

She continued shouting these absurd words, challenging me

to—what? agree with her? believe in her? I bumped into, and ignored, Ahmad in the hall. He stopped in front of Andi's room. I heard him open her door, then I heard the shouting stop.

Not the stunning victory I'd hoped for.

26

RITALIN FOR THE HEART

Andi had a nightmare. Angry men with baseball bats came through the window; they wanted to hurt the children. She tried to make them stop, really she did. Or rather, she hid while Ovidio shot them with his gun. I ran to her room when I heard her cry and grabbed her to me. She crumpled against my chest, a reluctant, shuddering ball; she would not be consoled. Ahmad, wearing only his pajama bottoms, came to the door. I told him about the dream.

Damn your daughter's Oedipal fantasies, he muttered. Andi pulled away from me, reached for him with both arms, her face smeared with tears. He took her from me and swayed with her, his arms strong against her back, his face nuzzling her neck, murmuring things till she fell asleep, still in his arms. Behind them, floating in the corners of the wall, lit by glow-in-the-dark stars, portraits of Ahmad and me, looking younger, more optimistic. I left Ahmad to put her back to bed and felt cold inside. When had I become superfluous?

From my bed I stared at the Corot poster on my wall, made strange by flashing avenue light. I'd made a vow when Andi was born: she'd be the center *and* the circumference of my life, its organizing principle and its limit. I would never abandon her, not in thought, word, or deed. I'd be everything my mother wasn't. Nothing would ever ground my girl: I'd make sure she flew to her big heart's content. Was I a bad role model? Was Connecticut better for my baby?

I've never been good at second-guessing myself. When that still small voice tells me to look at my life, I turn up the stereo, find anything to do but. The psychologists haven't come up with a cure for what ails me: there is no Ritalin for the heart.

I kicked my blankets to the floor. Time to *do* something. Organize under the kitchen sink, flush the coffeemaker with baking soda. As I left my room, something crunched underfoot: a Popsicle-stick throne Ahmad had made for Tink—a throne, flattened now by my big foot.

What do you think, Tink? I asked, the hall nightlight illuminating the shape of things. Should I move to Connecticut? Will I lose my daughter if I don't?

Tink kept his counsel, proving his wisdom, yet again.

•

The next morning, the spices were in alphabetical order and Andi was none the worse for wear. She was playing with the Lewinsky paper dolls and singing "Home, Home on the Grange," which is how Pammy insisted the song went. She'd already eaten—I saw the remnants of grape jelly omelet in the sink. As I made eggs for myself, I imagined the New York things we might do: pizza picnic on the Staten Island Ferry? Counting seagulls on the Circle Line? Inventing Mongolian ancestors at Ellis Island? But Andi had a better idea. She ran into the kitchen wearing a frilly dress Aunt Emma had sent her. Pammy had invited her overnight; she wanted to go *now*. She'd already filled her backpack with essential toys and, I hoped, some underwear.

Whoever heard of going to a sleepover at ten in the morning? I asked. And why did she want to go so far from her mama?

She's only upstairs! Andi said, giving me the look seven-year-olds cultivate that says, Where did I find this mother, is there any chance I can take her back?

I thought you didn't like Pammy.

What're you *talking* about?

Did you have enough breakfast?

Pammy's mother bought Drake's Cakes! she said mysteriously.
Oh, I said. Does Drake bake a good cake?
There was that look again.
Okey doke, I said. Eskimo kiss!
We rubbed noses and off she ran.

27

FALSE FRIENDS
AND TRUE

I found myself looking out the bedroom window at Benny's side dis-play, wishing I were a birdwatcher and could produce binoculars. What did I hope to see? Benny and Psychogirl smooching by All Things Green (books on the environment, money, and "envy man-agement")? Ahmad was hum-singing along with Glenn Gould in the living room. Maybe he thought he could draw me out, pretend noth-ing had happened, pretend he wasn't playing Connecticut tug-of-war with our little girl. He needed to apologize: confession, contrition, reparation, change.

Benny, Connecticut, the possible addition to our family—I needed help sorting it out, but where? Once upon a time, I'd have called Jeanette, Jonah's sister. She was the one friend other than Ah-mad who'd stayed true when I had a child. Some dropped me; others changed the subject when I talked about cracked nipples, the miracle of life. I hadn't felt the loss, because I had Ahmad and Andi—I had my family. But Jeanette became a *better* friend then, visiting when Ah-mad was teaching so I could shower, bringing me chocolates, telling somewhat relevant stories about her Dotty's colic, never asking when I'd lose my baby weight. We didn't have much in common except high school in Rome, and Jonah, but I enjoyed our confidences and the girly things we did—like getting our legs waxed and watching the weepies. She wasn't great at managing her own life, but she was terrific at managing mine.

My stories ended that. She hadn't minded "Tibet, New York," about Jonah's last days—it had moved her, even, she'd said so more than once. But in "Domino," my most recent, published a year ago, I'd imagined us in high school: Jonah at fourteen, defacing a portrait Ahmad had made of me, my Botticelli hair flying wild, and jerking off in a tree as he watched T. and me making out in a copse. I made things up to "tell a deeper truth"; Jeanette said I'd made Jonah out to be a pervert—why would I do that? She wouldn't return my calls.

When Ahmad went to his studio, I grabbed a book from his bookshelf: *Poverty and Landlessness*. Tiny print, grainy black-and-white photos—it was perfect! I called Jeanette, said her daughter Dotty had left a book last time she'd babysat. I'd be in the neighborhood, should I maybe drop it off?

Oh, Jeanette said. Sure.

•

I brought Romei's "Screen" with me and reread it on the downtown bus—the crashed parties, the rendezvous in the park. I stalled in the consummation scene, stared at it as we bumped down Broadway, came to myself only after we passed Fairway. I elbowed my way off and walked back up to Seventy-ninth. As I waited for the crosstown, I kept staring at the page. Something wasn't right.

False friends! The passage was littered with them. Words in one language that trick you into thinking they're related to words in another (like Andi, who appears related to Ahmad, but isn't). Like *fame*, which in Italian means not fame but hunger.

When the crosstown arrived, I went straight to the back and looped my arm around a pole. Had false friends insinuated themselves into Romei and Esther's Eden? No. Were they reflected in the mirror as Romei posed in the clothes he'd "liberated" from his friends' closets? No. They were only here, in the consummation scene. Baffled, I got off at Sixty-eighth and Third. Had Romei meant to do this? He must have. But why? Was he testing me, daring me to make a novice's mistakes?

C'mon, Shira, I thought as I walked up Third Avenue. Why would he do that? Surely he was making a point about the lack of correspondence between the character Romei and his English-speaking love. Interesting, but who would notice but me? I couldn't make his plays on words evident in translation—once translated, they'd disappear. (No one would look at the word *bookstore* and think, *Bookstore is libreria in Italian, which doesn't mean library*—what is that crafty poet up to!) Romei's joke would be visible only to the reader of Italian, and only if he were thinking about how it might translate.

Was it my imagination? No, because there they were. Ten classic examples on one page alone.

But I had arrived at Jeanette's building, a freakishly tall stack of condos on East 70th. I pushed the pages into my mom-bag.

Jeanette had moved here from Brooklyn Heights, determined to start anew after her divorce. She'd tossed everything she'd purchased with her ex, and redecorated every room except Dotty's, which Dotty, at the tender age of twelve, had refused to cede to her mother's stencils and window treatments, preferring instead to cover her walls with anything that might remind her of her uncle—or rather, her memory of Jonah or, increasingly, her memory of having had a memory of him: photos of Tibetan *tangkas*, monkey-headed gods, reproductions of his paintings from a gallery catalogue, a photo of him holding baby Dotty on his lap, blown up to poster size.

Jeanette thought it *fetishistic*, creepy even, but put up with it because, as her therapist said, we all grieve differently.

How could I forget him? Dotty asked one day. Uncle Joe was everything to me, but now all I remember is him looking like this, she said, pointing at the poster-size photo, or that, pointing to framed photos on her bookshelf.

That's life cutting you some slack, I said.

It's not right to forget someone you love, she said.

You were only seven, I said. Give yourself a break.

So the divinities came off the walls, replaced by teen idols, boys I didn't recognize, with longish hair and doe eyes and, later, Che

Guevara, images of the people united, never to be defeated, marching toward their bright, socialist-realist future.

Jeanette eventually combined her interior decoration mania with real estate work, entering the renovate-a-crummy-building-and-sell-it-for-a-killing business. Only she joined the bandwagon a moment too late and, I suspect, applied too bourgeois a taste: her renovations didn't appeal to the Lower East Side set. She declared bankruptcy, but in the process found a new beau—a master carpenter (her term, not his) named Georges, whom she called her Silver Lining, as in, there always is one. Georges was plump and affectionate, except when he disappeared, returning days later all glum and taciturn. It's just his way, Jeanette said, forgetting that this had been her ex's way as well. Soon she was back to selling real estate and happier than ever. Or she was last time I saw her.

I barely recognized her when she came to the door. She used to have what you might call *big hair*, but she'd cut it short—a mistake. She was wearing a white blouse with a red-piped Peter Pan collar, puffed sleeves, a red knee-length skirt, and a ruby pendant in the shape of a heart.

Like the new haircut! I said, when she said hello but didn't invite me in. Very smart!

Thank you, she said, and almost smiled, but remembered herself.

Does it have to be this way? I said. Really? We were friends once.

Jeanette shook her head, as if dismissing me. Do you have the book? she said. For a crazy moment I thought she was asking for Romei's pages, that she'd been ordered by the Great Man to get them back.

Right! I said, and reached into my bag. *Poverty and Landlessness.*

Thanks, Jeanette said. I'll give this to Dotty.

She's a fine girl. You deserve maximum credit.

Thank you, Jeanette said, looking inside the book and smiling.

I could use some pointers right about now.

Andi?

Yes, I said, and before I knew it, I was sniffling into my *MOM!* handkerchief. I'd intended to grovel with more dignity.

Jeanette sighed.

You'd better come in. And take this, she said, handing me back the book. It's Ahmad's. See? she said, and pointed to the frontispiece, *From the library of.*

Oh, I said, wiping my nose on my Barnard T-shirt. No kidding.

•

Jeanette pulled out the Chex Party Mix and made us strawberry daiquiris. Never too early for drinks, she said, as long as we call it brunch.

I told her about Mirabella, Connecticut, the choice it seemed I'd made.

Ahmad's in a tough spot, she said. He doesn't want to lose you, or Andi.

Why would he lose Andi? I said. He'll only lose her if he moves to Connecticut!

It's not that simple, she said, and pulled a Marlboro out from under the coffee table, lit it with a gold lighter that read, *Saleswoman of the Year 1996.* She kept a pack scotch-taped there, available for "emotional emergencies." Listen, she said, after offering me one (I said no), maybe you won't move to Connecticut, maybe it was wrong of him to use Andi to get to you, but she's part of his life. Whatever you decide, you'll have to come to an arrangement.

She sucked on her cigarette, closing her eyes in bliss.

He can offer her so much more than I can, I said. What if she refuses to live with me?

Jeanette smiled: she knew I was thinking of Dotty. When Jeanette's ex got custody, Dotty kept returning to Jeanette, sometimes in the middle of the night, carrying toys and, ever sensible, a store of apples in her knapsack.

Andi loves you. You're her mother.

It's not that simple, I said.

Yes, it is.

It is?

Yup.

I took that in.

I meant what I said about Dotty, by the way. You should be proud.

Dotty is a worrisome child, Jeanette said. She wants the condo association to organize a gold cooperative for Y2K. Can you believe it? We should convert our savings into gold and buy a safe together. These are people who can't decide what color to paint the foyer!

Dotty's got her head on straight. She'll be fine.

She *is* good, isn't she? Jeanette asked, smiling slightly, as if not to tempt fate.

Speaking of apartments, Jen: two bedrooms in Manhattan. With a study—what are we talking? We'd need a real kitchen, of course. And two bathrooms. Eventually Andi's going to need her own bathroom.

Jeanette just looked at me.

You don't want to know.

I do, I said. At least I think I do.

She named some numbers.

I'm not talking Fifth Avenue, Jen! I'm talking my neighborhood, so Andi doesn't have to change schools.

Jen shook her head.

That *is* my neighborhood?

That's Harlem, honey. Up and coming, or so they say.

Maybe I will have one of those cigarettes, I said, trying to laugh. It had been a long time since I'd looked for an apartment. After I left my husband at thirty-five, I moved in with my father; when he died, I went to India. I came home pregnant, and Ahmad took me in. It had been since I was a grad student! Twenty years!

I don't handle the kind of properties you'd be looking for, Jeanette added. No margin in it. I could possibly introduce you to someone, if it comes to that.

I nodded halfheartedly as Jeanette lit our cigarettes two at once, Leslie Howard style.

So, she said, as if getting to the point, love interest?

Jeanette despaired of seeing me properly coupled: singleness such as I'd enjoyed much of my life was not, she assured me, a state favored by nature.

No, I'd invariably say, blue food is not favored by nature, but the she-lion hunts alone!

Jeanette bristled at that: she often served blue food.

Between cigarette-induced coughs, I confessed to confusion about Benny.

(He sounds nice, she said. He's taken, I said. What's taken can be untaken. *Jeanette!* All's fair! I didn't want to explain how I couldn't compete with someone like Marie, how one man couldn't be interested in both her and me. He's lying to me, I said. He deserves a chance to explain. Is he cute? and so on.)

Okay, the rabbi's out, she eventually agreed. Anyone else?

I shook my head.

Shira! You gotta get out there!

I've suffered from a lack of female guidance, I admitted.

You want female guidance? I'll give you female guidance!

She stubbed out her cigarette and inspected me.

Stand, she said. I complied. She looked pointedly at my midsection and said, You're spending too much time at Cuppa Joe's. Only a true friend would tell you.

I looked down, pressed my hands against my belly, acknowledged there was more give and take there than there used to be.

More? she asked. I nodded meekly. What kind of bra are you wearing? From the looks of it, it's one of those athletic bras that smush you down.

I looked down again.

No, I really am this small.

Jeanette *tsk-tsk*ed me. No one's ever that small, she said, and gave me a short course on miracles. Push yourself up by your bra straps!

Isn't that deceptive?

Poor dear, she said, shaking her head. Men are beasts. They're wonderful, adorable beasts, and we love them, but they need to think they're getting titties, *big* titties.

Even if they're not?

Especially if they're not.

I didn't understand, but promised to think about it. Then we made more daiquiris.

You know my ex has prostate cancer, Jeanette said, as she dumped frozen blueberries into the blender. Did Dotty tell you?

Dotty doesn't talk about her father. Is he okay?

I don't think so, she said, reaching for the rum, which was still on the counter. I bear him no ill will, you know. I should. I should want to pull his fucking prostate out with my teeth.

Ghoulish, Jen! I like it!

She cracked up as she reached back inside the freezer for ice. But I say, live and let live. Ever tempted to rake your exes over the coals? she asked, tearing open a packet of daiquiri mix.

I knew what she meant: Would I defame one in a story?

You know what they say? I asked.

Tell! she said, and poured what must have been a quart of Nutrasweet into the blender.

If you put an ex in a story, give him a small you-know-what and make him impotent. He'll never say it was him! No one gets sued!

From that elevated point, we ascended farther, discussing size in general—one of us claiming it made no difference, the other claiming it made all the difference in the world—then size in particular, as in our exes, the hypothetical endowment of movie stars, politicians. All in all, an edifying afternoon. When I left, we promised to have lunch, watch weepies over what Dotty once called "white" ice cream, and never fall out of touch again. (Yes, that's how we referred to our falling out, as a *falling out of touch*.) Because we were true friends, true-blue friends! Drinking true-blue drinks and eating true-blue food!

These were hysterical concepts, so we clung to each other at the front door, shouting and laughing. I was still laughing as I descended in the elevator. *True friends, blue friends, true-blue false friends!* And was struck sober on Third Avenue.

Maybe there were no false friends in Romei's work. Maybe the false friends were true friends. Was this possible?

Taxi, Miss?

I stared at the doorman.

Casino, yes: in Italian, *casino* means mess, and Romei's home is a mess, but bedding Esther is also a gamble. Yes, Esther's body is *caldo*, or warm, but maybe in another sense it's cold. Romei felt *fame*, but perhaps his greatest hunger was not for Esther, but for fame. Why mention the *libreria*, the bookstore-that-isn't-a-library, if not to suggest that the couple didn't know if their story was borrowed or bought, a one-night stand or something that would last? When Esther decides that Romei is simpatico, does she in fact mean *nice* or does she think he feels sympathy? Does he? He does!

It was as if Romei were writing in two languages at once, as if two stories were playing themselves out together, one reflected in the mirror of the other. Words that appeared related, words that usually confused readers with their non-correspondence, were miraculously made cognate, reconciled by the all-powerful poet—but why? To suggest that as ill-advised as this coupling appeared, it was also good and right?

But why the sleight of hand? Only the translator, if she were lucky, or maybe (maybe!) the rare bilingual reader, could rescue significance from this mirror. And what did the translator care?

This translator cared. This sort of thing had not been done before. It was marvelous! Everyone would have to know! I would let them know! I'd write an introduction! A Translator's Note! A wise and learnéd piece, delicate in its approach, tensile in its construction. An introduction to be photocopied and cited by graduate students everywhere!

My heart was beating with excitement.

Yes! I said to the doorman and, to his astonishment, walked away.

28

MIRACLES ARE POSSIBLE

Andi called from Pammy's the next morning to say she'd been asked to stay the day; I confirmed this with Pammy's mother, who assured me that Pammy and Andi together were less trouble than Pammy alone, and could Andi stay the rest of Pammy's natural life? Till four, I said.

I took notes on true-blue false friends in my Door Number Two notebook, then, pleased with my labor, decided to check out Labor Day sales for advanced bra technology: miracles were possible, I now knew, and I needed a miracle. For the next rough beast who came slouching along.

Where to go? I recalled a photo of my mother laughing and holding a Bergdorf bag, her conical breasts lifted and separated. She would have known where to buy a nice, if not a miraculous, bra.

An assiduous woman with a Slavic accent appointed herself my minder, assuring me through the swinging doors of my dressing room that all I needed was a little "support." She had a professional's disdain for squandered femininity.

This was when Romei called.

You have receive these new pages, he said.

Thursday, I said, dropping the bras and covering my breasts with a forearm.

No, I think is Wednesday.

I think is Thursday, I said, picking up my T-shirt and holding it to my chest. Four days ago.

Ivana's gold pumps were pacing tense little steps on the other side of the swinging doors, as I fingered one crimson, one black satin, one front-closing, one strapless.

You are not working? You say you work on no other.

I *am* working, I said, and sat down on the little blue bench, careful not to prick myself on a pin. Of course I'm working!

What you are thinking? he asked.

Again with my opinion?

I was glad, I said, that in the character of Romei you brought Dante's adulterous desires out of the closet. It's always bothered me how Dante could call pure and honorable his love for a married woman.

Hurrumph, Romei said, or something like it.

You asked for it, I thought. Full disclosure.

You're honest now about your deception then, I said, or rather, your character's deception. I admire that.

You understand nothing, he said.

I understand a few things, I thought. One thing is you're nuts.

You understand nothing of this story I telling, he continued. You think you know every thing, but you know nothing of what is happen next.

I'm sure you're right, I said, and thought, *What's to understand? The whole world knows how this story ends!*

How is your little daughter? he asked then. She is fine?

Andi? She fractured her wrist.

Fracture her wrist! You must be careful! I am not receive this photograph. You are sending?

You only just asked for it! I said, realizing that somehow I'd agreed to his request.

Outside the dressing cubicle, Ivana sighed, loudly.

You will fax this thing to me.

No can do, I replied.

You have not a—how you say—scanning device? But you are American! You have every kind of machinery!

He was trying to be charming.

Listen, I said. I'd like to leave my daughter out of this if you don't mind.

She is intelligent, like her mother?

Of course, I said, not catching the flattery till it was too late.

Reading? Maybe writing little stories?

We try not to pressure her.

We? Who is we?

I'd like to make an appointment to discuss some questions I have, maybe next week?

Ivana, sensing my call would never end, clacked away from the dressing room.

Don't trouble me with this thing. Make a note and send the translation.

Romei! You said the end of the year!

This is good. I would like the end of this month. I send you more tomorrow.

You must be reasonable, Romei!

What am I—engineer? There is no time! I am busy. Goodbye, and he was gone.

I felt unaccountably abandoned in my cubby—with its florescent lights and stray pins and mangled hangers, the faint sound of a machine somewhere registering something, the closed-circuit cameras, the ghosts of other women who'd prayed for miracles. Romei would never answer my questions! He had no respect for my profession, no respect for *me*.

I put my cotton bra back on, and my T-shirt. There would be no miracles today.

29

ROSH HASHANAH, MY ASS

The sky had turned the color of dishwater, so instead of walking off the chocolate croissants Jeanette had seen clinging to my thighs, I took the M7 up Amsterdam. When I got back to Slice of Park, I checked my messages:

Jeanette was glad I'd stopped by.

Someone named Asante was looking for Ralph. A matter of some *emergency*.

Benny wanted to talk:

I know this isn't something you understand or believe, he said, but we're supposed to atone during the High Holy Days. The rest of my life's a mess, but I'm hoping you and I can make things right. Please? Call, or stop by the store.

When I was writing "Rose No One," the Paul Celan story, Benny told me Rosh Hashanah was the birthday of the world—a perfect time, Rose thought, to begin again. Benny had helped—providing biographical details, offering variant translations of key Celan lines, challenging me to do better, and publishing the story eventually, though he'd said he wouldn't. No one had ever taken such an interest in my work. Remembering this made me sad. We'd gotten along so well then. And now?

I looked over my shoulder at People of the Book. I'd made mistakes; if there was a moral bean-counter in the sky I hoped he'd be generous with me. Jeanette had been generous—more than generous; shouldn't I be generous as well? So Benny was a friend of Romei's and didn't tell me, big deal! Maybe he didn't want to get involved in our professional relationship. Weird, but okay.

Unless he already was involved.

Could it be? Had *Benny* referred Romei to me?

It made sense. They knew each other; Benny had given Romei my number. Benny was a literary guy—he knew lots of folks. Maybe Romei asked if he knew a translator. Maybe Benny hadn't wanted to admit such a large favor. His involvement would explain why Romei had taken a chance on an unknown—he'd trusted Benny's judgment!

All Benny had wanted was to do something nice for me!

I stood up again, ready to apologize. We could begin again, I thought, but then:

No. He couldn't have given Romei my name! He didn't know about my Dante translation, he'd never heard of *Vita Nuova*.

Might he still have recommended me? And I just happened to be an expert on an obscure work of Dante no one but me has ever read? Too large a coincidence.

A drop of rain landed on my nose.

I had it all wrong. It wasn't up to me to reach out to Benny. It was up to him to come to me, to come clean. He hadn't, he'd had his chances and he hadn't.

Rosh Hashanah, my ass.

30

INTO THE ITALIAN SUNSET

The next morning, we sent Andi off for her first day of school. Ahmad knelt beside her, straightened her jumper, and handed her a notebook and pen—a foot-long pen with a red-knit pom-pom dangling from its end. He insisted it was his family's tradition to give third graders notebooks so they could record their observations. Because they were "old enough" now, whatever that meant. Andi nodded solemnly, her eyes wide. I glared at Ahmad as Andi walked out the door clutching her notebook—looking, no doubt, for something to observe.

How like Ahmad, to show me up with school supplies!

•

More pages had arrived overnight, as promised: more "Screen," a whole page and a half.

I didn't want to read a scene in which a radiant Esther proclaims she must be free, free, *free*! Her husband begs her to stay, her child weeps in a corner, but proud Esther will not be moved! She walks with Romei into an Italian sunset. Or so I imagined, as I settled onto the loveseat.

Romei surprised me.

Esther and her narrator have not spoken of the future. Like all literary lovers, they live in an eternal present. In a poem called "Au(to) bade," they curse the arrival not of the dawn but of the child's school bus. So it's a shock—to them and to us—when they return to Esther's one day to find the apartment empty, the husband not in Palermo as planned, the child not in school, but both of them gone, their clothes gone, the jewelry given to Esther by her husband gone, her passport gone. All that remains, besides Esther's clothes: her translation, a canceled bankbook, a manila envelope she doesn't recognize.

Inside the envelope, photographs of the happy couple dating back to the fall; also, a letter from a family friend, a lawyer, assuring Esther that she'd forfeited her maternal rights and her rights to spousal support, begging her for the sake of all concerned not to press the issue—not that she has the money with which to return to the U.S., much less hire an attorney: her husband has left her penniless.

You have what you want, a note from him says. Now live with it.

Reminiscent of Dante's karmic economy, the punishment horribly fitting the crime, this note suggests that our lovers are now in Hell. Be careful what you wish for!

And with this, Romei shifts from the present to the past tense: the narrator and Esther plunge into time, out of their lyric self-absorption, into something far more dynamic.

I imagined that at this point they turn to each other, knowing they are stuck with each other, their dream become nightmare. Game won and lost, they had their cake, now they had to eat it. I imagined they return to Romei's silently, having lost their ability to speak. I imagined this but didn't know: the section ended with the envelope and the note.

For the first time, I found myself feeling something for Esther and Romei—I wanted to read on. Yes, the husband was the injured party, yes, he had a right to be angry. But his revenge was complete and irrevocable. It didn't allow for the possibility of change! Esther couldn't explain herself, or consider what she might lose. The coldness of it curled my toenails.

When my telephone rang, I answered it, unguarded.

They say we're obligated to ask three times for forgiveness, Benny said. Then the sin is on the head of the obdurate one.

Come over, I said. I'll make us some tea.

PART FOUR

MUSE

31

WATCH THE
DING DONG, DEAR

Benny and Andi arrived at the front door together.

You're Andrea, right? I could hear him asking from the hallway.

I'm not saying, Andi said. I looked out the peephole. She was squatting in her Paddington raincoat and rain boots, rooting through her backpack with her good hand, I assumed for her keys. Raindrops hung from the tips of Benny's beard.

Good girl, Benny said. Your mama must be proud of you.

She is, Andi said, pulling out a mashed Ding Dong. Do you know her?

I do if you're Andrea.

You're trying to trick me, she said. I'm not stupid.

Benny was still laughing when I opened the door.

•

I introduced him as *Uncle Benny*, which Andi didn't appreciate. She'd put her Ding Dong on a piece of Ahmad's china, and was eating it on the couch with a knife and fork.

I know him already from the store. Why does everyone want to be my uncle?

Because you're such a great kid, I said.

If you say so.

Then we heard about her new teacher, Mrs. Chao, who was *very* nice. Look! she added, and extended her cast so I could see additional names written in grape and apricot.

Are you going to have Ovidio sign?

Mo-omm! she protested, making at least three syllables of the word.

Watch the Ding Dong, dear—we don't want it on the sofa.

For some reason, this cracked Benny up.

Is he okay? Andi asked when Benny couldn't stop laughing. His beard jiggled, his long legs stretched out around the legs of the coffee table. Whaaat? she asked, smiling. What's the joke, Mom, tell me!

I was giggling too.

Mo-omm, tell me! Then Andi was laughing, Benny was howling and holding his stomach.

Watch the Ding Dong, dear! was all he could say.

•

That was great, he said, when Andi went to wash her plate. Laughing is better than sex, had you noticed?

Well, it's less complicated, I said, thinking that was the strangest thing I'd ever heard.

Then from the kitchen, a shattering: china smashing on an Italian tile floor.

Oops, I heard my daughter say. Oh, no.

Shit, I said.

Ahmad's antique Russian porcelain. Andi shouldn't have been using it. I should have stopped her. I was so happy to see Benny, I hadn't registered what she was doing.

You okay? I said as I went to her.

She looked up, unable to move. Her feet were bare—on her toes, sparkly blue nail polish. She looked scared, crouching, as if ready to leap. Her lower lip trembled.

Don't move, I said. I'll get something to sweep that up, but before I could turn, Benny had swooped Andi into his arms. She began to wail: Put me down! Put me down from here! pounding him with her good fist till he placed her a safe distance from the broken plate.

Put me down, she continued screaming, even though she was down. I ran to her, china crunching under my Birkenstocks, and wrapped my arms around her.

Sweetie! What is it? She was sobbing, great huge sobs, and pounding me. Sweetie! I said, holding her tight, making a confused face to Benny over her shoulder.

Maybe I should go, Benny mouthed to me. I shook my head. Andi was still sobbing.

Sweetie, it's okay. Benny was just moving you so you wouldn't hurt yourself.

I don't need another father! she wailed. Tell him to take his hands off of me!

Benny's over there, I said, mystified. You're okay. Benny's my friend. He'd never hurt you.

I'm going, Benny mouthed again. I nodded.

Ahmad's going to hate me! Please don't tell him I did this! Please don't tell him!

•

That evening, a tear-streaked Andi, coached by her mother, apologized. Tell him what you did, tell him you're sorry, you'll find another plate, you'll never play with his porcelain again. Confession, contrition, reparation, change. It worked for Dante, it can work for you.

Ahmad loves you, I told her. If you say these things and mean it, he'll forgive you.

Can't I just write him a note?

No, my love, you can't.

What about a poem?

I blinked.

You can write him a poem, but you still have to say these things.

Are you sure this works? she asked, her good hand on her hip. Have you ever done it?

Have I ever apologized? Of course.

139

No! she said, exasperated. Has anyone ever apologized to you? Has it worked?

Of course, I said, though I wasn't sure that was true. But it did work. Ahmad sat Andi down on his knee, and together they sang "Tomorrow" in crooked harmony.

My family.

Ahmad tucked Andi in. I thought maybe it would be a good time to talk about Connecticut, but I had unfinished business with Benny.

Sorry, I said to him over the phone. I don't know what came over her.

No, I'm sorry.

You did the right thing. You did what I should have done, instead of going off to find a broom. I don't know what I was thinking.

She doesn't know me—I shouldn't have touched her.

We've been under some stress.

You handled her well.

I did? I asked. It was crazy how grateful I felt. You think so?

Sure. You let her know she was safe and loved. And forgiven.

Ah, I said, remembering.

Listen, can you come over?

To the store? I asked. I could see it out my window, its lighted display, Benny's apartment above.

No, my place. We'll drink, we'll talk, we'll drink.

It had been a long day, the pans from my *tagine* were still in the sink. It was raining cats and dogs—only a fool would go out.

I'll be there in five, I said.

32

SECRETS OF
THE CONFESSIONAL

It was my first time in Benny's six-room, third-floor walk-up. Cheap metal bookshelves lined the walls, holding poetry, Judaica, how-to manuals (how to fix a VW Bug, how to build a yurt). In the kitchen, shelves of vegan cookbooks, jars of grains, lentils, pastas in various shapes, a three-tiered spice rack containing ingredients I'd never heard of—asafetida, galangal. A *mezuzah* in every doorway. His furniture had been purchased from the Salvation Army or found on the street, but it all had a certain interest: a chipped, gold-brocade loveseat; a table fashioned out of a butter churn. Between bookshelves, artwork from early issues of *Gilgul*—artists I didn't know then but certainly knew now; also, totemic pictures of patterned Hebrew letters. On the floor, a Chinese carpet of inestimable value. The effect was one of both rootedness and chaos.

I felt immediately at home, plopped down on a royal blue couch. Benny put on Meredith Monk, got us some Maker's Mark. In mismatched shot glasses, cut crystal.

Must be a busy time for you, I said, with the holidays and all.

Hmm, Benny said, enjoying his bourbon. He was sitting on a loveseat, wearing gym shorts, *tzitzit*, and a shirt that read, *I climbed Mount Parnassus*; he'd stretched his long, bare legs out on top of the coffee table. He was waiting.

The bourbon warmed the back of my throat, my stomach.

You knew Romei and you kept it from me, I said.

Benny said nothing. He was still waiting.

I wasn't going through your stuff. There was a kitten in your annex.

I still hadn't said what I needed to say.

Look, I said, putting down my glass, you took the photo off the wall and you hid it under your desk, I'm guessing so I wouldn't see it. It wasn't dusty; it hadn't fallen there.

Ah, Benny said.

You wanna tell me what's going on?

I can't, he said, and removed his legs from the coffee table.

I beg your pardon?

I hid the photo. I wish I hadn't. I didn't mean to hurt you.

You're not going to explain? I was flabbergasted.

I can't, he said, leaning forward and swirling his drink in his glass. Secrets of the confessional, as it were.

You're Romei's rabbi? I asked, stunned. I thought he was Catholic.

Not exactly.

I stared at him.

Not exactly, he's not a Catholic, or not exactly, you're not his rabbi?

Would you be prepared to trust me, just as I trusted you weren't going through my stuff?

You're *Esther's* rabbi?

It shocked me to think of Romei's muse as a real person, someone who looked to Benny for spiritual direction.

This is exactly the position I didn't want to be in, he said, standing. Once standing, he didn't know where to go.

Why on earth would Esther have a rabbi in New York if she lives in Rome?

She doesn't speak Italian. Also, she buys books from me; it's a two-bird, one-stone thing.

All these years, she doesn't speak Italian?

Benny shrugged.

What's she like?

Shira, this is exactly what I can't do. I can't talk about her, I can't talk about either of them—please don't ask me.

But you couldn't have referred Romei to me. You didn't know about *Vita Nuova.*

True. Can I get you more bourbon?

I recognized the strategy—I often changed the subject when I wanted to distract my daughter. It didn't work with her either.

Wait! I said, as Benny started toward the kitchen. Wait!

Benny turned.

I don't believe this, I said. I looked around: Was it the bourbon? The unfamiliarity of my surroundings? It can't be, I said. Romei referred you to me, didn't he?

Benny looked miserable, he didn't want to answer.

You solicited my first story all those years ago, you said you heard me read it at Trixie's. "Confessions."

I did.

Why did you go to the reading?

I often went to readings. I edited a literary magazine, remember?

Was Romei there?

Benny didn't reply.

I need to know, Benny! It's possible to lie by omission.

He was there. He told me about the reading. I went because he invited me.

I tried to remember who else had read that night. It was nearly ten years ago! Paula, the tired language poet? Franky, the funky fabulist?

Can we leave it at that? Benny asked.

It's weird that Romei saw me read and didn't mention it. Did I talk to him? I asked.

Could he have been part of the crowd swarming the tahini millet balls? I wondered. A lurker in the macrobiotic reading nook?

He couldn't have! I said. I'd have recognized him, right?

I'm going to get more bourbon, Benny said. When I get back, we're going to change the subject, okay?

I was distracted when Benny returned. *Romei? At Trixie's?* But Benny's face said, *We're changing the subject, right?*

Feeling better about the holidays? I asked gamely.

I guess I deserve that, he said as he settled back into his loveseat. What?

No, I'm not feeling better. The holidays are difficult. I'm angry; I can't get over it.

Angry about?

The usual, Benny said, and he began playing with his beard, as if pulling at loose threads. My father, you know. The way he treated us. Me. I can't get over it.

Ah, right—I remembered. The great Nazi hunter. He made fun of Benny because Benny was skinny and studious. Called him *ghetto Jew*, asked if he would have walked willingly into the gas, gave Benny barbells he knew Benny couldn't lift. For Christmas, no less. Yes, the family celebrated Christmas. Benny was what you might call a self-made Jew.

His father had been dead a dozen years.

When I was in therapy, we decided I don't *want* to forgive him. Every year I tell myself I do, but the truth is, if I let go, who would I be? Don't answer that.

I thought about this, stretched my legs out on the coffee table, where our toes nearly met.

You don't seem angry, I said.

That's 'cause you're not going out with me.

I thought of crazy Marie.

What do you do? I asked. When you get involved, I mean.

Jesus, he said, not looking at me. What don't I do? Then he stood, walked to the kitchen, returned with a bag of blue corn chips, opened it with a pop, muttered a Hebrew blessing, and passed me the bag. Nothing's as boring as the blatherings of the self-obsessed, he said finally.

I'll tell you what I do, if you tell me what you do.

You first. You're a woman of courage; I am a lowly worm.

Benny!

Inspire me, he said, leaning back.

I do nothing, I said, swirling the bourbon in my glass so I wouldn't have to look at him.

That's cheating! You don't do nothing.

I do nothing. I don't get involved.

You're not seeing anyone? I don't believe it!

Not since my divorce. Not really. Not in any real way.

That was ten years ago! It's possible to become a virgin again, if you don't do it enough.

I didn't want to get into the distinction between *getting involved* and *doing it*. In fact, I'd done it rather a lot.

Your turn, I said.

Benny shook his head, leaned back again.

I get involved. One after the other, he said, sometimes more than one at a time. I take them under my wing, treat them like baby birds. When they try to fly away, I get angry. *Very* angry.

You, angry? I can't picture it.

I *say* things, he said, looking away. Bad things. I tell them they're artistic frauds, they suck in bed, whatever it takes. I usually know just how to get them. The joke is, they're never as vulnerable as I think. They bite back—which I guess is the point. At least, that's what Sigmund said.

His name was *not* Sigmund!

That's what I called him. To be hostile.

To his face?

That's what I paid him for, right? To absorb my displaced Oedipal rage.

I watched my toes for a moment, wiggled them, realized what I was doing and tucked my legs under.

I'd rather be alone than go through that, I said finally.

I'd rather be dead than be alone. You're not eating your share of chips.

Knowing the pattern doesn't help?

I can't get off the bus, Shira. I can't change who I'm attracted to. I'm on a Circle Line, trying to revisit some primal scene with Pop so I can give it a happy ending. But I can't change the ending: it's ordained. Like me, he added, giggling. Then he sighed and looked at his knees. There is no new life. Not for me. Life for yours truly is an endless, cycling loop.

145

Can't you short circuit it? I asked, trusting that he'd forgive a mixed metaphor.

Insight hasn't done the trick, he said. Forgiveness. That's the answer.

Hmm. What would you say to yourself if you were a member of your, uh, congregation?

Benny laughed.

I'd say, as a Jew—a *professional* Jew—you have to believe in return! *T'shuvah*, the guarantee that, repentant and ready to make amends, you can break the cycle. That's what new life means for us, our burden and our blessing. If I follow the cycle of weekly Bible readings, monthly new moon celebrations, seasonal festivals, I'll never find myself trapped in a circle: I'm on an individual and collective spiral, endlessly revisiting the same meaningful lateral coordinates, presumably on ever higher planes. That was quite a sentence, he added, wasn't it?

When I do that, Ahmad says, "Real people don't talk like that."

Here's to not being real people, Benny said, extending his glass. I clinked and waited for him to continue. He seemed lost.

You think forgiveness is key . . . , I prompted.

Yes, and we've established that this is something of which I am not capable.

You know, I said after another pause, I don't think everything *can* be forgiven.

What would it take for you to forgive your mother?

Case in point.

Well?

Off the top of my head I'd say nothing. There's nothing she could do after forty years to make up for forty years of doing nothing.

Nice chiasmus!

Thank you.

Not even if she were on her death bed and asked for forgiveness?

If she wanted absolution, she should talk to the Pope. Billions of people are going to Rome next year to ask for indulgence. I'd say, join 'em. Assuming she's alive, which I doubt.

You think she's dead?

Why not?

You think that because she's absent: you can't imagine her.

When I was a kid, I imagined she was dead. I found that easier than admitting she'd left us. She'd been assassinated on her way to the airport.

Assassinated?

There was a spy subplot.

Benny laughed.

What did your father say?

I knew if I asked him, he'd crumble like stale bread. He was always so sad.

So you know nothing about her—not even why she left?

I'm pretty sure she joined the circus.

You never tried to contact her?

No interest. No idea where she is. I don't even know her maiden name.

What was her first name?

I stared at him.

Eleanor. Can we change the subject?

You think she's Catholic? You said that bit about the Pope . . .

She went into churches and lit candles. I assumed so.

Your father didn't talk about it?

Religion didn't interest him. He cared about archaic Archaic statues, quiet drinking, getting blown by the maid. What else? Scrabble.

I picked up my glass, was disappointed to realize it was empty. I held it anyway, my finger worrying the chip on the bottom.

He never remarried?

He never went out with anyone. Not more than once.

That you know of.

He didn't, I said, aware of how defensive I sounded. I found myself wishing I had a Marlboro, a whole pack of them, taped under the coffee table.

That hardly seems healthy.

He was taking care of me! What's wrong with that?

A man's got to have a life, no?

He seemed content.

You said he was sad.

He was both.

What would it take for you to forgive him?

My father? I asked stupidly. What's to forgive?

I've made mistakes, he'd said before the nurse wheeled him away. *Please don't hate me.*

We'll talk about it later, I'd said, thinking there would be a later.

Forgive me, he'd said. Contrition, one-size-fits-all. No confession, no reparation.

You sound angry, Benny said.

I'm angry. What's your point?

I don't have a point.

Oh, I said.

I'm just trying to understand.

Oh.

Benny took a moment to sip his drink. You know, he said, if my father had taken just one step in my direction, I'd have jumped over the abyss to meet him.

Well, I said tightly, you're a better man than I.

That's not what I meant, Shira.

What did you mean?

What I meant was, all I ever wanted was one stupid gesture, one lousy pat on the back—it could have been anything, it wouldn't have mattered. I'm such a cliché!

He pulled his legs off the table, leaned forward, put his elbows on his knees, his face in his hands.

He was your father, I said. You loved him.

I leaned over, touched Benny's shoulder. It was trembling.

Shit, he said, and got up. I need a drink.

•

Sorry, he said when he got back. How's the work going?

He'd brought the bottle and sat next to me on the couch so he could pour for both of us.

Slowly, I said. You sure you can talk about this?

Are you being sarcastic? Benny asked. His eyes were red.

No! I swear!

Of course I can talk about it.

Okay, I said, and told him how I kept finding what seemed like references to my stories in Romei's pages: images, the odd phrase.

Benny crinkled his nose.

Odd, he said. Why do you suppose he's doing that?

I liked that Benny didn't second-guess me. Did he trust me or did he know what Romei was capable of?

I was hoping you'd tell me, I said.

Me?

Yes, you. Why not you?

What do *you* think?

I haven't the foggiest.

I'd like to think he read your work and was unconsciously affected by it.

Not likely. He's way too self-conscious a writer. He put those images there on purpose.

That sounds reasonable, Benny said. How does it make you feel?

You sound like Sigmund! I said, laughing.

Sounds like he's trying to manipulate you, elicit a reaction of some kind.

Interesting, I said. I hadn't thought of that.

What's your reaction?

Well, I said, it confuses me, it makes me angry, like he's stealing. And mocking me, because who am I? I'm just the translator!

Does it affect how you read the story?

How I read the story? You mean how I feel about his characters?

I guess. Whatever.

They pissed me off from the start . . . , and I told him how I believed Romei was writing a self-serving piece to justify his adultery, how Esther seemed less a muse than a sloppy projection of his fantasies. Then I thought about the last section, their defeat by the husband, how that twist had defeated my expectations as well as theirs. Maybe I didn't hate them after all.

I don't know, I finally said.

So Dante embeds poems from an earlier time into his narrative, and Romei embeds bits of your work. It's as if yours were the original work, the proof-text!

The what?

The proof-text. The original authoritative bit of Bible that "proves" a rabbinic argument.

You're drunk. That makes no sense whatsoever.

Benny shrugged.

Right on both counts, he said, and pulled a handkerchief from his gym shorts, looked at it puzzled for a moment, then blew his nose. In what context does he quote you?

You name it, I said, then thought about the images: Romei blocking the sun as Esther sits on her bench, Romei watching Esther from a tree in the park, Romei throwing stones at her window, Romei kissing her for the first time on the neck. Scenes of seduction, I said.

Interesting. Does this speak to you in any way?

You think he's using my words to seduce me? I whispered.

I don't know, Benny murmured, frowning. He loves his wife.

I stared at my shoes.

Maybe it *is* a manipulation, I said. He mind fucks his translators to keep their interest. There are probably dozens of mind fucks in there, bubbles of real life injected into the veins of his "autobiography."

Inject a bubble into someone's vein and they die, Benny said pensively. I learned that on *Columbo*.

The more I thought about my theory, the more I thought it had to be. The false friends, the "borrowed" images—all addressed to the translator.

I don't know if I can go through with this, I said, shaking my head. It's too weird.

You have to! Benny said. It's important!

Wow! This may be more important to you than it is to me.

Benny shrugged. We were both a little drunk.

You want to know what happens next, right? he asked.

I didn't know what he was talking about, but I lacked the energy to investigate.

I have to do the dishes, I said, struggling to get out of his deep plush cushions.

Stay with me, he said, grabbing my arm so I couldn't stand.

I beg your pardon? I said, plopping back onto the couch.

Stay with me, he said, but he was looking in front of him, not at me.

You want . . . Oh! No! No, I'm sorry. Benny?

He let go of my arm.

I'm sorry, he said, still not looking at me, putting his hand back in his beard. My bad.

Shall I see myself out? I asked, trying to remember where I'd left my raincoat.

No, he said, but he didn't get up. I stood, wandered through the living room, the hallway, found it in a hall closet.

Forgive me? Benny said, almost inaudibly, when I was almost out the door.

Everything, I said, not looking back. And I did.

•

He called as I was walking out the building's front door.

Don't say anything to Romei, he said.

I thought he was talking about his botched seduction, but no, he was probably talking about Esther, the reading, what we'd said about the Great Man.

No problem.

He's my patron saint, you know.

I didn't know, I said, confused. *Gilgul*?

Maybe. He said something else, but the 116 bus passed.

Benny? I asked, but he was gone.

33

BALD DONUTS

I woke up feeling lousy, my brain an airless closet.

Ahmad was slumped at the dining room table, his coffee long gone cold.

I wouldn't forgive him without an apology, but I'd give him every opportunity.

Morning, I said, aware that I was shuffling. Andi get off okay?

Ahmad grunted.

I feel like shit, I added, thinking this might cheer him up.

Coffee's mud by now, he said, reflectively.

We lapsed back into silence. Maybe he was thinking about Mirabella, her crazy plan to export their sons to America. Maybe he was thinking about dew on a suburban lawn, the simple pleasures of Metro North.

Andi thinks you have a thing for Benny, he said almost grimly. Do you? I remember, vaguely, you thought he was cute?

No! I said too quickly. Can you see me with a rabbi?

What's wrong with rabbis? Ahmad asked with a half smile.

Everything's God-this and God-that! I said, and poured myself a double.

I'm at People of the Book a lot and I've never heard Benny talk about God.

If you're a rabbi, you believe in things, you have certainties.

Like Dante, with bagels.

Exactly. Then there's the ritual, keeping up with the Yiddish-isms . . .

You keep up with the Joneses, why not the Yiddishisms?

We couldn't have a life together. It's obvious.

Ahmad shrugged.

Besides, he's seeing someone.

Ah. There are donuts in the kitchen, but Andi and I ate the good ones.

I was ravenous, I realized. I brought the box to the table, though it contained only what Andi called *bald* donuts, barely worth the calories.

I looked for the Philosopher's Tea the other day, I said, but couldn't find it.

The box was empty; I threw it away.

Really? I asked, hoping Ahmad couldn't sense how crestfallen I was.

A scanner arrived, by the way. I insisted to DHL that I was Shira Greene.

I laughed.

Hey, I said, I think I know why Romei is so interested in translat-ing his work into English!

Oh? Ahmad had surrendered again to his hazy gloom.

His wife doesn't speak Italian, can you imagine? Benny told me.

Again with the Benny, always with the Benny. How does he know?

Oops! I shouldn't have said. He knows Romei, and Esther. Don't say anything.

You're confusing me, Shira. It's too early. I heard you come in last night, by the way.

(I may have tripped on the umbrella stand; I may have repri-manded said umbrella stand.)

Be careful, he said. I don't want to have to pick up the pieces.

There's always another umbrella stand, I said, knowing that wasn't what he meant at all.

Ho, ho, he said, but not in a jolly way.

I picked up a bald donut.

I haven't heard from her, if that's what you're wondering.

Really? I asked.

Not since I agreed to cooperate.

You must be on email day and night, I said.

The time difference doesn't help, he said.

I'm sorry, I said.

Ahmad shrugged.

No Connecticut if Hassan stays where he is, right? I wanted to ask, but didn't.

I've made a cock-up of my life, Shira. Mistake after mistake. I look back, though, and don't see how I could have done differently.

You've done good, Ahmad, I promise!

Maybe, he said, maybe not. If I ever lost you guys, if I ever lost Andi . . .

Why would you lose us? Why would you lose Andi?

He gave me a sharp look, then softened.

Right, he said. Why ever?

It wasn't an apology, but it would do.

34

THE CHARMING CHIASMUS

I went online and found an email from Benny: *Thanks for the visit. Sorry if I acted weird. Love trouble. (Don't you love that section in* Vita Nuova *where Dante talks about love as if it were susceptible to reason, then concludes that love makes him unreasonable?)*

It was true! As Dante writes poems of love, he muses: love is good because it keeps us from thinking vile thoughts. But it's also not good because the more faithful he is, the harder his trials. He writes a sonnet, then, saying he's confused, his theme is confusion.

There was more: *I've left a present for you. In the lobby.*

I ran downstairs like a child. There, in a padded envelope, *The Song of Songs*, Ariel and Chana Bloch translation.

Excited, and hungry, I brought it to the Eight Bar.

At night, the Eight Bar was a blues club where dapper old men played harmonica and called other old men up to the stage: *Sonny Boy, is that you? Stormin' Eddie, get up here!* while awestruck undergrads looked on, clutching their collectible albums. I'd been something of a regular before I became a *loco parenti*. I found a booth in back, well beyond the reach of drunken darts, and ordered a junior-size Junior Wellsburger.

I'd read my share of scripture in grad school, but of the *Song* I knew only what Bernard of Clairvaux had said of it eight and a half centuries ago. Bernard, because he was Dante's biggest crush, able to travel farther in Paradise than even Beatrice herself. In his lifetime, Bernard was best known for his eighty-six sermons on the first two chapters of the *Song*—yes, eighty-six sermons on a mere eighteen verses, sermons about the redemptive power of love, the intimate relationship between Christ and His flock. Bernard was clear that the *Song* was not an erotic tale. No, it was the *very opposite* of an erotic tale! There was nothing carnal about that book, he insisted, *nothing whatsoever*.

Reading the *Song* now for the first time, I could see why he needed eighty-six sermons to make his point. For a description of purely "spiritual" love, the *Song* is all about the senses. The sound of a lover's voice, the singing of birds. The vision of a lover's beauty. The taste of milk, honey, and wine. Lovers' bodies exuberant—dancing, running, bounding, chasing—and luxuriant—embracing, leaning, resting in bowers, on couches, in beds. All of nature flowing, flourishing, flowering.

And the lovers, the Shulamite and her "king": they believe in each other, they believe in themselves; they do not hesitate, they will not hold back. It was hard to imagine a love story more different from that of *Vita Nuova*. If Dante only *looks* at Beatrice, if he only rarely hears her speak, and certainly never tastes, touches, or smells her, these lovers revel in senses that blur boundaries (two points, no longer clearly separate, become one point, which is the point).

The *Song* has two heroes, moreover. Neither is a symbol, an idea of perfection, neither waits patiently or in peril while the other fulfills his destiny. Quest is unnecessary: in their happy world of lyric fulfillment, they have no need for heroes or new life, no need to look behind Door Number Two.

My beloved is mine, and I am his. Close enough to *I am my beloved's and my beloved is mine.* The source, I was beginning to understand, of the inscription on my father's wedding ring.

I called Benny.

I am my beloved's and my beloved is mine, I said.

It's a bit early for declarations, he said.

Where from? I asked.

The charming chiasmus? he said. King James, *Song of Songs*, 2:16. *Ani ledodi ve dodi li.*

Nicer in King James than the Bloch version, I said. Thanks for that, by the way.

What's that? Benny was talking with someone who wasn't me. Be right there, pumpkin. Sorry, Shira, gotta go.

My heart beat too quickly, tears welled.

Benny's pumpkin. His voice, speaking to her, was kind, it was gentle. Had anyone ever spoken to me that way? You don't get to be pumpkin shagging your boss, not if you're a temp.

I could (almost) imagine Benny and his Maid Marie luxuriating in their fragrant bower, Benny making plaits of Marie's green hair as she strained to finish her word find. But I couldn't imagine myself there. I tried! I tried to imagine myself—with Benny, with *anyone*—shooting spikenard or dropping myrrh, but I couldn't. I could imagine desire, I could imagine seasonal flings, but not tender reciprocity, not the charming chiasmus. Even at fourteen, when I danced for T. in the chem lab, I was no Shulamite—I called myself Salomé, veiled even then. When I imagined love now, it was Love Lite I imagined— or, more often, the end of love: waiting at the airport, the ring on T.'s finger, my father being rolled away.

Prelapsarian Shira, innocent Shira, Shira before T., Shira before marriage, the *Shir haShirim* Shira was gone, the Flying Girl grounded.

I looke down, was startled to find a Junior Wellsburger sitting cold on an oval plate, next to a side of Jimmy Witherspoonbread. Freshmen were tossing darts, drunk already, or pretending to be. I found I'd lost my appetite.

35

WHAT COMES AFTER ONCE UPON A TIME?

I finished trotting "Call" and "Screen," and this is what I found: aside from the echoes in Romei's first poem, my lexicon of oft-repeated words contained just one entry: Romei's omnipresent *penna* (his pen, wing, man of letters, writer). Had I missed something? He repeated the usual articles and prepositions (*I* figured rather frequently; *she* almost as often), but nothing substantive—no important nouns or modifiers. As if the New Life involved finding a new word for every situation, as if nothing I'd ever done could help me now.

I was working on the park bench scene, when Ahmad stuck his head in the study.

Our precious needs help with her homework, he said.

Huh? I asked, not looking up. You help her.

I'm due at the Temple of Learning.

After dinner. Tell her I'll help her then.

Shira, Ahmad said, raising his voice, she needs help now! You need to help her now.

I looked up. Ahmad was holding a wastebasket overflowing with crumpled paper. I pulled out a paper ball. Laboriously perfect block letters, *Once upon a time . . .* then an error, a "t" that slipped below the line, scratched out furiously with a dull pencil.

They're all like that, he said. She's been at it for an hour, apparently.

Andi was seated at her little desk, her face grim with concentration, her Observations Notebook closed under her elbow, her children's dictionary open to *P*.

You already have homework? I asked. You've only been in school three days!

Exactly. It's all downhill from here.

I leaned over her shoulder to see what she was writing, then pulled up a chair.

How do you spell *precisely*? she said. I can't find it in this stupid dictionary.

How about you tell me what you want to write, I'll write it down, then you can copy it.

Mrs. Chao says we can't copy.

She means you have to make it up.

I *am* making it up.

What's your story about?

It's about once upon a time there was a boy named Ovidio . . .

You're writing about your friend?

It's about once upon a time.

Sweetie, I don't think it's a good idea to write about your friend. He might not like it.

It's my story. Ahmad said it was okay.

He did? Well, maybe it depends on what you write. What happens to him?

I don't know. I've only written *Once upon a time*. I keep making mistakes. Look! she said, and swirled around, then swirled around again. Where's my wastepaper basket? Where is it?

Ahmad took it.

Wow, she said, shaking her braids. He's always playing tricks on me! I think that's what he does best.

I laughed.

If Ahmad goes to Connecticut, I think I should go with him.

I stopped laughing.

Why? Why do you say that?

Because he'll be lonely there without me.

Why do you think that? I asked, and had to keep myself from crying out, *What about me?*

Because I'm the only one who likes what he likes.

Conservative economics? I thought. *Picking up boys at barber shops?*

Don't you think I'd be lonely without you? I asked.

No, Andi said, applying pencil to paper. You've got Benny.

Benny's just a friend. Besides you're my baby.

I'm *not* a baby, Andi said, putting down her pencil and looking at me, exasperated.

You'll always be my baby.

She rolled her eyes, but I could tell she was pleased.

Did I spell *Ovidio* right? she asked, leaning into me, her braid tickling my thigh.

Yes, sweetie.

She squinted at me.

I'll ask Ahmad when he finishes his stupid class.

You're spelling it right, I promise.

You could just be saying that.

Why would I do that?

So you can go back to work.

I'm staying right here while you write your story, I said, putting my hand on her shoulder. That way you can ask me anything you want. Okay?

What do you think happens after *Once upon a time*?

I wish I knew, princess, I wish I knew.

•

Andi read her story out loud at Friday Night Dinner: Ovidio lived in a cave where he hid from his mother and father. Sometimes his mother fought with his father. That's when he went to the cave. Ovidio had a broken nose but he wasn't nosy.

I had to bite my tongue while she composed her masterwork, not to influence her. At one point, I took a break in our bathroom, looked at Mr. Bubble, her Winnie the Pooh shampoo, and wondered: Was Andi okay? Was the friction between her *loco parenti* scarring her for life? Did she need Sigmund? My funny, my beautiful, my startling child! My baby—look at her!

The Polaroid Ahmad had given her was on a shelf. I snapped a shot of her hunched over her desk, the tip of her tongue sticking out as she crossed out yet another word.

Mo-omm! she cried. Look what you made me do!

But there she was now, smiling, triumphant, standing behind her uneaten dinner, peas hidden inexpertly under some mashed potatoes. *The End.* We clapped; Ahmad gave me a look.

Mommy says it's spelled right, she said to Ahmad, but I think you should look.

He scanned the page.

It's perfect! he exclaimed. I have never seen such perfect writing!

See, Mambo! I told you.

Know what *Chao* means in Italian? Ahmad asked.

Don't, I said, hiding my smile behind my hand.

What? Andi asked. It means food, right?

No, it means hello and goodbye both.

Only if you don't know if you're coming or going, my baby said.

36

RIGHT! WRITE!

It was Friday evening. Ahmad was telling Andi a bedtime story, and I was in my room, looking out at People of the Book. It seemed ages since Benny and I had talked, though it had been just two days. I shouldn't, I knew, but I did: I pulled out my cell phone.

Marie answered, wanted to know who was calling.

Tell him it's Hester Prynne.

Who?

I spelled it for her. She put the phone down, didn't ask if I could hold.

Shabbat shalom! Gut yontif! Benny finally answered.

Kasha varnishkes! I said.

Who is this? Benny asked.

Shira! Who else?

Shanah tovah! Happy new year! Can I call you after the weekend? It's not a good time.

Locusts? I wanted to ask. Frogs?

I'm getting ready to close, he said. Rosh Hashana.

Rosh Hashana! I said. Too bad! I mean, congratulations!

Benny laughed.

Happy birthday of the world, I blurted.

Thank you, but it starts in an hour and I've got a sermon to write.

Right, I said. Write! Ha, ha.
I got off the phone and stared at myself in the mirror.
Watch out, Shira, I said. Watch out.

37

BY A CLEAR STREAM

The next morning I found a fax from Romei, a new section titled "Muse." And a note:

You say Dante experienced love only in his imagination. You are right, of course, to an extent. His dreams and visions, and therefore his poems, are inspired at first by illusions (the figure of Love, his screen ladies). But increasingly he locates his muse outside himself.

His English was better than he'd let on! If he alienated every translator in town, he could easily translate his *Vita Quasi Nova* himself.

The later poems in Vita Nuova *are inspired or commissioned,* he continued, *by ladies, the brother, various pilgrims, the mysterious visitors. These are not constructs of Dante's imagination but "real" people, and the poems he writes for them reflect an increasing engagement with the real. His later poems praising Beatrice also represent an advance on his earlier, more self-centered work. As his love grows, so does he.*

Yes, I thought, burning my mouth on my coffee, after Beatrice is dead and more of an idea than ever!

Your rigid judgments do not allow for the possibility of change. To put it in terms you should understand: what good is a story if nothing happens?

Where is this photo of Andrea?

I laughed and scanned the photo I'd taken of Andi at her desk, then faxed it to Romei, together with a note:

Yeah, whatever. So Dante accepts commissions, so he is inspired by "real" people, so he has a "muse," whatever that means. So he stops writing woe-is-me poems. This doesn't mean he changes—not really. This doesn't mean he learns how to love.

Then I said, What the hey, and mailed the photo to Aunt Emma, or Elisheva, as she now called herself, though this would mean receiving a photo of her in return—in the scarf she wore so the West Bank wind wouldn't wig out her wig.

Which inspired me to find my daughter. She was at the dining room table, coloring in her Insects of the World coloring book.

What kind of bug is that? I asked.

A green bug.

Is that its scientific name? I asked.

Mom!

Up, child! I exclaimed. It's time to exercise your limbs. Come! Where's Ahmad?

In Brooklyn, fixing his car. Come! First-to-get-to-Joe's-while-also-checking-both-ways-before-she-crosses-the-street gets a happy-face cookie!

Once at Joe's, I had to grab Andi to keep her from stepping on the twins, who were playing with the Barnard student's shoelaces. I got a double for me and a coconut dandy for Nate, who, oddly, was nowhere to be found.

Andi ate her cookie while leaning into me on our Riverside Park bench.

It's pretty great living here, isn't it? I said, my arm around her. When she didn't reply, I elaborated: the playground, Joe's, Cohn's Cones.

Can I have an ice cream later? she said.

I considered that a victory. Sure, I said. Then she asked for, and I produced, a Handiwipe from my mother's bag of tricks.

Bye! she shouted, waving furiously, as if she were off on a polar expedition.

Don't run, I cried pointlessly, thinking of her cast. Then I arranged everything on my bench—Romei's pages, Andi's pail and shovel, her Observations Notebook, my iced mocha, Andi's Wonder Woman Band-Aids, a jumbo pack of goldfish.

165

The Hudson glimmered. I closed my eyes, heard the trickle of the fountain behind me, imagined myself as Esther on her bench, smiled to think that a singular Romeo might someday watch me from a tree: Benny, for example, his long legs dangling from a branch, playing a flute like an oversize sprite.

Down girl! The only woman Benny wanted anywhere near his flute was narcoleptic Marie.

So what was Romei's task now? At this point in *Vita Nuova*, Dante addresses poems to his muse. He runs into her at a party—his entire body throbs, he is abandoned by his spirits, he leans against a fresco for relief. The ladies laugh at his distress, not understanding the cause of his transformation. But this sighting occasions more poems—poems about romantic anguish in which the figure of Pity frequently appears.

Then Beatrice injures him by not saying hello. Heartbroken, he tells the ladies who surround him that while his joy once lay in her greeting, now he must locate it in something that cannot be withdrawn. His new path? Words of praise! He resolves to write not of romantic anguish but of the perfections of Beatrice.

Like most of us, Dante finds change easy to talk about, but the prospect overwhelms him. He dithers, he's beset by fear and trembling. Finally, while traveling by a "clear stream," he receives a first line . . . The result: a *canzone* describing Beatrice's perfections.

So what would Romei do? Esther was his muse, presumably. He'd praise her, right?

Not exactly.

I'd thought that Esther and Romei, once "liberated" from her husband, would be speechless. In fact, their first act is to dine *al fresco* in Trastevere, Esther's Samsonite propped against a wall covered with obscene chalk drawings. Romei avoids her eye, tosses crumbs to urchin cats, sketches nonsense syllables onto a paper tablecloth. He imagines himself a poet Picasso, whose scrawled words will one day pay for dinner, for he is down to his last lire.

Esther, meanwhile, cannot sit still: she spills wine, complains of pains in her hip, gives her ragú back to the waiter, insists she'd ordered *carbonara*, though she doesn't eat pork. She tastes her *penne*, vomits them onto the cobblestones.

Yes, more *penne*, not filled by Esther this time, but voided, *spennar*, like Icarus.

You will live with me, Romei says, as if this is a comfort. She wipes her mouth on the tablecloth, looks at him in horror. He looks back at her in dwindling light as if from a mountain top, imagines words falling from her mouth, heavy and broken—and from these on the tablecloth he fashions poems. A blotch between lines three and four represents a smear of sugo, between six and seven, a drop of wine, or so a sidebar explains.

In the days that follow, Esther's languor, attractive in a lover, is revealed as pathological passivity: she is by turns depressed, hysterical, withdrawn. The passion that brought them together proves no stronger than a wishbone, snapped in two by Esther's loss, the rigors and banalities of everyday life. Esther refuses Romei her bed, brings men to the flat—foreigners, thieves, CIA operatives. She acts not out of desire, nor to make Romei jealous, but to give form to her despair. When the men finish their business, she sends them off and crawls onto Romei's lap, babbling, her words slippery and disconnected. He croons at her—in Italian, Romanian too. Her babbling, his crooning (increasingly insincere), neither understood by the other, is the subject of another poem, a long-limbed Whitmanian knock-off, the wind knocked out of every line. The Song of Me-Me-Me taken to its solipsistic extreme.

Housekeeping is a nightmare. Esther can't cook, her habits are slovenly. She takes the pittances Romei earns from interpreting, from acting as guide to visiting journalists, and spends them on imported Rice Krispies, fat loaves of American bread. Their phone is disconnected: she's been calling overseas, calling everyone she knows, trying to find her husband. No one will help: even her mother has disowned her. Romei shouts at her in Italian: get up! get up! Curled on a couch, unmoving, she asks in English if she should take up crochet. *Croce?* Romei wonders. *Croce?* The cross? Does his Jewish wife wish to convert?

They know so little about each other. Esther is allergic to cigarettes; Romei *always* smokes when he writes. Esther is a morning person; Romei likes to sleep in. Romei, despite his slow start, is swollen with ambition; Esther has only her past.

She is difficult, complains of wrist pain, leg pain, she sells her mother's pearls, forgets to attend job interviews. Awaking with a rash across her nose and cheeks, she stays in bed, pretends she is a child in Connecticut. Romei grows tired of her babbling, her complaints, her wild-eyed wandering. There are circles under her eyes, as if she hasn't slept, yet she spends whole days in bed. Romei urges her to continue her translation. It's a lie, she says, the *Song of Songs*, translation, all of it a lie. He agrees but thinks her lazy. One morning she presents him with a handful of her hair—did it fall out or did she pull it?—he finds he doesn't care: it's her fault, surely, something she has brought upon herself.

Their bond is a negative one: held together by the drama that brought them together, his guilt and sense of obligation, her inability to imagine anything different, they live a life of crossed purposes, missed opportunities, swallowed outrage and, not incidentally, squalor. But Romei writes. Out of this impossible relationship, out of their perpetual misunderstanding and disappointment, Romei, no longer "blocked," discovers the anti-vocabulary for his art. He writes, she wanders, falls to the ground, he writes. She is his muse, his anti-muse.

A poem that comes close to announcing Romei's poetics of distance and incomprehension includes an outrageous scrambling of the Celan line I'd featured in my story, written here not in German but in what I guessed was Yiddish: *Then, when only nothingness stood between us, nothing brought us together.*

To make clear the poet's identification with this poem, he writes it as an acrostic, each line beginning with a letter from his name: R-O-M-E-I.

A pattern emerges, the couple's version of normalcy. Esther takes typing lessons from an expatriate Scot, finds work in English-speaking offices, but always she is forced by drowsiness, by ever-shifting aches and pains, whose fluidity and unpredictability torment her more than their effects, to quit these jobs, though Romei suspects it's the daily demands—the clothes that must be pressed, the long journeys by tram or bus—that wear her down. A disbarred doctor offers her a diagnosis over wine—hysteria, of the Freudian variety, he says, and suggests sex with a vigorous man.

The couple develops friendships with other marginalized types— a surrealist painter displaced by the Spanish Civil War, a schizophrenic actor, a heroin-addicted banker who leaves gold coins in Esther's underwear drawer. Homosexual brothers: black dancers from Georgia. An amateur archeologist from Duquesne, in search of an underage wife. Esther types, the two attend parties, drinking fests in public places, Romei writes.

And thus, the years pass: Romei publishes a book of poems, and another. Esther dresses in men's clothing, wanders late at night. Romei's work is translated, he travels to consult with translators and publishers, leaving Esther in the custody of a friend, a poverty-stricken academic, a costume designer, an art restorer who can be relied upon to buy toilet paper and make polenta. Daily life is marked less by hysteria, more by courtesies, occasional kindnesses that betray the fullness of their resignation. Their intercourse is defined by what they do not discuss: Esther's loss, the choice they did not make, which was to be together.

With extraordinary timing, Andi pulled on my sleeve.

Hello, my darling, I said, reaching for her shoulder.

You look funny, Mom.

Moms do that sometimes. You having fun?

Have you been reading my Notebook? she asked, squinting at me.

Never! I would never read your notebook! Your notebook is private!

I'm just asking.

I couldn't help adding: You could share it with me sometime if you wanted.

Andi rolled her eyes. Good thing we brought Band-Aids, she said, pointing to a scrape I couldn't see. I kissed her knee, once, twice, thrice, and held her tight.

It's okay, Mambo! she said, pulling away. No need to go bananas!

I watched her run away, *sans* Band-Aid, watched the glimmering

Hudson, and awaited my share of wisdom. These pages were no gift to Esther. To invert Dante's poetics of praise, Romei had spared her nothing—he'd stripped her bare, exposed her as an hysterical, nymphomaniacal, cross-dressing hypochondriac. He dug his *penna* into her pain—her tears now the ink that filled his pen—and to what end? So he could play the martyr? What purpose could he have but injury? The modern meaning of *libello*, Dante's "little book," was libel. How could she bear to read this defamation? I felt a traitor's desire to soften the language, to protect Esther from Romei's vituperation. But I couldn't. Who was I? The translator. I was no one.

38

ALWAYS WE RETURN
TO DANTE

The next morning I awoke late. A note from Ahmad advised me that Andi was upstairs at Pammy's. Again? Surely it was Pammy's turn to come here, but I wouldn't insist. Pammy was what Ahmad liked to call *an expert*: spinach makes you fat, childhood is incomplete without a parrot. My adulthood was complete without Pammy.

I visited the Flying Girl, who was in good form, flying over the head of the artist's crazy mother. What was Romei doing? I asked. Did he hate his wife? What was his game? Would Ahmad move to Connecticut? What would Andi and I do then?

You're pondering imponderables, the Flying Girl said. Go get lunch.

I got a hot dog from Cohn's Cones' beach menu, decided to take it for a walk—up Broadway, past Abdul's, past the Eight Bar, then west to Riverside Drive, where I stopped at the Skating Park to watch mad young men turn upside down on their boards. I was heading to Grant's Tomb, apparently, where Ahmad and I had walked every day when I was pregnant, talking about the future—how the world would begin again when she was born. We didn't talk about the future these days; we didn't talk about much of anything.

I was nearly at the Tomb when my phone rang.

Who is the child's father? Romei asked. He didn't say hello.

I beg your pardon?

Andray-a. Nice photograph, but who is the father?

You are unbelievable! I said. My daughter's father is none of your business!

He is Ahmad from this last story you are writing? I like this story!

He was referring to "Domino," the story about Jonah as a boy, the story that made Ahmad's face go white, that made Jeanette stop talking to me.

Oh, I said. Well, thank you. But, no. Ahmad isn't her father.

I found a bench facing the Hudson and sat down. In front of me, industrious, red-faced people jogged or roller-bladed along the Riverside Park path.

She looks like a good girl, Romei said, writing like her mother.

Yes, I admitted, looking for my *MOM!* handkerchief. She's writing a story. About a boy at school.

She is loving this boy?

The thought made me laugh: like Dante loving Beatrice at her age. Was it so impossible?

She empathizes with him. He's had a hard life. She confuses herself with him, maybe.

She is also having the hard life?

She thinks so . . . But that's a long story.

I felt a strange urge to share with Romei the story of Connecticut, of Mirabella and Jonah, and all our hurts—he was so avuncular! Except he wasn't, not really.

You too, maybe, are writing a story?

I am *not* writing a story. I'm working, like I said. Just working.

The muse is not with you? There is no *fidanzato* who inspire you?

I laughed and wiped Indian-summer sweat from my neck and brow.

Men may *amuse* me, I said, but they do not *muse* me.

This I cannot believe!

"Domino" was a bear, I said. The last story I ever wrote. I'll probably never write again.

A *bare*? You mean you hide nothing?

Bear, *orso*! I mean it was difficult. But, yes, it was also rather bare.

You do hide, if you refuse to be with a man.

You have too little knowledge of my life to make that judgment with, I said, too flustered to take care with my prepositions.

I mean *you* in the impersonal sense of *one*. This is the American way, no?

You don't mean *you* in the impersonal sense, but I forgive you. Besides, if I hide, it's no more than Dante does.

Always we return to Dante when we want to understand our life! Romei said.

Is that *we* in the royal we sense, the you-and-me we, or the impersonal we?

Wee, wee, wee! the poet cried. All the way home! This is American, no? A game played with the children's feet?

Maybe it was Indian summer or the hotdog napkin still in my hand—a memory struck me, of little Shira on the beach, skin roasting, sodas warming nearby, bathing suit sticking like a reassuring second skin. Screaming with glee as someone, her mother, wee-wee-weed up her fat little thigh, little Shira laughing till she wee-wee-weed in reply. And my mother, smiling a sun-kissed smile, calling me babydoll and, caking my legs with sand, picking me up and running me to the sea. I couldn't have been more than two. Baby Shira laughing with her mother? Was it possible?

Yes, Romei said, after a pause that seemed to respect my silence. Dante is fearful, this is true. But he has a muse. Beatrice motivate him, she inspire him.

He was referring to my fax of that morning.

Beatrice cause Dante to change, he continued. Because of her, he *choose* change.

He changes his aesthetics, I said. First he writes about romantic anguish, then he writes poems of praise. Is that change? At the end of the book he decides to write not just lyric poems but narrative. What kind of change is that? Who cares?

Is still change, Romei said, and he sounded grumpy about it.

We were going to have to agree to disagree.

You've written a *bare* tale about your muse, I said. Would you tell me why?

Bear, meaning *difficult*?

Meaning *not hidden*.

I tell you already, I hold no interest in poetics.

What *are* you interested in? This story is no gift to Esther.

You are wrong. This is the biggest gift I give my Esther. You will see. Send me when you can. Goodbye.

Wait! I have questions!

You were at Trixie's! You heard me read! Why didn't you tell me?

I think this is all. Goodbye!

Infuriating man!

•

Ahmad was in his studio; Andi was back early from Pammy's. Pammy, it turned out, needed "alone time."

You guys fight? I asked.

No. They'd disagreed about how to punish Tink. Andi said he should sit quietly and think about what he'd done; Pammy thought he needed a spanking. Andi said spanking was *uncivilized*. Which was when Pammy slammed the door and said she needed alone time.

Does Pammy's mother know you left? I asked.

She gave me an apple.

You upset?

About what? she asked.

39

GOOD ON PAPER

I was awakened the next morning by the telephone. *Someone get that,* I thought, then realized it was my cell, Brahms's "Lullaby." Andi had been at my ringer again.

Veronica! Benny said.

Veronica?

Betty? he asked.

Benny?

You don't read comic books, do you?

I was supposed to call you, wasn't I? What day is it?

Dear me, I woke you, didn't I?

We made a plan: Benny would cook, I'd bring wine. I went back to sleep, half aware that dinner sounded rather like a date.

•

That afternoon, I lay on Andi's bed and wrote a quick running translation of "Muse." I shouldn't have been surprised to see paronomasia sprinkled all over the couple's tragic victory, like shots on a Cohn's cone, but I was. Paranomasia: words that are unrelated but sound alike, placed in proximity for the fun or pleasing sound of it. Kissing cousins-in-law, couples that look good in public (or on paper) but aren't, in fact, compatible. Not *croce*/crochet (false friends), but a *place for the plaice* or *traditore-traduttore*. The *heart's hurt*, if you stretch it.

It made a certain sense. Esther's loss is Romei's gain: she deteriorates as he, inspired by his anti-muse, finds his Nobel/ignoble voice. By reminding us of the lack of "true" correspondence between words that appear connected, Romei underscores the lack of affinity between his lord and lady.

Or so I wrote in my Door Number Two notebook. Then I read over my notes—about the *Song*, the false friends, Romei's poems— and found that it was good.

I was, and would for a short while remain, the world's leading interpreter of Romei's *Vita Quasi-Nuova* (or whatever he was going to call it). Should I expand my Translator's Note into a definitive monograph? I should! I could see it now: Talks at sexy Italian conferences! A dissertation-cum-bestseller! Graduate students shouting me half-caffs at the Hungarian Pastry Shop!

Spirit aloft, I called Jeanette to finagle an invitation to watch the three Eves: *The Lady Eve, All About Eve, Three Faces of Eve*. I even put on lipstick and a low-cut blouse, so she'd think I'd made progress.

Where're you going? Ahmad wanted to know, looking me up and down.

I winked—it was my scheduled night out: let him wonder! But he wasn't playing.

It's been days since you put Andi to bed, he stage-whispered. She'll be so disappointed!

I looked at Andi sitting on the floor, absorbed in her crayons.

You're nuts, I said.

Maybe I said it loudly. Her head jerked up; she looked anxiously at me, then Ahmad.

You look pretty, Mommy. Don't you think she looks pretty?

It seemed very important to Andi that Ahmad think I look pretty. I raised my eyebrows, dared him to agree. When he didn't, I walked over to my daughter and kissed her on the head.

Thank you for thinking I look pretty. I take after you.

•

Jeanette greeted me at the door, a cosmopolitan at the ready. She confided during intermission that she was going through The Change.

Fasten your seat belts, she said, it's going to be a bumpy night!

PART FIVE

DEATH

40

YOU DON'T THINK
THE APOCALYPSE
CAN HAPPEN

Every so often we indulged Ahmad's craving for things Russian. Sometimes this meant Brighton Beach, *solyanka* in the shadow of the Cyclone. More often it meant midtown and the Balalaika. Fish eggs didn't agree with Andi, or so she said, so when Ahmad and I went out, Jeanette's daughter Dotty babysat. Dotty was eighteen and postponing Harvard to volunteer for U2K, a Y2K-preparedness group; she'd go to college in January, she said, if there were any colleges left.

Andi had organized her school stuff to show Dotty, her Pretty Princess backpack leaning against a tower of textbooks, Tink, newly rehabilitated, standing guard on top.

Guess what! she said, taking Dotty's hand as soon as she walked in the door. Ahmad's going to buy me a bike! A pink one, with a basket for Tink!

Ahmad! I said.

Every kid should have a bike, he said. He was trying to do jovial, but Ahmad didn't do jovial.

Every kid in Connecticut has a bike, Andi said. I'm going to be every kid in Connecticut!

Honey, I said, trying to control my voice, we're not going to Connecticut.

Aw, Mom!

You'll thank me later.

I doubt it. Is there apple picking in Manhattan?

I stared at her.

I didn't think so, she said.

I shook my head and turned to Dotty.

How's the Y2K business?

I brought a list of everything you'll need, she said, digging in her backpack. Then she saw my expression. Poor dears! she said. You don't think the apocalypse can happen! Even if our government cared for us, which it doesn't, it could never untangle our dependence on computers. She read to us from a list: Canned food, and don't forget a manual can opener. Twenty pounds of wheat per person, per month; a grain mill; ten pounds of soybeans. Food-grade plastic containers. We're vulnerable, she said, but we don't have to despair! There's a great safe-house site on the Internet . . . , and she was digging again in her backpack.

We managed to slip out, eventually. Reservations, I said, though the Balalaika always had room for Ahmad.

Of course, Dotty said. We can talk about this later.

No dessert for Andi, Ahmad said from the door, unless she finishes her corn. And make sure she doesn't get her cast wet when she brushes her teeth. She splashes.

I couldn't visualize this, but let it go.

And we were off! Just three stops to the best borscht in all Manhattan.

I loved the Balalaika, the Dr. Zhivago soundtrack notwithstanding. Ahmad would flirt with gawky Anton, who'd mumble to hide his buck teeth: he'd ask about girlfriends, make Anton blush and smile and cover his mouth with his hand. After dinner, Ahmad would join Gorky in wild Russian dancing: he'd squat and thrust to the vast amusement of the Balalaika regulars, rough-looking chaps who drank their vodka neat at the bar. Breathless, Ahmad would laugh with the waiters, exchange jokes in Russian. Soviet humor, he'd say, wiping his eyes. Untranslatable.

We'd left Indian summer behind us and were back in steaming July; evening, if anything, had only made it worse. Ahmad was walking briskly; I could keep up only with an occasional hop, skip, and jump. Early years in Pakistan had taught Ahmad to love the heat; Manhattan hadn't quite done the same for me. We descended into the subway and it became clear we should have cabbed it. The humidity was rainforest grade. Before we reached the platform, I was wiping sweat from my forehead and neck. Around us, everyone concentrated on not moving, their hair pasted onto their foreheads, or they fanned themselves without commitment.

I followed Ahmad to the end of the platform. Near us, a Columbia student huddled over a copy of *War and Peace*, marking the margins with a mechanical pencil. A mother with a double stroller hummed abstractedly with her Walkman while the younger of her children pointed excitedly at something on the tracks. I hoped it wasn't a rat.

Moisture, moisture everywhere, and not a drop to drink. Ahmad wouldn't look at me—not a good sign. He pulled a bottle of Evian out of his bag, took a swig, replaced it without sharing. Perspiration had accumulated inside my bra, on the small of my back. I wiped my face again and wondered why I never thought to bring water of my own. And watched Ahmad, as if I might find some clue to his coldness in the wrinkle of his shirt, the angle of his tie.

What's wrong? I finally asked. I was tired, my blouse was sticking to my chest. I didn't want to battle.

What makes you think something's wrong? he said, still not looking at me, as our express roared into the station.

There's obviously something wrong, I said, following Ahmad onto the train. The cool inside should have been a relief, but it wasn't. Is it Mirabella? Something at work?

Not now, Shira, Ahmad said, sitting neatly in the one available seat, hands folded on his pressed-together knees. I clutched a steel pole as we started hurtling south.

What do you mean, not now? We need to talk about it, whatever it is!

Shira, he said, looking at me finally, you need to get *off my back!*

I won't! I said.

He made as if he hadn't heard, but the vein at his temple was pulsing.

Was that your final answer, by the way? he asked.

Was what my final answer?

You told Andi you weren't going to Connecticut. I'm asking if that's your final answer.

I told you already we weren't going!

You were going to think about it, is what you said, for Andrea's sake.

I'd never said that, but the car was screeching to a halt. Seventy-second Street. People pushed past me, squeezing right and left, some making a sudden rush for the exit when a local pulled in across the platform.

I waited till we'd pulled away. Ahmad was studying graffiti etched into the Plexiglas windows behind me.

Listen, I said, I know you're in a tough spot . . .

Save the fake empathy, Shira. You want to be in New York so you can be with your boyfriend, even though being in Connecticut, being together, is better for our daughter.

My boyfriend? What boyfriend? What are you talking about?

You'd give up everything for him, wouldn't you? You'd give up our family, you'd give up Andrea's happiness. That's the one thing we said we'd never do, or had you forgotten?

I don't have a boyfriend! You're out of your mind!

Ahmad shook his head—sadly, as if disappointed with me.

If you're not willing to do what's best for your daughter, Shira, then you don't deserve her.

I wrapped both hands tight now around my pole, so Ahmad wouldn't see them shake.

You don't think I can raise Andi on my own? I said, trying to keep my voice steady.

Keep your voice down, he said, though I hadn't been shouting. What I said was, if you're not willing to put your daughter first, then you *don't deserve her*.

What are you saying? I said. Say what you mean!

Ahmad said something I couldn't hear over the crackling

loudspeaker—then we were at Times Square. More pushing, more squeezing and shoving. When the train pulled away, I could see a seat some distance away, but I didn't move.

What did you say? I asked.

I *said*, I had to go to Andrea's school today.

You what? I maneuvered a few inches closer to his seat. You had to go to Andi's school?

Mrs. Chao asked to see us.

See us? About what?

Ahmad drank some water, put his bottle back in his bag.

She sent a note home with Andrea.

Andi came home with a note?

You were on your hot date. She gave it to me this morning.

My hot date? Was he talking about Jeanette? I'd been tired and tipsy after the third Eve, it was Ahmad's turn with Andi this morning, so I'd stayed over. Too late for me to call, but I'd had my phone with me had anyone tried to reach me, which they hadn't.

I didn't have a hot date! What's going on here? I said. I sensed betrayal, smelled it, like old blood.

Someone has to be there for our daughter, someone has to be responsible. It has to be me, doesn't it? It always has to be me.

Tell me why you had to go to Andi's school!

Ahmad's face was an infuriating blank; my arms and knees were shaking.

What is going on with my daughter? I said, my voice rising again.

I'm waiting for you to stop shouting, he said.

Fuck you! I shouted. The people around us went quiet, looked to each other for reassurance. If Andi has a problem, I said, lowering my voice, you need to tell me what it is.

Ahmad crossed his arms against his chest.

Tell me! I shouted.

Know this, Shira. I will do whatever it takes to make sure no one ever hurts our daughter. Do you understand me? Our stop, he said then, standing and smoothing his pants. You coming?

People began flowing out the door—people with suitcases, large bags, a woman with a cat box, young people, their hands locked, a

Chinese grandmother holding a grocery bag in one hand, a child's hand in the other. I stared at Ahmad, watched him shrug and exit without me.

I clung to my pole and pinched my arm, savagely, to keep myself from crying. He thought I was seeing Benny, and for this he was becoming crazy? Calling me a bad mother? Saying I didn't *deserve* my daughter? Of course, I'd seen it before: Ahmad attacking—when he thought he was losing something, when he had lost something. It clearly wasn't me he was worried about losing; if it was Andi, he might try problem-solving with me instead of issuing ultimatums and manipulating our girl behind my back—or, radical idea, he might wait till he'd heard about Hassan! It was nine months till summer: What was his rush? But then we were at Fourteenth Street. I allowed the crowd to carry me onto the platform. Hundreds of bedraggled passengers swarmed past me to this exit or that, many already checking their cell phones. Ahmad had gone to the Balalaika, I was sure of it; did he think I'd double back and join him? I wouldn't.

I pushed through the turnstile. Seventh Avenue and Twelfth Street. The Village—well outside my Comfort Zone. The Stations of my Loss, I called it; I never came down here. It was just there, on Fourteenth Street, that Jonah walked in front of a cab, crossing the street to meet us. Ahmad had said terrible things to me that night as well. He waved at Jonah from across the street, but it was me Jonah watched as he stepped into that road, the picture of the flying girl in his hand, me he was looking at when he was hit.

And it was here, at St. Vincent's, that he died.

And over there, south of the Vanguard, my father's place, where I broke up with T. Where my father and I moved after we returned from Rome without my mother. A new apartment for a new life, he'd said, face grim. Where he was rolled away: *I've made mistakes*, he said. *Don't hate me.*

Ahmad thought I was a bad mother? A *bad mother*? My father and I waited at the Rome airport. At Kennedy, a light snow falling, we waited some more. I was Andi's age when my mother left us. Despite the blankets on my New York bed, the sun shining through the window, I was always cold, I felt myself on an ice floe alone, floating farther and farther from the shore. My father saw none of this. Go back to bed, he'd say, slouched dull with grappa. Wrapping his bathrobe tight around his chest. Leave your daddy alone, he said, you need to leave your daddy alone.

Later, I threw things from my bunk, breakable things, dolls with china heads, souvenir ashtrays he brought back from his trips, then tiptoed through the shards, daring my skin to break. Until the neighbors complained about the noise.

It's nothing, I said, hiding my scarred toes under a blanket. The neighbors are crazy.

Good, my father said, and left the room, fishing in his bathrobe for a pipe.

When I was older, I tested the elasticity of his not-being-there. I stayed away nights: I could always find a boy in Washington Square, a man even, to take me home. When I returned, I found him sleeping, his arm slung over his easy chair, glass in hand, grappa staining the carpet. If he'd tried to stay up, he hadn't made it.

At my father's funeral, Emma, newly Orthodox, wearing stockings with visible seams, a wig too dark for her pale face, said, Never question your father, he always did right by you.

I wasn't aware he'd done anything for me, I said.

She slapped me.

Your mother wouldn't care for you! she said. She wouldn't nurse you, she wouldn't touch you! I had to fly in from California, you and your colic. Your father put up with a lot!

After the funeral, I found letters my mother had written him before I was born. *They smelled like her!* I burned them unread. And threw my father's decanters, his ashtrays still filmed with ash against the wall, threw his papers, the minutes from his precious Archaic Greek Research Organization meetings, his statuary photos into the flames, his books, in Latin and other ancient scripts into overflowing boxes, dragged them onto the street. His wedding ring—he'd saved his wedding ring!—with its improbable inscription, I sent to Emma. Then I screamed for him, I screamed *at* him, at both of them, for always leaving me so alone. Then swept up the shards, mopped the grappa from the floor.

She did this to us, she abandoned us, she turned my father into a drunk. Ahmad knew something about bad mothers? He knew nothing about bad mothers!

A Directory Assistance robot connected me to Angeline Chao. I was sorry to bother her, but Ahmad-this, and missed-messages-that, and what had her note been about?

She'd been concerned about Andi's story, she said. She'd wanted to make sure everything was okay in our happy home. Ahmad had charmed her. It was no big deal.

You're wrong, I thought. It's a big deal, a very big deal.

41

THE HERO'S DESCENT

I slept little that night, imagining the worst: Ahmad and I no longer speaking, the metamorphosis mural on Andrea's wall whitewashed, replaced by lifelike portraits of Ahmad's four sons, pensive, their chins jutting out in the noble Pakistani style. Ahmad ensconced in his Connecticut mansion, Andi and I at the Y, Andi noting my shortcomings in her Observations Notebook, crying for Ahmad as once I'd cried for my mother: only Ahmad can draw her bath, only Ahmad can tell her what to wear. I am helpless to comfort her: I don't want *you*, she says, I want *him*. Blaming me, leaving me, walking to Connecticut, a store of apples in her knapsack.

I'd made a wrong turn, somehow; the connective tissue that bound my life had become fragile: under pressure, it threatened to tear apart. The lives of others were held together by a mightier gravity, I thought: they orbited their suns happily, their moons securely in place, tugging at their tides in love and gratitude.

Too many metaphors for such a late hour, but I was at a loss. How could I have thought Ahmad and I strong enough to be *loco parenti*? Friends for six months at fifteen, reacquainted for a few hours at thirty-five; both times he'd turned on me. This was Ahmad, this was who he was—did I think he'd changed? People don't change!

Dreams flickered like clouds: temp jobs I'd had, the flash of T.'s ring, which was my father's ring. Buttoning my blouse on Fourteenth Street while Gal Monday through Friday filled my former desk with

189

soybeans and food-grade plastic containers. I was climbing a mountain, Andi behind me. On top were incredible wonders, but Andi was falling behind, I could feel the pull of her suffering: Sweetheart, come on, the top is just there! Wait! she cried. Wait for me! Come along! I called. But she was falling! Hurtling toward earth, my baby, my little child! Like Icarus dropped from the sky, my flying, my falling girl! I reached for her, but my arms weren't long enough. I screamed for her, but my scream wasn't strong enough. I called for Ahmad, for anyone, I flailed my arms, hoping to grab onto *something*. But Ahmad wasn't there, he'd never been there, not for any of it—I was as alone as I ever was, as alone as I'd ever be, floating on that ice floe alone. I threw myself off the mountain after her, but Andi was gone. I awoke to find that I was crying.

42

HEAD OF THE
CANONICAL CLASS

I didn't get up till Andi and Ahmad were gone: my body was too heavy, my eyes too raw. I heard the call of the Flying Girl, but I wasn't in the mood. I brought "Screen" to Joe's, and ordered a cinnamon bun, thighs be damned. I asked Joe if he'd seen Nate.

Who? he asked.

I chose a seat by the window, nodded at the black man with the deformed hand. Out the window, everything was as it always was: people mucking through sidewalk bins at the Dollar Store, ladies patting their hair in the Love Drugstore window. Bike messengers threading through traffic, buses exhaling at the light. It was as it always was, not as it was supposed to be. It was supposed to be new.

Without enthusiasm, I returned to Romei's poem about the babbled phone calls—Romei calling Esther, her husband also on the line, their fractured voices speaking Italian, English, Romanian, language become Romei's screen.

I made a note in my notebook: *Ask Romei about the Romanian, or find someone to translate it.* Then saw what should have been obvious: if I translated the Italian and Romanian into English, there'd be only one language on the page, not three. The *terza rima*—or Romei's approximation thereof—would collapse, as would the meaning of the poem.

The poem was untranslatable.

Shit. I put the folder down and looked around. I must have looked like I was looking for something because Joe ambled over. His wife was leaning, unconcerned, against the counter, the twins where she could see them, pulling each others' hair and laughing by the jukebox. Fine white flour dusted the hair that tufted from his shirt. I was glad for his company, but he didn't stay, just suggested I try the sachertorte. This from the man who used to bring me baked goods, unconcerned about crumbs between the sheets. He'd been sweet and light, like all my affairs, like Clyde, who'd recited dirty limericks and called me his lemon drop. How I missed them—kind of. I wanted more now—maybe. But I wasn't capable, was I? No man could inspire me to change, as Romei suggested. There would be no charming chiasmus.

I opened my Door Number Two notebook, wrote halfheartedly about *terza rima*, then stopped. My nerves felt brittle from too much caffeine, too little sleep. I wanted to rest my head on the table and dream—about sexy Italian conferences, poets claiming my time till 2020—but turned instead to "Screen": Romei joining Esther and *lo sposo* for dinner, pretending to be an expert in the Bible.

And saw that he'd done it again. Syllepses this time. A figure of speech where a word is placed once in relation to at least two others, each instance suggesting a different meaning: *He bought the sales pitch and the Brooklyn Bridge. She caught hell and a cold after staying out in the rain.* All untranslatable. A figure of speech used here (I guessed) to show the divisions in Esther's world, the different things she meant to her two very different men. I pulled Romei's earlier books out of my bag to see if other translators had been faced with this challenge. They hadn't. I knew they hadn't.

My head was thudding. Everything about this work, *absolutely everything*, was untranslatable. Not just individual poems, not just the occasional phrase or play on words—but everything! The false friends, syllepses, paronomasia, the goddamned pantoums. An extended family of monkeys could try for all eternity and never manage to translate even one line.

I felt broken. And had the irrational feeling that this had been

Romei's purpose—to break me. Not to compose a prose-and-poem work as gift to his wife, not to produce a work establishing his rightful place at the head of the canonical class, but to write the ultimate untranslatable work, to prove that I was right about the futility of translation and, in the process, break me.

43

LIFE FOR DUMMIES

I trudged back to the Den with groceries, then called Benny, ostensibly to confirm dinner.

He's not here, Marie said.

I was wondering about dinner, I said. Do I bring red or white?

He's out of town, she replied.

How about I try him at home? I said, and hung up. Then lay on Andi's bed, staring at her metamorphosis mural. *Can I offer you some change? No thanks, I'm fine the way I am.* Was I fine? I didn't feel fine. I felt like an odorous object. I'd failed, just as I'd known I would fail.

The Flying Girl called out to me in her stupid Flying Girl voice: Visit me! We'll talk!

What if I don't want to talk? I shouted back.

That shut her up.

When Andi returned from school, I was still on her bed.

Have you been reading my Observations Notebook? she asked.

Never! I said.

That's my bed, you know.

I know, lovebug. Snack?

Of course, Andi said, plopping her Pretty Princess backpack onto her desk.

I got her Kool-Aid and a pink thing with coconut, and sat by her at the dining room table as she ate.

Pammy was angry with Martina, she told me. Martina had spilled

Pammy's Jell-O into the sewer: green was Pammy's favorite flavor and she wouldn't share. Martina explained that she'd done it by accident, which Pammy accepted, though Andi didn't see how you could kneel down in the road and scoop Jell-O into a drain by accident. So now Pammy was angry with Andi.

You guys are friends again. I hadn't realized.

We just had a fight, Mom, weren't you listening?

I meant from the other day, sweetie. You said you had a fight the other day.

Andi looked at me blankly.

What about Ovidio? Does he play with you, too?

How can he if he's not real?

What do you mean, not real?

How can he if he's just a story? she asked, perplexed and licking the pink off her fingers.

A story? I asked, equally perplexed.

Don't tell me you've never heard an Ovidio story! she said, shaking her braids. Were you raised by wolves?

I shook my head, amused by my daughter, and leaned over to kiss her cheek.

Ask Ahmad, he'll tell you one.

I'll do that, I said. She'd finished her pink thing; I reached for a remnant on her cheek.

How about a movie! I said.

She squinted at me.

I'm not going to any stupid Samurai movie, she said.

Understood. Your choice.

Hmm, she said, and, delicate chin in hand, pretended to deliberate: The Thinker with magic marker fingers, Kool-Aid lips.

I'll go to *Toy Story II*, but only if I can have Raisinets. My own Raisinets, no sharing.

You drive a hard bargain.

And the aisle seat, she said, hand and cast at her hips.

Don't push your luck, I said.

•

I made my escape that evening as Andi described the high points of *Toy Story II* to Ahmad—before he could ask where I was going or tell me I was ruining our lives.

It was still light out, but People of the Book was dark. The boys with boomboxes, even the drunks, were gone. Reflexively, I looked across Broadway for Nate; he still wasn't back. Where was Benny? His last-minute message had been clear: *Meet me at the store, not the house.*

I banged on the door—no answer—then saw him approaching, a grocery bag in each hand. He had a black eye, a cut down his right cheekbone.

So what did you decide? he said instead of kissing my cheek. Red or white?

What happened?

Were you trying to cause trouble? I ask because I told you I was making pasta. Pasta goes with white, right?

Uh oh, I said, leaning against the shop window.

She chased me down Broadway, throwing books.

I put my hand to my mouth, then looked down the street as if I might find them there.

I ran like a coward.

She chased you down Broadway?

Up Broadway, actually. Throwing books. Dummy books, must have been a whole case of them . . .

A case of the Dummy books!

Don't you love that? Benny said, half smiling, hand in his beard. *Salt Mining for Dummies, Agitprop for Dummies* . . .

Dental Hygiene for Dummies . . .

For some reason, this cracked us up.

She thinks you're the devil, he said, putting his bags down. She sees things—ghosts, spirits, she sees people's intentions, like auras around their heads. Yours is green, in case you didn't know; it means you're up to no good.

Exorcism for Dummies, I said. Benny smiled and dug a key out of his pocket. She said it was either her or you. I had to choose.

You're kidding!

Relationships for Dummies, he said, inserting the key in the lock.

Marie had wrecked his store. With the force of a whirlwind, she'd pushed books from their shelves; knocked the antique cash register and smaller bookcases to the ground, then left the door propped open. Marla was missing, two kittens had been crushed under a pile of dictionaries.

Benny had gone looking for Marla. The kids in Slice of Park pointed to the China Doll: chop suey by now, they said. He offered them ten bucks to help find her; they laughed. He went back to the store, locked the door, and cried.

Then he buried the kittens in Riverside Park, said Kaddish without a minyan.

I buried them with a book about Africa, he said, so they could dream about being big cats. I once wrote an ode to Marla in which I imagined her a cheetah trapped in a housecat's body. One of the reasons I failed as a poet.

He took a nursing bottle from the grocery bag, filled it with milk, and tried to feed one of the two remaining kittens. But the nipple was too big. I picked up the other, plopped it onto my lap. It stuck its chin out bravely, started wobbling toward the abyss.

You wanna know what I said? When she asked me to choose?

Not really, I said. The kitten squirmed in his hand; drops of milk dribbled down its face.

I said, at least *you*, Shira, were literate, at least one could have a civilized conversation with *you*. She never finished high school, you see. She's dyslexic; she's terrified people will think she's stupid. All year I've been training her to do battle in the New York art scene. *You can do it! Now what's the difference between a Warhol and a Jasper Johns?* It took guts for her to work in a bookstore. Yup, I really got her.

Oh, Benny!

I'm a credit to my race. I'm sure you're proud to know me. Want to know something funny? He put the bottle down, the kitten back in the box. Baruch, he said. My Hebrew name.

Hebrew name?

The name by which I'm recognized when I go up to Torah. You know.

No, I don't know. What's funny about it?

It means *blessed*.

Oh, I said. I take it you don't feel blessed.

Benny just laughed.

Full disclosure? I said. I've been feeling rather miserable myself.

But Benny was slumped over his arm, sobbing.

I loved her. I really thought I loved her!

Could have knocked me over with a feather.

•

Not my finest hour, he said finally, lifting his head. Lucky you: you get to witness this.

How about I help you clean up? I said, my hand on his shoulder. We could get takeout from the Eight Bar. It'll be fun.

I'm thinking of closing the store.

Well, you'll have to till we get it cleaned up. We should be able to do a lot of it tonight.

I mean for good. Work on *Gilgul* full time—I've got backing for four issues. I can't help thinking that if I can change the structure of my life, the deeper things, the more difficult things, will also change. Easier to stay away from paranoid rageaholics if I don't work with them, right?

Sure, I said. You'll just hire them to copyedit, I thought.

I could work a regular business day, get myself a life.

Ooh, I said, a life! What's that?

Life for Dummies, he said.

44

NINE LIVES

We worked a few hours, trading songs as we reshelved. I knew the torch songs Ahmad's ex had taught Andi, also "Eensy, Weensy Spider" and your basic Raffi medleys; Benny knew Clapton's early solos, songs from the Yiddish theater. We'd been at it an hour when Benny dropped his books and ran to the back of the store. I lost sight of him, then heard an anguished cry. He returned holding Marla in his arms. She was frothing at the mouth; she looked half dead.

That crazy bitch stapled her paws together! he said.

She had, front and back. We put her in her box, rushed her with the kittens to an all-night vet on Broadway, where we learned that Marla had probably been left on a top shelf: she'd fallen a substantial distance and, missing the use of her legs, had been unable to break her fall. She was bleeding internally, all nine lives simultaneously at risk.

Never seen anything like it, Dr. Ghosh said, then disappeared with Marla into an exam room. An assistant fed the kittens with an eye dropper.

I should have found her sooner! Benny said.

I held his hand, but wasn't sure he noticed.

It's my fault, he kept saying, my fault!

Not your fault, I said, thinking, *It's mine.*

She said the cat was possessed, Benny said, shaking his head. I should have known!

Marla died at around ten. Nothing to be done, Dr. Ghosh said. You say it could have been anyone in your store did this?

Benny nodded. Dr. Ghosh offered to take the kittens, find them a home. Benny nodded again, and we walked into the rain.

With quiet words, I offered to make dinner. I poured water into a heavy pot, was about to light the stove when he appeared and wrapped his long arms around me, buried his beard in my shoulder. I turned, put my arms around him, lost my face in his sweater.

I'm so sorry, I said, then realized that I was crying, we were both crying, for our big mistakes, and small, the people we hurt as we stumbled along, the endless recycling of our same old shit, the torment we put ourselves through as we ran in place, trying to escape— what? I didn't know, but then Benny started kissing me, and I kissed him back, not sure what I was doing or why. Then an image came to me, not from memory but from "Confessions": Ahmad kissing Shira at fifteen, Shira thinking about T. but kissing him back—also, a line from that story: *I knew nothing about myself—who I was and what I wanted; this, it seems, made anything possible.* Young Shira had made nothing but mistakes. I pulled myself out of Benny's arms. We were both breathing hard.

Not a good idea, I said.

Benny's eyes, soft and wet, became small and stonelike.

Benny? I said.

You know what you are? he said, but I knew his game. I didn't know what my soft spot was, but I was sure he did.

Your bullshit won't work with me, I said, because I knew it would. My heart drummed in my chest as I tried to squeeze past him. He was blocking the door, his body a dead weight. Let me pass, I said, holding my hands in fists so he wouldn't see them shake. His face crumpled.

I'm sorry, he said, hanging his head, but still he didn't move.

It's fine, I said, lying again. I'd like to pass. Let me through. Thank you, I said, as Benny, dumb with sorrow, turned to let me by.

Call me? he said.

Sure, I said, lying for the third and final time.

45

UNDERSTANDING

It was my morning to get Andi off to school. She wanted to wear a frilly dress; I let her.

Ahmad and I still hadn't talked. We hadn't even made eye contact since that night on the train.

Ahmad, I said as he passed me in the hall. He pretended not to hear.

Ahmad, I said. I don't have a boyfriend. Really.

He shut his door.

I've done as we always said we'd do, I thought. I've kept my affairs out of the house. My family is everything, you're everything. Ahmad? I'd never do anything to hurt us. Come out. Please! We'll talk about Connecticut. I promise, we'll talk.

I said none of these things. I stood at his door, hand on the jamb as if feeling for tremors.

He and Andi left together, Andi looking over her shoulder with a worried expression. I blew her my usual hurricane kiss, sent with all my motherly might; she, as usual, pretended it landed with great force on her cheek. But she knew nothing was usual.

Still wearing my father's bathrobe, I brought my coffee to the study. Romei's next section had arrived, together with a faxed photo of Romei in a too-small chair next to a hospital bed, where a small woman—Esther, presumably—lay lost in her bedclothes and a tangle of tubes. Above Romei on the wall, a crucifix. On a table to his right, a laptop, a printer, a fax machine.

He was working in his wife's hospital room? His wife was dying and he was writing?

Of course: the next pages of *Vita Nuova* were about death (or, as Romei put it, more precisely, "The Harrowing"), when the hero makes his obligatory visit to the underworld. Poor Dante! The poetics he'd stored against his ruin were about to collapse. First, the death of Beatrice's father—a small death by cosmic standards, but when Dante learns of it, he grieves so much (for her sake) that the ladies who attend her speak of *his* grief, *his* suffering. He is so grieved he becomes *gravely* ill. On the ninth day, so weak he cannot move (corpselike, in other words), he understands that his beloved, too, will one day die. He envisions her death, and his own. Birds fall from the sky, the earth trembles, the sun grows dark, and the stars begin to weep, as Beatrice's soul, accompanied by angels, ascends to heaven. His cries break through his dream, he is crying!

He looks dead! say the ladies—as if we'd missed the point.

When he rises from his sick bed, at long last, he thinks he can return to Life as Usual: he writes poems of praise, he prattles on about figures of speech—but Death stalks him, pulling him ever deeper into understanding, eventually taking from him everything he holds dear, which is to say, his muse, his sense of purpose, his artistic certainty, his faith in love—for Death has his eye on Beatrice: she will be the next to go.

Her death is noble, as it happens, but anticlimactic: it can't compete with the one Dante has imagined for her. So he doesn't write it, saying, instead, that it isn't relevant to his theme. Whatever that means.

I didn't want to read about Romei's harrowing, or what passed as such. Esther's illness, the loss of hope. There wasn't enough hope to go around. I wished I had some PT.

I thought about dusting Andi's Nancy Drews, or going to Cuppa Joe's. Instead, I visited the Flying Girl.

You're being a child, she said.

Speaks the child! I said. What do you know about the loss of hope?

I feel hope, she said, so I can imagine losing it.

I wish I could be like you, I said.

You are me. Silly rabbit! she said. Go! Read what the man has to say.

I brought the pages to Andi's room, wrapped myself in her quilt. But again, Romei—or should I say, Esther?—surprised me.

She left him. Twenty-five years after her husband left them, she left Romei. While he was in Kiev, being feted by the Writers' Union in a language he couldn't understand (an absurdity that occasions a villanelle: Romei asking repeatedly for an interpreter, his hosts replying in nonsense syllables borrowed from what we understand to be a Ukrainian nursery rhyme). He returns to find Esther gone, her suitcase and favorite clothing gone, her passport gone, mementos from her lovers gone. A note on the fridge reads: *Gone to the U.S. Back soon.*

Her first visit to the U.S. in a quarter century. Romei can't imagine what occasioned this trip—and for *trip* he uses *scampagnata* for its suggestion of "an outing in the countryside" (*campagna*), an irony that points to his unwillingness to read the irony of Esther's note, to accept that she has left him. Frantic, concerned, he thinks, for her safety, he contemplates going after her—but where? The U.S. is a big country, and he's due to read in Dubrovnik. She has to have gone to New York. He sends a telegram to the one person there he considers a friend.

Benny. Called here, with quaint brevity, *the bookseller*. He begs Benny to look for her, tells him she's unwell, hints at emotional instability. Benny develops a plan to flush her out, a colloquium on the *Song of Songs*. Poets, biblical scholars, a translator, even an artist or two. Romei promises to foot the bill when his ship comes in.

Benny and Esther have never met, so Romei must describe her. But he remembers only what she looked like at thirty, he has to *imagine* what she looks like now. He doesn't know what she likes to wear, how she does her hair, he's haunted by images of the distant past— Esther chewing her finger on a park bench, watching him watch her, standing elegant and tall, a highball in her hand, pushed up against a wall, responding to his kisses, *yes, yes*, vomiting on the cobblestones. In a mad flurry, he writes up these scenes, *scenes we recognize because we've read them before*, and faxes them to Benny, so he might, through them, recognize Esther.

Benny has a better idea: he asks all who attend to wear a name tag.

And there she is, Esther Romei. Wearing stirrup pants, a silk top the tentative color of an April sky, a scarf over her hair. She doesn't look unstable, she looks radiant, talking with her friends—a laughing man named Kendrick Weiner-Peshat, whom Benny remembers from a Midrash conference; a rotund woman named Miriam Remez, who may be a poet; rabbinical students named Marty Drash and Hannah Sod, holding notebooks, pens, tubby bottles of Perrier.

You are mistaken, Romei says when Benny calls. That is not my Esther.

She sends her regards. We're having dinner tonight.

Thus began one of the strangest stories I have ever read.

Benny feeds Romei information about Esther, her vibrant life in New York, the classes she takes—classical Hebrew at the university, Talmud at a women's yeshiva. One gets the sense that, amused, she feeds Benny stories to pass on.

Romei is stunned. This is not his Esther! Who is this woman? How can a person change so much, and overnight? She has to have met another man! The idea sickens him. He takes to his bed, or so he tells Benny. Esther laughs: she is not changed, not one bit. Silly man!

In daily faxes, Benny assures him that Esther is well, she's cut her hair short, taken up photography. They meet at Joe's to discuss her translation, which she's picked up again: she frets about the *hapax le-gomena*—words that appear just once, making their meaning difficult to determine.

Romei is such an ass, Benny observes: How could he let this woman get away?

Romei accuses Benny of having an affair with his wife.

Don't be absurd, Benny says.

I'm coming to get her, Romei says. I'll cancel the Goethe-Institut readings.

Don't, Benny says. I strongly advise you not to. She doesn't want to see you.

What's his name? Romei raves, and calls Benny *Galeotto*, using Dante's language to accuse him of introducing Esther to a paramour.

You're jealous, Benny writes, but of what? You know nothing about your wife!

Romei slumps into a chair. Benny's right. Esther is a stranger—a fascinating, enchanting, mysterious stranger, who's left him, probably for good. He sits a long while in his chair, not shaving, getting up only to piss in the sink and to admit Emilio, neighborhood vintner and one-time lover of Esther. He brings table wine, *pizza rustica*, souvenirs of Esther for night-long drinking sessions that leave Romei dehydrated and sentimental.

His imagination is useless. He sits to write but the paper laughs at him. Fool! What do you see when you open your eyes, when you walk out the door? Yourself, obviously!

Does she have money, he writes finally. I'm about to sell the English rights to *Baby Talk*.

It turns out Esther has been left something by her mother, who on her death bed had regretted having disowned her. Esther went to the Hebrew Home, accompanied by her rabbi; she cried when the matron said they'd disposed of her mother's effects. Naturally we thought she was alone, fifteen years with no visitors. Besides, there was only a book or two, some photos—yes, one may have been of you, how were we to know?

Don't send money, Benny says, send something else. She may not be unresponsive. I think she still loves you.

Heartened, Romei shaves, kicks Emilio out the door, tries to imagine what he might send.

He can think of nothing.

What about some poems? he finally asks.

Heavens, no! Benny says.

Disheartened, Romei thinks some more.

Give me a hint, he says eventually.

Jesus, Benny says. Can't you think of a way to tell Esther you love her? You do love her, don't you?

Romei, to his astonishment, realizes he does. He flings open the door to his apartment, strides into the piazza, is stunned by the sun shining onto his face, through the water of the fountain, glinting off the tesserae on the facade of Santa Maria in Trastevere. Last he knew it had been winter. But no, it was June! In a fanciful passage reminiscent of one of Calvino's folktales, the mendicant Romei asks a series of unlikelies for advice on how to win his Esther back.

Force her to stay, says Efesto, the crippled blacksmith.

Buy her something extravagant, says Hera, the drag queen.

Take her on a second honeymoon, says Mercurio, the travel agent.

Massage her feet, whispers Cytherea, the "comfort woman." Tell her she's beautiful.

She knows she's beautiful, she will not be told what to do, she can go anywhere and get for herself anything she wants—why would she need me? he asks. What can I possibly give her?

What about understanding? Benny says.

But I *don't* understand, Romei says.

Exactly! Benny says.

Romei pulls his chair up to the table, does the only thing he knows how to do: he writes. A rambling letter in which he asks Esther to come home: he'll change, he says, he should be given another chance—but his words sound flat and whiny. He writes a dialogue between them, which quickly becomes a monologue in which Esther berates him for his inattention, his mistaken assumptions, his infernal self-absorption, asks why on earth she would ever want him back. People don't learn new tricks, she says in English, especially not an old dog like you.

This is not the offering he wishes to make. Esther already knows that he's an ass. He puts down his pen. How to understand, how to offer understanding?

He picks up his pen.

I am Esther, he writes. I am fifty-five. I am beautiful, but I don't know it.

He will write her. He will write her skin, her pleasures, her habits and desires. He offers her stories he remembers her telling—about a brick house in Connecticut, a terrier named Sire, a roommate who dated Jack Kerouac—and when he runs out of stories, he interviews ex-lovers, colleagues at the school where she worked. His reputation as an eccentric disposes them to answer his questions: does she give change to the mandolin player; is she popular with the students; what did she do during her lunch hour; does she prefer pistachio or *nocciola*. He gathers facts, trivial and profound, also the answers to questions he didn't think to ask: she plays practical jokes, she has nightmares about being trapped in a trolley with no brakes.

Benny helps.

Does she have green eyes or blue? Romei asks.

Brown, Benny says.

She tells of the loss of her family, her anguish, her feelings of impotence, all magnified by Romei, who is so exiled from his own loss that he can't help her. He writes of the panic she feels during one of her episodes, he tries to imagine what it would be like to have your body turn against you, to suffer ailments you cannot understand, to lose your hair, to awaken with rashes across your face, to be unable to move, so great is your fatigue.

These "first-person" reflections are mixed eventually with third-person views of Esther in New York. He imagines her in Talmud class, describes with loving attention her comments about oxen falling into pits, which detail, tossed off in a line or two, must have required hours of research. He rejoices in the success he imagines for her: the rabbi, stern-faced, pulls his pointed beard and mutters, *Excellent, excellent*; Esther flushes with pleasure. She wishes she—

But the section ended here, mid-sentence. Had Romei not sent the ending? Did he win her back? He must have, because there she was, but how? How had he done it?

I sat up on Andi's bed, took a deep breath. Esther had to have been touched by this effort—it was monumental. She'd be overwhelmed by his devotion, his deep interest in the specifics of her life. She loved him, Benny said; of course she'd give him another chance!

I was rooting for Romei—how had that happened? I found his borrowing of her first person convincing—moving, even: the lover walking in the footsteps of the beloved, demonstrating his willingness to adopt her perspective, wanting to understand. He'd mingled their first-person accounts rather as the woman and man share their stage in the *Song*—except his first person had become a third person, trailing behind her. As if he didn't merit a first person, as if self-effacement in service of the beloved was, finally, the point.

I liked Esther, too, now, laughing and learning her way through the City, I admired her bravery, her resourcefulness, I liked Romei for making me like her. She'd come alive, finally, not through praise, or exposure, but through detail and an empathic, imaginative leaping. But where was Romei's harrowing? Yes, he realizes he's been a fool, he even takes to his bed in a parody of Dante's suffering. Unless the harrowing was Esther's? Maybe now that their points of view had mingled, the story no longer belonged just to him: Your harrowing is my harrowing?

I brought the pages back to the study, where two more awaited me. According to the time and date stamp, they'd arrived a half hour apart—and another was on its way! Romei was writing his pages on the fly, writing a single draft and faxing it to me! Not pausing for breath. What other explanation could there be? Unbelievable—not just because of the cheek involved, but because the writing was so damned good. But why?

Finally, I understood.

Romei wasn't interested in publication—given what he'd written about his wife, and himself, he'd probably never intended it. He was writing for himself, to help him "cope" with his wife's illness, so he wouldn't have to look at her ravaged face. He wasn't *talking* to her as she lay sick in bed, he wasn't holding her hand—he was writing! Given the rush he was in, and the look of her, she was likely dying. Maybe he wanted to give her this testament, this "gift," before it was too late, translated into her native tongue. She didn't speak Italian, we knew that already.

With this thought came more understanding, an answer to the question, why me? If Romei didn't care about publication, if he only wanted a translation he could give his wife, he wouldn't need a pro. He'd need a competent friend-of-a-friend, someone who'd keep his story in the family, as it were.

Why not be straight with me? Did he think I wouldn't be interested if fame and fortune were not attached? He didn't know me—maybe I wouldn't. Also, from what I could tell, she didn't have a lot of time. Pros by their nature have places to go, people to see—I was probably the only semi-qualified translator available at a moment's notice—a translation SuperTemp! Happy coincidence that Benny knew how to find me.

Why all the funny business, then—the images from my stories, the mind-fucks, the bubbles of real life? He must have been trying to keep my interest. Flattering me after a rocky start. He didn't want to waste time finding a replacement.

Pretty simple, really.

46

THE FLAME OF LOVE

Romei might hope for new life through this unlikely love letter, but for me, there could be no new life without publication. No authors lining up, no Translator's Note praising the poet. Come Y2K, I'd be back at the prosthetics charity, or its Connecticut equivalent.

I needed to get out of the house. Ahmad had left a message saying he'd pick up Andi after school, so I brought the three new pages to the Eight Bar.

I sat in back where it was quiet and ordered a Hot Fudge Brownie McGee. I might not become famous because of Romei's gift to Esther but, in Benny's words, I still wanted to know what happened next.

We are still with Esther in New York. She is sitting with Benny in People of the Book, leaning forward on her folding chair, discussing Midrash. She quotes Rabbi this and Rabbi that, using her imagination to fill in the blanks left by the Author of the Text, who demands that we be partners in creation.

Midrash, we're told: Story written between the lines of biblical narrative.

Together, Esther and Benny translate verses 8:6–7 of the *Song*, discarding traditional versions.

First, Esther reads aloud from King James: "For love [is] strong as death; jealousy [is] cruel as the grave: the coals thereof [are] coals of fire, [which hath] a most vehement flame. Many waters cannot quench love, neither can the floods drown it . . ."

No, they agree, that's not it! That's not it at all!

Not strong, but *ferocious*! "Love is ferocious like death."

They do not translate *Sheol*, leaving the word as is to preserve its sense of the underworld, with its implication of suffering *beyond* death, an implication lost in the dead-end translation of Sheol as *grave*: "Love is ferocious like death, its jealousy cruel as Sheol."

Love and death conflate here: love finds its identity in the underworld, love is our harrowing, "its sparks, sparks of fire." Sparks, not coals, Benny insists. To recall Isaac Luria, he says, mysteriously.

They debate whether *shalhevetyah*, the *most vehement flame* of King James, includes in its fiery body *Yah*, the psalmists' Name for God.

Esther laughs: Of course it does—look, there it is!

"A great God-flame," they decide then, God's name not absent from the *Song* at all, but inscribed in love's fire, where it belongs. "Love is ferocious like death, its jealousy cruel as Sheol, its sparks, sparks of fire: a great God-flame!"

"Great waters cannot extinguish this flame," one of them suggests, the great waters being nothing less than the *mayim rabbim* of creation, the primordial waters which, according to some, predate creation, the waters God separates to allow for distinction—between two subjects, a subject and object—the waters that separate Romei and Esther. Or, better, "not even the great waters of creation can extinguish the great God-flame which is love."

Romei was writing his own Midrash, opening the sealed story of his wife, imagining what he couldn't know about her, her secrets and illusions, her beliefs and silent moments, writing between the lines of her life. And writing about the *mayim rabbim* when from across the great waters he receives a call that changes his life.

Esther's in the hospital, Benny says. Kidney disease, brought on by a condition called lupus. Romei must come at once.

47

THE ENEMY WITHIN

Lupus: when the body can't distinguish self from enemy, when it attacks its own cells and tissues, thinking them foreign bodies. From the Latin for *wolf*, because of the characteristic butterfly rash, which gives a "wolflike" appearance. Only ten percent of "lupies" have a parent or sibling with lupus, and only five percent of their offspring get the disease, usually between the ages of eighteen and forty-five, the first symptoms often appearing in pregnancy. Esther's lupus is systemic, the most serious kind, as it affects the internal organs. The result: flares that can last for years, followed by periods of remission. Esther's symptoms included hair loss, joint pain, extreme fatigue, facial rashes, and now renal disorder. Her ANA test came up positive, but a syndromic diagnosis would have been possible years before, had Esther seen a competent doctor.

Her condition is serious, but she'll be okay, this time. She wants to go home.

Romei packs his bags, the page ending mid-sentence, also mid-page.

Was the break intended to make clear the gravity of the disruption, or had the work itself been interrupted? What could interrupt Romei as he wrote by his wife's sickbed? Only his wife's sickness, I supposed.

•

As I walked home down Broadway, I thought of Esther, how small she looked in that photo, like a child, her face barely visible among her crumpled bedclothes, and felt tenderness for her. It was hard to believe I'd despised her before—what had *that* been about? I'd send Romei a fax when I got home, ask him how she was—I should have done it ages ago.

I was surprised to find no one in the Den. Ahmad said he'd pick Andi up after school, so where were they? Was something wrong? Another conference with Mrs. Chao? Something worse? It wasn't like Ahmad not to call if he were late. My fingers felt prickly and light. Two hours? I tried calling but he didn't pick up his phone.

Before I could call again, I heard the sound of keys turning in our several locks.

Where have you been? I asked as Andi burst into the room holding bags from Gap Kids and Saks, tugging a bike with training wheels. I pulled her to me, causing the bike to crash against the wall. I was so worried! I said as she wiggled from my grasp.

Mom! You're being weird again.

What's all this? I asked Ahmad. He also was carrying bags: his were from FAO Schwarz.

A bike and some clothes, Andi said. What's it look like, a toaster?

Don't get smart with me! I said. I am *not* in the mood.

No need for that, Ahmad said.

No need for any of this, I said, gesturing at the excess tumbling out of the bags.

Andrea needs it for school. You didn't do enough shopping.

Andi's got plenty for school. I just went through her clothes!

Look, Mom, Andi said, holding up a pink satin dress that must have cost a fortune.

Why don't we agree to disagree, Ahmad said.

I'm sorry, I said, trembling, that's not good enough. I am Andi's mother and, like it or not, I am capable of giving her what she needs.

So you say, he said.

Don't you start! I said, raising my voice.

Well, you're not, really, are you?

I froze. Something was coming—I could feel it.

Andi, leave the room, please, I said.

I don't want to leave the room. I'm always leaving the room!

Go! I said, and when she didn't move, I gave her shoulder a little shove. *Go!*

It's not right! she shouted, and slammed her door.

Lovely, Ahmad said. Just lovely!

What is it? I insisted. You said *I'm not*. What am I not, exactly?

Not capable of giving our daughter what she needs.

What is it you think I haven't given her? Frilly dresses? Expensive toys? Are you trying to buy her? Do you think this is some kind of competition?

Ahmad was moving in for the kill, I could feel it, and I hated him for it. I hated his smugness, his will-to-damage, I hated him with trembling hands and pounding heart for whatever he was about to say.

You think I'm talking about *things*? he said, feigning disbelief. You can't support her, this is true. You've never earned enough to care for her. We can agree on that.

I'm sick of your insinuations! Tell me! What haven't I given her?!

You're selfish, Shira! I've said it before. You like to claim you're the opposite of your mother, but you are as selfish as she ever was.

How can you say that! What have I not given my daughter? *Tell me!!*

Love, for a start. You have no idea how to love her! You've never loved anyone but yourself. I don't suppose Benny knows this yet. He will.

Rage coursed through my body, pure as the purest drug, it rushed through my veins and gathered behind my shoulders like an explosive. It took everything I had to control myself, to not say, You know something about love? Roger, the only boyfriend you ever had, left you because *you're not capable!* You haven't seen your children in a decade! It's not like you've *tried* to see them! Tell me what you know about love!

I didn't say these things, of course. There were places one didn't go, places I wouldn't go.

Benny is not my boyfriend, I said. I don't know how many times I have to say it. Or why I have to say it.

What about understanding? he said. Andi's unhappy—do you have any idea why?

Unhappy? Andi? Uncertainty surfaced on my face before I could stop it.

You didn't know, did you? Well, she is, and I have proof, all the proof I need. He looked meaningfully at Andi's Observations Notebook, in the basket of her new bike.

You didn't!

How could he? Read her private thoughts? Had he given her the notebook just so he could spy on her, on us?

It's all there, he said, still affecting detachment. How unhappy she is, what she thinks of you, everything.

You're sick! I shouted. I'm going to tell her exactly what you did!

You *would*, wouldn't you? he said, shaking his head. It doesn't matter. She knows there's no room for her in your life. We talked about it this afternoon.

What are you talking about! I screamed. You talked about what?

Connecticut. My lawyer's working on it. Custody, if you decide not to come with us.

You're crazy! I shouted. Anger pressed against my chest, a terrible white-heat. She is not going to Connecticut. You can't have custody! You don't have any rights!

I asked her this afternoon—she's made up her mind: she's coming with me to Connecticut. That'll be enough for any judge. That and your staying out all night, your inability to support her. You can't even make it to her parent-teacher conferences! Besides, why would you force her to stay with you if she wants to be with me?

She doesn't have a say! It's not up to her. *I'm her mother!*

Have you got money for lawyers? I didn't think so.

I rushed at him and pummeled him. Fists high, I attacked him.

You frustrated, cold-hearted, son-of-a-bitch bastard! I shouted as I slapped his arms, his face—and hated him, for turning my daughter against me, for wanting to crush me, for being so good at it. He didn't move, just collected my blows like trophies. You deserve to lose everything! I shouted. You deserved to lose Roger, and Jonah, and your children; you deserve to lose Andi! You deserve to be alone, you pathetic, horrible, disgusting man!

Mommy! I heard Andi sob. Don't hit Ahmad!

48

A BRILLIANT SOLUTION

———————

The energy that had frenzied my limbs evaporated. The shame of what I'd done settled into my body. I left the room, I left my crying child.

Everything Ahmad said about me was true. I was selfish, I did think only about myself. I wanted Benny—he was right. It didn't matter that I was incapable, it didn't matter that we would crash and burn, and Andi would get hurt. It didn't matter because I only thought about myself. Connecticut might be better for Andi—I couldn't see how, but shouldn't I have been willing to consider it? I was no better than my mother. My baby knew it now, she knew it; she'd made her choice. I could give up writing, I could give up men, but I couldn't rid myself of my mother's taint, which was *my* taint, which was an inability to love and be loved. There could be no new life for me—no Romei, no Romeo, no deus ex machina could arrive out of the blue to make everything, to make *me* better.

I pounded my bed with my palm. I wanted to hurt myself, rake an X across my chest, score my skin and scar it; I'd take pleasure in the hemorrhage, nothing could clot my hateful blood. I huddled into myself and sobbed.

Time passed, I didn't know how much. I couldn't unball myself. My eyes were "destroyed," to use Dante's phrase, my face a sodden wash. I became aware of a calm outside my door. A quiet, like the silence after a child has left a room. I wrapped the silence around me, like a girl on the shore, wrapped in a towel, blue-lipped and reflective. I'd let my daughter see me scream and curse like a she-wolf, I'd let her see me attack Ahmad with my fists. Then she saw me walk away, defeated. I didn't know which was worse.

Was I willing to give her up without a fight? I was not! Andi was mine, she was *mine*, the best, the only part of me!

I sat up, felt the chenille under my hand, the rag rug under my feet. Then stood by the door. Nothing.

I needed a plan. We had to *go* somewhere. I'd been in dreamland, never imagining that Andi and I might actually have to find a place to stay. We needed a place to stay, but where? Jeanette could take us for a day or two, but she had no guest room. Benny? We couldn't stay with Benny. I could, at least, do my work anywhere, Romei's money would support us for a while, half a year, even.

Rome! We could go to Rome! If I were there, Romei would have to publish, I'd make sure of it; Andi could go to my old school. For a semester, while I sorted things out. We could even stay, if we had to. I could meet all the new writers, maybe get a teaching gig—anything was possible!

I tiptoed across the living room to the study, scribbled a fax to Romei: Could we come to Rome, could we come *now*, maybe even today, Andi and I? It was an emergency, he shouldn't delay, he should reply ASAP—then I went to find my daughter.

But Ahmad had beaten me to it.

I'm taking Andi some place where she'll be safe. My lawyer will be in touch.

Like a heroine in a romance novel, I fell in a dead faint.

•

When I came to, my cell phone was ringing. I sprang to the phone. I'd do anything! Admit I was selfish. Move to Connecticut. Become a lifelong celibate. Anything!

Yes! I said breathlessly.

Romei seems to think you're in some distress. May I be of service?

Benny! My fax must have been more incoherent than I'd thought.

Yes, I whispered. Come over. Please.

Two minutes later, he was there.

49

TOPEKA

He's crazy, I said, my face in my hands. He's taken my baby!

Does she have a passport? Benny asked. He was sitting stiffly next to me on the couch.

What? I said, lifting my head, then felt my heart try to push its way through my chest. Oh God! I cried, and ran to my room, where I found her passport in my drawer.

Benny took my hand when I returned.

I don't mean to scare you, but he could have gotten her another. Are you willing to take that risk? Though I'm not sure who can stop a father traveling with his daughter.

He's not her father. He's not her real father.

Benny looked surprised, but didn't ask.

If there's even a possibility they might disappear, you have to call the police.

The police? I said, withdrawing my hand. You're kidding, right?

I looked mutely at Benny. He walked some steps away, mumbled into his phone.

I'm talking to a lawyer, he explained to me, his hand over the mouthpiece. He says that we can explain to a judge that Ahmad is not Andi's natural father and get an injunction preventing him from taking her out of state. It only takes effect after it's been served, though, so we'd have to find him before he left. Once we got her back, we could get a restraining order. Did I get that right, Marty?

Looking at me, he nodded.

It wasn't that simple, I thought. Ahmad said his lawyer would be in touch. If he'd spoken to lawyers, he'd know this already. If he wanted her out of the state, they'd be there by now. If he wanted her out of the country, they'd be on a plane. But he couldn't, he couldn't!

He didn't plan this, I murmured. Tink is here. Her suitcase. Her Nancy Drews.

It's kidnapping, Shira. If Ahmad is not Andi's natural or legal father, he has no right to take her out of the house without permission.

He always takes her out without permission.

This is different.

I can't send the police after Ahmad! I mumbled. That would be crazy!

But you just said . . .

I can't. He couldn't.

Benny mumbled thanks into the phone, then came to sit with me.

I can't think about this, I said, shaking my head.

You have to.

Andi's fine, she has to be. *Duplicate passport, on a plane to Karachi, my daughter in* purdah. *Growing up without me, hating me, blaming me.*

You have to call him, Benny said.

He won't answer, I murmured, looking at my hands. I tried.

Then leave him a message. Convince him to come back.

I hate him, I said. I never want to see him again.

He's your friend, Benny said.

He's not my friend, he's never been my friend. He won't pick up—I've tried.

Take my phone. Call him. He won't recognize the number. And if he doesn't pick up, leave a message.

I called him a pathetic, horrible man. I hit him, Benny! I said he deserved to lose Roger, he deserved to lose his sons.

No one deserves to lose a child, Benny said.

No, I said.

I sat a while, holding Benny's hand, squeezing it.

That's what I have to tell him, isn't it? I asked.

Benny nodded.

I took his phone.

It went to voicemail.

I took a deep breath. The deepest possible breath.

Ahmad, I said. You need to bring our baby home. You're scaring her—she can't understand what's happening. You can't separate us, you can't keep us apart. You can't keep a child from her mother, no matter what you think of me. If you do this, you'll be no better than Mirabella. Think about it: *Mirabella!* Think about what she's done to you! Are you willing to do that to me, to bring more suffering like that into the world? You can't do that to me, or Andi. You can't do that and think you're better than she is, or better than me. Andi needs her mommy. Oh, please, Ahmad! I feel like I'm bleeding to death. Bring her back to me!

I looked at Benny, my hands holding my mouth, as if to keep the hurt inside. He took the phone from my hand.

You did good, he said. You did real, real good.

I shook my head. I hadn't. To melt that man's heart I would have needed words of fire; all I had were words of stone.

I'd like to put my arm around you, Benny said, looking miserable, but I don't think I should.

I looked up at him. Then I was crying into his chest, his hands stroking my hair, the line of my jaw. I don't know if he moved to me or I to him, but we were at it again, Benny murmuring my name, I clawing at his buttons. As our clothes came off in a ritual stream to my bedroom, I knew that I didn't know what I was doing, but I didn't care: I might disappear, my insides might evaporate if not tamped down by Benny's loving hands.

I tried to imagine my daughter, safely sleeping; I moved my body as expected, whispered Benny's name, grateful for his tender mercies, thought of Esther's madness when she lost *her* child, thought maybe my madness wasn't so bad. As Benny rocked into me, I thought of flying, of being lifted despite myself—as in that Celan fragment, *through the nothingness we reached each other*—of flying across the abyss, as if toward him, naked like a newborn, a flying girl, like Esther's flying girl.

As Benny moaned, I stared past his shoulder at his skullcap,

Mother Mary blue, on my clock radio, the clock blinking twelve noon, twelve noon, though it was well past midnight.

Two flying girls. Two girls in Romei's mirror, one reflecting the other.

Oh my God, I said, pushing Benny off of me. No! Jesus!

Shira! he half shouted, his coital dream cracked open like a cantaloupe.

You knew! I said, staring at him, horrified. All along, you knew!

One flying girl, there had only ever been one flying girl.

With the precision of film rolling backward, the pieces shot back into place, the shattering of my life became whole.

PART SIX

TEST

50

THE FLYING GIRL

I tried to get Benny to leave, but he wouldn't. I accused him of being Romei's patsy, his puppet, his hired thug. Romei was bankrolling *Gilgul*, wasn't he? Benny would do anything for that magazine! He'd fuck me to get information about my fucking so Romei could put it in a scene where he fucks his wife! Romei was a sick bastard, they both were! Benny had to get the hell out of my house, but he wouldn't.

When I know you're okay, he said, holding the sheet up to his long, skinny chest, reminding me that I was naked before him, flailing and shouting.

When you're okay. When Andi was home, is what he meant. Andi!

I sunk back onto the edge of the bed.

Shira, Benny said, putting his hand, always warm, on my shoulder. I shook him off.

Get out of my bed, I said. I don't care where you go, just get out of my bed.

I love you, he said.

Liar, I said, but he didn't move, so I grabbed the nearest item of clothing, which was his shirt, and slammed the door behind me, focused my rage on Romei. I wrote him a fax in big black letters: *Let me guess!* I wrote. *The great Romei, the ever glorious, ever victorious Romei, wants to be a superhero and give the daughter back to the mother. Only the mother doesn't care and the daughter won't go willingly—he knows this because Benny's told him so—so he uses story, the daughter's medium, to capture her attention, to try to steal her empathy. He uses her words, her images to bring the story closer, to convince her she's "just like" her mother. His calculus is simple: daughter forgives mother, mother forgives Romei, no one has to repent, everyone sleeps cozy at night. Right? Wrong!*

I sent the fax and stared at the hateful machine, which had only brought lies into my home when I had dared hope for something more, and realized: it *had* been Romei's intention to break me. You think it's not possible to create intimacy between author and reader? You think translation is shameful and shamful, the *traduttore* always *traditore*? Let's put my money where your mouth is. I'll write a great, ground-breaking book, which you'll want more than anything to share with the world—only you won't be able to, I'll make sure you can't: the book will be untranslatable, every word of it untranslatable! You'll try, translator SuperTemp, you'll do everything you can to prove yourself wrong, you'll sweat and strain. You'll lose sleep and develop all manner of theory—because you will have decided that you *want* that intimacy. Author-reader, translator-author, woman-man, mother-daughter—there is no difference, once you accept what they have in common, once you decide they're possible, desirable, worth the effort and risk.

Horrible man!

But he wouldn't give up, would he? Men like Romei don't take no for an answer. He'd keep sending pages! They'd spill out onto the floor, an infinitude of A4, taking over the study, slipping under the curtained door, into the kitchen, out the window, onto the street, through bus doors, onto the laps of dockworkers, au pairs . . . One reads how Eleanor changed her name to Esther, to celebrate, or at least mark, her new life—or, more likely, took her Hebrew name when she realized that, like it or not, her new life had begun.

Another reads how we left Rome suddenly in snowy March, not at the end of the school year as I'd assumed.

A third reads how Eleanor experienced her first lupus episode after delivering her only child, leaving the child in the care of Emma, her sister-in-law.

A fourth reads how Eleanor named her child Shira, after *Shir haShirim*, hoping the girl would experience a love that she, Eleanor, had despaired of experiencing.

A fifth reads how it hadn't been my mother who'd left us, no, *it had been my father who'd left her*—and he'd had a chance to confess and hadn't.

I hated them all. I went to Andi's room, lay down on her bed, smelled her Andi pillow, looked up at her metamorphosis mural, imagined a new constellation there, a mother turned into stars to spare her the pain of losing a child. I put the guilt quilt into my mouth and screamed.

After that, the world was an empty vessel. I waited, but nothing happened.

I tiptoed back to my room. Benny was still there, upright on my bed. He hadn't moved.

Why did you do it? I whispered. He held out his arms to me, as if to say, *please*.

I couldn't go to him. He put his face in his hands and wept. I left him there.

He hadn't tried to defend himself. He'd absorbed my anger, he'd looked at me and listened. He hadn't been ruined by my anger, then or before. He held out his hands, he told me he loved me.

Strange.

I circled the Den, went back to my room.

I want to show you something, I said. He followed, naked, wiping his eyes, into Ahmad's studio, where the Flying Girl hung above the drawing table.

That's me, I said.

I know, he said, taking my hand.

You recognize the drawing from that story I wrote?

From you, he said. I recognize you.

I took that in.

When I realized Ahmad had taken Andi, I wanted to come in here and destroy this. It's his favorite thing in the world. I wanted to smash the glass and smear the picture with my blood.

But you didn't, Benny said.

You know why?

229

Tell me.

Because it means something to me, the Flying Girl. Remembering myself as someone who once knew how to fly. Do you understand?

That's how I see you every day.

You see me as the Flying Girl? I whispered.

He nodded.

You can hold me now, I said, shivering, and then the front door opened.

•

I ran to the living room, as Andi, bleary in ragged braids, trudged through the door, wearing pajamas and her Pretty Princess backpack. She was guiding her bike with her good hand, Tamika upside-down in the bike's flowered basket, her long brown legs forming a V for victory. I ignored Ahmad and flung my arms around my girl. She let go of the bike as I grabbed her, and it crashed to the floor. Numb with fatigue, she didn't notice. Ahmad picked up the bike, leaned it gently against the wall.

Put some clothes on, Mom! she mumbled. Ovidio doesn't want to see you in the nude.

Ovidio? If Ovidio, or Ahmad for that matter, saw my backside under Benny's shirt, I could hardly give a damn.

I'm sorry, Shira, Ahmad said softly. I don't know what I was thinking.

His face was desolate with the knowledge of what he'd done. I said nothing, stared at him over Andi's shoulder, held my daughter closer, if such a thing were possible. Exhaustion, not affection, caused her to lean into me; I felt complete with her, whole and ferocious.

Will you ever forgive me? he asked.

Never, I said. Get out of here. You will never see either of us ever again.

Ahmad's hand floated to his heart, his mouth opened, he stared at me, tears maybe welled in his eyes, and with small, shocked steps he backed out the door.

•

Andi wanted Ahmad to tuck her in, but he was gone. In any case, I insisted.

I'm glad you're home, I said, but she was sleeping.

Ovidio wants eggs Benedict for breakfast, she mumbled, turning onto Tinky Winky. Room service comes on a rolling table.

It was only after I'd watched her a while, the movement of her ribcage as she breathed, the way she curled in on herself bringing Tink to her cheek, that I remembered Benny, alone in Ahmad's studio. I found him sleeping on the daybed, covered by a kilim he'd pulled from the floor. I could have let him sleep, but I didn't want him there when Andi awoke. There would be no more surprises for my baby; from now on, she could rely on me absolutely.

Sorry, I said, pushing his bony shoulder gently with my palm.

His eyelids fluttered, he reached for me, as if by reflex. I fell gratefully into his arms.

•

You should have been able to do what I couldn't, he whispered. A minute had passed, or maybe an hour. He was unbuttoning my shirt, kissing my collarbone, each of my ribs. You have a chance to make things right. You have the opportunity I never had. It would be good: I know her, I know them, I know you.

You don't know me, I said, dropping back my head.

I know you, he said, kissing the nape of my neck, under my ear, smoothing his hands from my waist to my shoulders.

You don't know me, I said, arching my back. You know nothing about me.

I know you, he said. You're my flying girl.

•

Andi woke me with a poke on the shoulder. The sun hadn't yet risen.

Ovidio wants waffles, she said, her braids even more of a wildness. Who's that?

I looked over, adjusted the kilim.

That's Benny. You know Benny.

Of course I know Benny. Why is he here?

He kept Mommy company last night. I missed you.

He was keeping you company in the nude?

Come on, sweetie, I whispered, grabbing Benny's shirt from the floor, astonished that he hadn't awakened. Let me make you some breakfast.

Ovidio, too, she said, twisting to get a last look as I led her out of the studio.

Of course. How many waffles does he want?

He'll share with me, she said, hitching up her pajama bottoms. He wants to know when we're going back to the Plaza.

Hmm, I said. Someday.

Today?

Not today.

He might run away, you know.

I looked down at my daughter. Did she know what she was saying?

Why would he do that? I asked, as gently as I could.

If Ahmad stays at the hotel, he might go there to live with him.

You think Ovidio might do that? and lifted her up onto the kitchen counter, my heart pounding.

He's a silly boy, he might do anything.

Try to convince him to stay, will you?

I'll try, Andi said, nodding her head solemnly.

I reached for eggs, flour, sugar.

But Ahmad isn't staying at the hotel, right? she said, almost as if it weren't a question.

At that moment, Benny tiptoed past the kitchen doorway toward my bedroom, hunched into his kilim.

Why doesn't anyone wear any clothes in this house! my daughter sighed, and I was off the hook. For the moment.

51

THE HERO DEFEATED

Ahmad moved out—temporarily, as a "gesture of friendship," or so he said in an email I read before blocking his address. He'd give me till Y2K to decide, three and a half months: reconcile or find other accommodation. No, he wasn't trying to extort forgiveness by threatening to throw us onto the street, Benny said. No one was going to be out on the street.

Ahmad had cornered Benny in People of the Book, he wanted *someone* to understand: Mirabella's plan had failed. It was Hassan, Ahmad's eldest: he wasn't interested in Ahmad, he wouldn't leave Karachi for the demon West. Faced with what Ahmad perceived to be my, uh, fast-developing relationship with Benny, he convinced himself that Andi would also fall from his life. He wouldn't lose another child. He'd been talking with lawyers about custody when we'd fought.

This is supposed to make me feel sympathetic? I asked.

He's trying to apologize, Benny said.

Confession, contrition, reparation, change—it didn't seem enough anymore.

You tell him he comes anywhere near Andi, I'll have him thrown in jail.

I don't want to be your intermediary, Shira. You need to talk to him.

Never, I said.

When I explained to Andi that Ahmad wouldn't be living with us any more, she pounded me with her good fist.

You shouldn't have hit him! she wailed. He'd be here still if you hadn't hit him!

I tried to hold her, but she kicked my shins.

It's not fair! she cried. You can see him anytime you want!

When I told Andi that Ahmad wasn't her real father, that her real father lived in India, she screamed at me: Liar! Ahmad's my real father!

At her birthday party, she picked at the cake. At night, she cried. When I asked what was wrong, she said, Nothing, her face smothered in tears. You're waking me up, you know that?

I thought I heard . . . something, I'd say, helplessly. Right, I'd say then to her silence. If you need me, I'm just down the hall.

I know that, she'd mutter. I'm not stupid.

I crept into her room when she was at school, to smell her Andi pillow, and stare at her Observations Notebook (*Do Not Tuch!!*), which she kept, though its edges were frayed, the koala on the front smudged. I picked it up once, opened the front cover, went no farther. Did she know I'd done this? I was sure she did, I was sure my guilt followed me, left tracks wherever I went.

She came home with a note: Her school was doing Career Days. Could one of Andi's parents attend?

I want Ahmad, she said. Everyone's doing a dad. Except Martina. Martina's dad's in jail. She doesn't have anyone else to ask.

What about her mom? I asked.

She doesn't *do* anything. Not like Ahmad. Ahmad knows the forty-first president! He was nominated for a Noble Prize.

Nobel.

Pammy's dad's got a bald spot, Andi said. And he was a Good Humor Man.

Almost as good as knowing a thief conman president, I said. And not quite winning a prize. I'll go. I'll be happy to.

Forget it, Andi said. Forget I said anything.

I tried to seduce her with stories, metamorphoses plucked from her wall. To convince her change was good. (*No change, thanks. I'm*

234

fine the way I am.) Never mind that for Ovid, metamorphosis is at best a consolation prize, meager compensation for what's been lost.

Go away, she'd say, I'm trying to sleep.

Not till I tell you a story.

I'm too tired for stories. I hate your stories. Your stories are stupid!

I absorbed her anger, breathed in her rage, allowed it to settle inside me, accepting it as her gift to me, and holding it there, as my gift to her; I'd learned this from Benny. Someday, I hoped, her anger would spend itself. If not, I'd still be there—I hoped.

I skipped the story of Niobe, her fourteen children sacrificed, and Phaethon, who flew his father's flaming chariot into the ground; I talked instead about Perseus, his flying sandals, the hero Heracles, whose bravery earned him a spot in the gods' Greek heaven.

With Aunt Emma? my baby asked.

What?

In heaven with Emma. Emma's in heaven, right?

Who said Emma's in heaven? Emma's not dead.

You told my Enrichment Facilitator she was.

Shit.

She told you that?

We sat in a Healing Circle. I had to Share Memories. Only I didn't have any.

What did you do? I asked.

I made something up. I said she took me to the park. And bought me things.

Your Aunt Emma isn't dead. I told your teacher a fib. It was wrong of me to do that.

If she's not dead, can I see her?

I don't know. (Maybe I made a face.)

Of course, Andi said, rolling away. Forget I asked.

What I mean is, she lives far away, but why don't we invite her for a visit?

Why don't you finish your stupid story?

•

My translation lay in medias res, preserved in the study like a crime scene, the pages in fact piling up: I wouldn't go in there but I could hear the fax machine churning. I imagined pages spilling like so much wasted seed, Romei's love's labor lost. Did he know I wouldn't read what he sent? He couldn't: Benny promised he wouldn't talk with him about me, but wasn't I curious?

I am in no way curious, I said.

I did wonder when Romei would tire. Maybe when Esther died, but I couldn't think about that, I couldn't think about Esther—her small, ailing body. My anger, once pure and unsparing, had been diluted by moments of compassion, interest, affection, back when I thought her merely a character in Romei's peculiar drama.

It wasn't her idea, Benny said. It was all him.

He lied to me, he used me, he made a fool out of me.

He had to try, what choice did he have?

I put my fingers over his mouth, told him never to mention Romei's name. And called Durlene from SuperTemps.

What are you looking for? she asked. *The usual*, I thought: *love, companionship, the American Dream*. The usual, I said, so she found me more of the same. Jobs stuffing envelopes, sitting in empty rooms waiting for the phone to ring, being paid by middle managers, always men, to listen to their fantasies of new life—as wildlife photographers, authors of best-selling novels drawn from the thinly disguised stories of their lives—*I could tell you stories*, they said, and invariably they did.

I temped in the Village. At lunch, I found myself walking to T.'s townhouse. The stunted tree I'd stood under in grad school had grown, but it was late-autumn bare and offered no protection. Still I stood under it, looking for T. through the blinds, arms crossed against my chest, shivering, waiting for light, movement, anything that might help me understand where I'd gone wrong. I'd spent years loving a man who didn't love me back, I'd squeezed everything out of myself so I could love him—and why? Why had I done that to myself? Was it easier, loving someone I never saw and couldn't have? I then spent years imagining love with someone I didn't know, someone who was *dead*, for heaven's sake, and wondering *what if?* What if I'd been dif-ferent? What if instead of saving myself for T., I'd noticed Jonah, what if we'd become friends, what if I'd been open to loving him? It was too late for Jonah—was it too late for me?

The figures silhouetted against the blinds told me nothing I needed to know. A woman left the house once, holding a bicycle. She stood on the sidewalk a moment, tall and willowy—she could have been looking at me—then she was joined by a laughing child. They climbed onto their bikes and glided away. T.'s happy family, his happy life.

My child was not happy. Mornings, I tried to get her ready for school, Andi struggling all the while—I don't want to wear *that*, it's too tight, too ugly, too green, too stupid—I losing patience sometimes, saying things I didn't mean. Andi would look at me, then, scowling and victorious—*see*, she seemed to say, *see*, this is who you really are!

After school, she read at People of the Book till I got home. Then I'd bring her to Joe's or Nice Cream, get her anything she wanted; I didn't worry about ruining her appetite, since she had none. When she asked, I lied and said Nate the panhandler had gone to the East Side where people were richer; when she asked if we could visit, I said, Sure, some day, and she rolled her eyes. When we got home, I cooked, and washed dishes, and tried to help her with her homework, though she said I knew nothing, what did I know about Eskimos, the hibernation of bears? She whispered with Ovidio, laughed at his jokes, jokes she wouldn't translate but which caused her to laugh uproariously and look at me out of the corner of her eye.

Her cast was removed; her shrunken arm grew plump again and brown.

•

Benny visited only when Andi was asleep or at school—she'd been through enough, I said. From now on, she could count on me. Saturday nights, Dotty sat and Benny made me a vegan dinner. I'd push tofu around on my plate, try not to share my worries.

Take the money, he'd say. Quit your awful job!

I'd returned Romei's retainer, left five dollars in my account for good luck. He rewired the full sum of my "fee"; he said I'd earned it. I wired it back, gave instructions to my bank.

When Benny pressed me, I told him to shut up or I'd leave the room.

Only there was no place for me to go.

I don't want any connection with that man! Can't you understand?

Benny would shrug, impatient, as if there it was, the solution to my problems.

You need a plan, he said. It's October. If you're not willing to settle things with Ahmad, you need to figure out what to do.

He's not going to throw us out. He'll lose the apartment if he does. I'll make sure he does. The university only gives apartments like that to *families*.

He had the apartment before he had a family, Shira.

I don't care, I said.

He can't stay at his friend's forever.

Yes, he can.

You're in denial.

I deny that.

But Benny didn't laugh. He was tiring of me, I could tell.

This is no relationship! he'd say.

I'd said no sex. He knew what Romei was doing, he'd played his part, how could I trust him? Besides, didn't he really want Sandrine, his new salesgirl, the candle artist from Spain: she wore an eye patch for no reason and spoke in tongues. She was organizing his books by color, it was *muy bonita* that way, much better for the store's *feng shui*. Benny thought she was *spiritual*; I thought, well, it's no secret what I thought. After a revival, she'd lay in bed for days while I called in sick and reshelved books in alphabetical order.

He wanted me to read *Shir haShirim* with him, said it would be good for us. I read Dante instead, *Vita Nuova*, as if it might tell me something about who I was and what would happen next.

It wasn't encouraging: after death destroys Dante's world, he writes poems of grief, then stops writing, stops living. On the anniversary of Beatrice's death, he sits idly, doodling and dreaming of her, when mysterious men stand suddenly before him. They observe his drawing, *say nothing*, and dissolve back into the text, their sole purpose having been to recall him to himself, to jolt him out of unconsciousness.

He writes again, but it doesn't go well. He resurrects his aesthetic-of-praise and it collapses—after just four lines! How to praise someone who's perfect *and* perfectly absent? He tries another version of that poem—finishing it, we suspect, because this time it's about *him, his* grief and lamentations—making it an artistic throwback. Hyperalert, he raises his eyes and sees a woman watching him, her eyes full of pity—what could be wrong with that? Plenty, because she isn't Beatrice; his interest in her is a sign of emotional and spiritual backslide.

The whole section is about backtracking, Dante's artistic, emotional, and spiritual regressions when he is unable to assimilate Beatrice's death.

This is the Dante I loved best: so human, so lost! Forgetful of his purpose, paddling without direction, sketching idly, visited by angels he doesn't recognize as such, seeking comfort in used ideas, infatuated by a pale imitation of Beatrice, rationalizing a love he must eventually reject, which comes unbidden when he must have despaired of ever loving again. He faces his greatest test here: how to survive the harrowing, the death of the woman whose life gave his meaning. By any measure, he fails, at least at first, for he is overcome by his greatest weaknesses—passivity, self-pity, desire, sophistry, a longing for emotional comfort, a narcissistic need to be seen, admired, and understood. I don't know that any of us could do better.

Was I unconscious? Backsliding? Where were my angels? What regressions would distract me from my destiny? Did I have a destiny? It was too late to become a Good Humor Man, or a Bad Humor Man, too late to win a noble prize. I was an old dog: I'd played out my tricks; there could be no new life for me. Maybe my destiny was *this*: raising a child who hated me, and crying myself to sleep at night.

So the weeks passed; autumn threatened to slip unremarked into winter.

PART SEVEN

RETURN

52

ICARUS DEFEATHERED

The Monday before Thanksgiving, Benny stopped by. Andi was in bed, and I was looking over brochures for Caron, an Italian manufacturer of passenger ferries.

Guess what? I said. I got a new job, starting next week. No more filing.

Good! he said. I brought the stories for you to read this afternoon.

I'd agreed to read stories for *Gilgul*, give Benny my opinion. For what that was worth.

I'll be earning more money, I persisted. Temp to perm.

Great! Benny said. I used the key you gave me, I put them in your study. The stories, I mean.

Thanks, I said, not realizing what he'd said. Do you want to hear what I'll be doing?

Benny nodded halfheartedly, so I told him how Luigi, Caron's U.S. sales manager, was so impressed that I could take dictation in Italian that he insisted I stay at least a month.

You had some papers in there, on the desk.

Huh? I said, looking up.

He was still standing, holding the end of his beard, a folder tucked under his arm.

Some papers. Your translation. It was there. I read some of it.

Ah, I said, putting down the brochures. You shouldn't have.

I know. It was there.

243

Uh huh.

Shira, it was beautiful, he said, sitting next to me. Really!

Which part? I asked, despite myself.

Esther and Romei at the restaurant.

Oh, I said. Shit.

I want to read it to you.

You what?

I want read it to you. Will you let me?

He'd opened the folder, my work was in there.

You'll stop at nothing, I said.

Listen, he said, putting his arm around me. Close your eyes and listen.

•

It was good.

I was surprised. I listened as a writer, a translator, a daughter.

We sat in silence a moment.

What's your point? I asked.

I want it in *Gilgul*.

No! You're crazy!

I'm not crazy. This is a major work by a major author. It would be good for you, too!

You just want Esther to see this . . .

This has nothing to do with Esther. Romei would never let her see it, out of context. She's too ill—what would be the point?

You're trying to manipulate me.

I'm responding to what you said.

You think you can get a grant for this!

Of course! And readers. The poet describes the genesis of his Nobel Prize–winning poetics—who wouldn't be interested? Better, he admits that his poetics arose out of his wife's suffering and his own self-centeredness, his inability to feel. That's powerful stuff. He discredits his entire life's work, calls it graffiti!

He does not! Where does he do that!

You don't see? Look, he said, riffling excitedly through the pages.

His first mature poems are associated with scribblings, obscene chalk drawings on a wall, his wife's nonsensical ravings, the inarticulate mewling of an underfed cat. His wife wipes vomit onto the tablecloth he uses as his page—not exactly subtle! His first poem is smeared with blood—tomato sauce, drops of wine—the blood of the suffering Christ. Again, not subtle.

I don't know, I said, wondering how I could have missed this, and explained about Esther's *penne*, how Romei's *penna* from the first section, filled with ink by Esther and resounding with the fluttering of writer/bird wings, became Esther's rejected sustenance, vomited to the ground like Icarus defeathered.

Then she's also vomited up the flying girl, the daughter we first saw flying like an airplane around her mother's park bench—if we understand the child to be winged.

I suppose so.

What did you think it was about? Benny asked.

I don't know, I said, wishing we could talk about something else. I was angry, I said. I thought Romei was engaged in a vengeful poetics of exposure.

Exposing himself? How could that be vengeful?

Exposing Esther. He made her ugly.

I'd have to see the whole thing before I could form an opinion . . .

No way! I said.

Look, here's the spot I've reserved for it.

He began sorting through *Gilgul* pages, and I found myself wondering: Had my feelings for Romei and his "characters" informed my choices as a translator? If I went back with a new perspective, what would I find? Electricity pulsed through my legs, a spring urging me, despite myself, to snatch his pages from their papery grave. Followed by the leaden thought: Why bother?

Here's the spot, Benny said, holding up some pages. Before Diego's novella, if you like it, and after Sandrine's piece. (Sandrine's "piece" was a black-and-white photo of some candle droppings. It looked like a deformed cow, but Benny insisted the "image" was not representational. Candles are a part of every major spiritual tradition, he'd said.)

You can't publish it, I said.

Why?

For all the reasons I've said: I don't want to, I don't want to, I don't want to.

Well, this is the spot. For when you change your mind.

Whatever, I said, too tired to argue. Coffee?

Hmmm, he said, distractedly, and started thumbing through his artwork. You know, Esther survived her crisis in September, but she can't last another six months. Her kidneys are shot.

Why are you telling me this? I told you I don't want to hear it.

I'm telling you because I'm going to Rome to see her.

My heart stopped, but I didn't skip a beat.

Have fun, I said.

Come with me. In a few weeks, around Christmas, when the issue's out.

No way.

He started examining a woodcut of a marauding bear.

How about I bring Andi, he said, holding the woodcut up to the light. A week, tops.

I gaped at him.

Are you insane?

Andi should get to know her grandmother, he said, putting the woodcut down and picking up a poem by a Latvian unknown.

Never! I said, throwing a mock-up of the masthead to the ground. It's never going to happen!

A too-deep intake of breath advised me that he'd prepared for this. You wanted this, he maintained. You wanted Andi to know her grandmother: that story you wrote about the artist—what's-his-name, Jonah, Ahmad's friend—and his mother, the one where Jonah draws the Flying Girl?

"Tibet, New York"?

It ends in reconciliation, doesn't it? The little girl . . .

Dotty, his niece.

Dotty sits on her grandmother's lap; the artist, long estranged from his mother, feels tenderness for her, perhaps because of this.

It's just a story, I said. Besides, you're misreading it.

Benny picked up the page I'd thrown to the ground, put it back on the table.

What about that other one, he said, where the daughter runs away.

Elena, I said, despite myself.

The reader knows the daughter blames her mother unfairly. The mother *invents* a grandmother for the daughter, so she won't have to do without. It's what you want.

Those are stories! They're not me. What kind of a reader are you?

They are you. I know you.

You don't know me!

We sat in silence a while, our limbs tense.

It's something Andi might not forgive, he said softly, when she's old enough to know what you've done.

What I've done! I said, jumping up again. That's precious coming from you! Oh no! I said, shaking my head. I don't have to defend myself to you! and turned, looking for my purse. I'm going to my room! Lock up when you go.

Benny jumped up off the sofa and, for the first time ever, shouted at me: Run away! Go ahead! You say you're protecting Andi, but you're not! You're protecting yourself!

I stared at him, he stared at me. His beard was trembling.

Jesus, I said, sitting down. Look at us! I laughed and pulled him back to the couch. You'd think we'd been married sixty years!

We looked at each other.

Even if I wanted to go to Rome, and I don't, I haven't been invited.

What are you talking about? he asked.

Esther, I said, aware that my lower lip trembled. She doesn't want me. She never wanted me. That's what you don't understand. She never made any effort to find me, she never sent a birthday present, she never called. One minute I had a mother, the next I didn't. Can you imagine what that's like?

Benny shook his head.

Can you explain her silence?

I've never spoken with her about you.

Romei makes excuses for her, he wants me to believe it was all my father's fault, and maybe it was, partly, but he can't hide her passivity, her indifference. You say she'd want to see me, but how do I know that? This whole thing was Romei's idea, it's always been about him, his ego, his desire to manipulate. He could write ten volumes and that wouldn't change the fact that she doesn't want me, she never has.

Are you saying you need Esther to invite you? Shira, she's very sick.

I'm saying it's too late. She could have found me and she didn't. Even after I was findable on the Internet, I always made sure my name was in the book. For twenty-five years I did this, so I could know her silence wasn't my fault. She's not sorry for what she did: she doesn't want me, she never did.

Benny put his arm around my shoulder, began to stroke my hair. I wrapped myself into him, breathed the heady smell of his armpit, traced the line of his collarbone with my finger.

Do you really think I'm running away, do you really think I'm scared? I whispered into his chest.

I think it's complicated, he said, still stroking my hair. I'm sorry about what I said.

I don't want to run away, I murmured. Really, I don't.

Then marry me.

I pulled away and looked at his face. His eyes were shining green and gold, his eyebrows were raised, as if surprised by what he'd said, yet his face was expectant: he'd meant it.

You can manage the store, he said. Start a reading series, a translation series, even. You won't have to work those terrible jobs, I'll make you fiction editor of *Gilgul* . . .

Are you offering me marriage or a job? I asked, stunned.

I'm asking you to spend the rest of your life with me, Shira. I love you, I want to take care of you, grow old with you . . .

No, I said, standing.

No? he said.

I don't need anyone to take care of me. I can take care of myself.

You know what I mean!

I know what you mean.

We can't keep on the way we are.

Maybe we can, maybe we can't, I said, staring at my Docksiders.

248

We can't. You say I'm your boyfriend, but you won't let me touch you. I can't be in the same room as your daughter. You won't even invite me to Thanksgiving! It isn't right. I can be patient, but I have to know we're moving toward something.

I shrugged, not meeting his gaze.

At least think about it? he asked in a thin voice.

I nodded, numbly, and gestured for him to go.

•

We couldn't continue? Not continue? How could we not continue?

I slipped on my father's robe, went to Andi's room, where she was sleeping at a forty-five degree angle to the wall. I straightened her quilt, touched her still, soft, satin cheek. She'd been through enough. I couldn't give her another father who might not stay. It was out of the question. Neither Benny nor I knew the first thing about love! I knew how to fly a flaming chariot into the ground, he how to enflame others. How long before I decided it was time to move on? How long before he used my pain against me?

Not continue? How could we not continue?

He didn't mean it, he couldn't mean it! I crawled under the guilt quilt next to my daughter, held her sleeping body close.

Mom? she asked, poking my shoulder. Are you dead?

It was light, and she was standing over me, wearing the outfit she wore to do her Canadian Air Force exercises: leotard, tights, and tutu.

I pulled the guilt quilt over my face.

Not yet, I said.

Ovidio spilled Cheerios all over the floor. And he says he isn't sorry.

53

NOT AS HE WAS, AS HE MIGHT HAVE BEEN

To appease Benny I agreed two days later to "learn" the *Song of Songs* with him, which, as far as I could tell, meant talking about it with him. It was the night before Thanksgiving and he arrived bearing gifts: cassava chips, heavy tomes, Jelly Bellies.

Froggy comes a' courtin'? I asked.

Yup, he said, and pecked my cheek.

Where do you want to start? he asked, opening one of his books.

At the beginning, I said. Where else?

There is no beginning or end in Torah. We start wherever you want.

Huh?

The Rabbis don't consider the Bible a linear narrative. The beginning informs the end, one story comments on another, all occur simultaneously. Everything is connected by an infinite collection of cosmic hyperlinks.

I don't get it, I said, but I like it. How about the *shalhevetyah*? I asked, taking a handful of bellies. The great God-flame? I was intrigued by your conversation about it with Esther.

With Esther? I never talked with Esther about *shalhevetyah*.

You know, when she came to New York and you found her through your colloquium and studied the *Song of Songs* with her.

Shira, I don't know what you're talking about. Romei said this?
Of course.
Why would we study the *Song*?
For her translation.
Benny didn't say anything.
What? I said.
Wow, he said, shaking his head. He said she was a translator? That's intense!
She wasn't?
No.
She wasn't translating the *Song of Songs*?
Benny shook his head.
He wrote that she left him. After twenty-five years, she disappeared, went to New York. You flushed her out by holding a colloquium on the *Song* at People of the Book . . .
Shira, this never happened.
You called Romei when she got sick. That's as far as his story got.
I don't know what to say. She never left him that I know of. I got to know her through him, I advised her on . . . well, I can't talk about that.
Shit, I said. The whole thing is a lie.
I'm a character in his story?
In this last section, yeah.
So much for my cover! he said, laughing.
It was after I realized you knew each other.
He and I had a conversation around that time, Benny admitted.
Yeah, and what did you talk about?
Not what you're thinking.
What am I thinking?
Shira.
What did you talk about?
Way back when, I told him a direct approach would be counterproductive . . .
Got that right, I said.
Later he said he wanted to include you in a project that would be good for you professionally and might make you, well, more

open to seeing Esther. I thought both sounded good. We didn't talk particulars. When he offered you the job, I had no reason to think it was anything other than a job. I never told him anything about your personal life.

He seemed surprised to learn I had a daughter.

He knew you were single. He's old-fashioned, he made assumptions.

We sat a moment, as I imagined what it might be like to suddenly learn you were a grandparent. I remembered the photograph I'd sent so easily, tried to imagine what it might feel like to receive it, to look at that beautiful face and know it was yours. And from nowhere, an image came to me, of my father, as he looked in those early photos, his face untouched by disappointment, his hair clipped Eisenhower short. Holding a swaddled infant, hunched over her, as if protecting her from air and wind, his grip sure, his face uncertain, looking up as if to say, how can I be trusted with this little being, surely I will drop her, surely I will fail her, but his face radiant, still—a trick of the light, perhaps. He was holding me—only now I imagined it was Andi he held, the granddaughter he didn't know, her eyes, alert from the start, straining to understand. I saw him through Andi's eyes as he gazed at us in wonder, the inchoate bundle that we were, his new life. He might have recovered some of his tenderness, he might have been able to see outside his own pain, had he been able to hold her, had he been able to hold my child.

You've done well, I could hear him say. I'm proud of you.

My father, not as he was, but as he might have been.

Shira?

Are you okay?

I shook my head.

Benny put his arm around me. My pores felt too open— memories, dreams, wishes passed unbidden through my skin like vapors. Forgive me, my father had said as the nurse wheeled him away. I thought because he'd not been much of a father. Because he hadn't told me the truth, I knew now, not even at the end.

If I had known you were dying, I might have asked about my mother. I might have asked about you.

Can you tell me about it? Benny asked, squeezing my shoulders.

I wanted to but his eyes were too open, they always were, my billboard artist of the heart.

Hold me, I said, and he did.

•

May I see what Romei wrote about me? Benny asked after some time had passed.

I couldn't speak. I wanted to say no but I couldn't.

Please, Shira? It's weird to be written about. Romei used me for some purpose, to get to you. You don't seem to know why. I'd like to see for myself.

It's not translated, I murmured.

You could do a running translation, couldn't you? How long is it? Not long, I admitted.

Please?

Of course. Get me the pages—the ones on the table, not the ones on the floor. I'll make tea.

Licorice, Benny said. Or twig.

You're crazy, I said, gazing into his serious face, his ragged beard. Chamomile, or Very-Berry.

As I waited for the water to boil, I could hear him humming a mournful tune, a wordless melody, his voice like a wounded clarinet. I tried to imagine him, my lanky, unlikely, stretched-out guy as a *character* in Romei's drama. I'd challenged Romei to treat Esther and himself as characters, then lost that perspective, assuming everything I read was "true." Yet it was false, possibly all of it. But true in a more fundamental way, at least for him.

Why turn Benny into a character, why bring him into the story?

Because he *was* in the story: he was in *my* story.

Jesus.

Romei was using Benny as he'd used my words and images, to lure me into his text. Benny as love's counsel, helping him snare the woman he loved, helping Esther understand the book of love. Benny the savior, the wise man, Benny as cupid, love's messenger, associated

253

everywhere only with love . . . I left the water warming on the stove and returned to the living room. Benny was sorting through Romei's pages.

You told him you were interested in me, didn't you?

I may have, he said.

I turned to go back to the kitchen. Incredible! Romei was trying to fix us up!

•

The Ukraine Writers' Union? Absurd! Benny said, and laughed. Romei's work was never published in the Soviet Union. It was everything they despised.

That had never occurred to me.

He turned a hostile audience there into an appreciative one, Benny said. Just as he tried to do with you.

I hadn't thought of that either.

He claims to have sent me those earlier sections? As if he'd written them in, what, 1987?

The names of Esther's Midrash friends! Peshat, Remez, Drash, and Sod? Those are the four levels of biblical hermeneutics: the literal, allegorical, moral, and symbolic. There's a Hebrew acrostic that refers to these four levels—*Pardes*, or Eden. He's trying to help us understand how to read his work!

More disbelief: He said we went to her mother's nursing home? We did no such thing! Esther's mother died in Esther's childhood home. And left her not a penny. It was your aunt, what's-her-name . . .

Emma?

No, Elisheva.

Same difference.

It was Elisheva who sent her the obituary.

Emma had my mother's address?

I guess so. You have another aunt?

Just Emma.

That's her, then. Your namesake.

I'm named after Emma?

No, sorry, your Grandma Melody. She never did a Jewish thing in her life, but she couldn't forgive Esther for naming you after her. She said Esther put a curse on her. Jews don't name their children after the living, but Esther didn't know that. She was just trying to make her mother happy. She wasn't a nice woman, your grandmama. Her Hebrew name, of course . . .

Was Shira. For *song, melody*.

I leaned back on the couch. I couldn't believe how devastated I felt. I'd thought my mother had named me for some higher purpose, to communicate something of her aspirations for my life, to instill in me through the magic of naming an aptitude for love. I'd found in my name a secret pocket of regard, a message left by her after decades of silence. I'd dared imagine a bond between us, based on this, something we held in common: the desire to love and love well. But no: I was named for her mother, who never forgave her for it.

Emma knew where my mother was and said nothing? I said.

You didn't ask.

I didn't ask? She hated my mother! Why would I think she knew where my mother was?

Blood is thicker than water. Or so I'm told.

Blood?

Sisters, Benny said.

Sisters? Emma is my father's sister.

Shira.

What do you mean? How do you know?

How do I know? Esther refers to Elisheva as *my sister Elisheva*. She's *baal t'shuvah*, right?

Huh?

"Returned" to orthodoxy. That's what they call themselves: "masters of return."

That's her.

She's there now, in Rome, helping out. She's been there since September.

Emma's in Rome? I asked stupidly. I couldn't incorporate this into my consciousness. I can't believe you know more about my family than I do, I said finally.

Benny shrugged. Nothing you can't learn if you want to.

What else do you know?

Benny looked at me, kissed my hand.

You look like Esther, he said, you look like your mother.

•

Eventually, Benny stopped interrupting.

It's beautiful, he said, when I finished the section where Romei describes Esther to herself. A complete fiction, but it says something true.

Like what?

Like about how we love.

By trying to imagine the other's experience.

By putting ourselves in their shoes, yes. About how Romei learned to love.

How he thinks I should love.

Obviously. Your grandmother's regrets, the too-late visit to the nursing home, these are not-too-subtle hints, when you look at them a certain way.

When you know it's fiction you can look at it this way. I'd assumed it was "true."

Then I realized another reason for including Benny in the story: so he could prove Romei's story a fiction, so I could eventually *interpret* it, make it my own.

Also, Benny said, how difficult the work of loving is.

I hadn't thought of that.

Romei's task of trying to see the world through Esther's eyes is gargantuan, he said.

And incomplete. He hasn't finished when he gets the call about her illness.

She *is* sick, Benny said. She does have lupus.

I didn't say *good*, because I didn't think that, but I was glad to know that something in Romei's story was real. Then wondered if this wasn't part of his plan: the one "true," unchanging, always-reliable fact, visible in the photo he sent me and verifiable by Benny: Esther's sickness unto death. Lest I forget. I was about to share this observation when I realized that Benny was crying into my translation.

I kept forgetting: Esther was a real person, loved by my love.

Honey! I said. I am so sorry! and lifted his face to mine; his tears now falling from my cheeks.

This isn't about Esther, he said, after a moment. It's about Romei. I wish you knew what he's really like. He's such a wonderful, loving soul. He wrote this section partly for me, you know. You don't realize this. It's his gift. You can't see this, can you?

I watched him, astonished, prepared to listen, to save my reaction, whatever it might be.

Benny said nothing.

Explain, I said. I'd like to understand.

He just shook his head.

54

THE INDISPENSABLE PIVOT

Later that night, Benny called.

I'd like to explain, he said.

Talk to me by the window, I said. I put on my father's robe and lifted the shade. Across the avenue, I could see Benny's backlit silhouette.

Romei made me important in Esther's life, he said. Her confidant, her study partner. He's given me something of her to hold on to, for after she dies. A vision of what I meant to her.

Oh, sweetie, I said, and felt myself begin to tear.

There's more, he said, and I could hear he was choking up again.

Tell me, I said, putting my hand on the glass, as if that would bring me closer.

It's terribly Freudian, he said, and laughed weakly.

Yes?

Well, he knows about my father, how my father thought I was . . . well, a loser, you know. He knows that I view him—Romei, I mean—as a father figure. Do you see what he's done?

He's made you the indispensable pivot around which his story turns. The one he turns to when he loses Esther, the only one who can help. The child as father of the man.

You see, he said.

I see.

I'm sorry I woke you, he murmured. I feel rather foolish.

I love you, I said, surprised to hear myself say it.

Really?

With all my heart, it seems.

55

HE'S BACK

We always celebrated Thanksgiving with Dotty and Jeanette. Jeanette and Ahmad would tug war over fixings, Jeanette preferring traditional fare—string bean casserole with cornflakes—Ahmad preferring the exotic: millet-shitake stuffing with chestnut-and-caper sauce. Jen stopped by a week before to make sure Thanksgiving was on, with or without the one who could not be named.

I'll take care of everything, she said, and got out her Day-Timer.

I can help, I said.

She considered this.

You make the cranberry sauce, she said, and started her shopping list.

I smiled. I didn't eat the stuff, and both Jeanette and Andi liked theirs from a can.

You can also do coffee, she said, looking up. Georges likes hazelnut. You bringing anyone?

Jen! No!

Aren't you seeing that guy?

What guy?

That rabbi guy?

I told you no!

Something about the way you said no made me think yes.

Well, kinda. I'm kinda seeing him. It's complicated, and I tried to explain.

He's crazy about you, she said. That's a good thing.

I don't trust him.

Trust? Who's trustable? Everyone's always hiding something, anyone can disappear, or disappoint. Not just men—everyone!

There is no absolute fidelity, I murmured. The translated one is always betrayed.

I beg your pardon?

Nothing. I'm quoting myself.

Shira, you have a choice: stay in and never get hurt, or get out there. Out there is much more fun, I promise you. So when are you and Ahmad making up?

Never, I said, and I don't want to talk about it.

I have three things to say to you, Shira, and you will listen. One: you look like shit, which means you're more upset than you say. Two: Ahmad's not perfect, he did a stupid thing. But it was one stupid thing, and he's your oldest friend.

One stupid thing? He didn't just take Andi for the night—he wanted to take her forever!

What does he have to do to make things right?

What's number three?

Andi needs him.

No, she doesn't.

Yes, she does. And she has a right to see him.

Whatever, I said. You said Georges likes what kind of coffee?

Do you have a plan for what to do if you don't make up with Ahmad?

I'm working on it, I said.

Jeanette gave me a look that said, You're not working on it and Y2K is a month away.

Hazelnut, she said, finally. Georges likes hazelnut.

When I woke up Thanksgiving morning, she'd used her spare key and was already in the kitchen. The apartment was redolent of turkey, and the table was set: yellow and brown crepe-paper turkey centerpiece, dried orange flowers, Thanksgiving horn o' plenty. If Ahmad saw this, he'd have a cow.

But wait! Six place settings? Andi, Jeanette, Georges, me . . .

Dotty might stop by on her way to see her father in the hospital, but unless Ovidio got his own spot, I couldn't figure six.

Jeanette?? I shouted. *Jeanette!* Because already I knew. Her explanation, whispered so Andi wouldn't hear, was simple: if I had told you, you might have gone elsewhere.

What was I to do? Deprive Andi of her Thanksgiving, take her to some lonely restaurant with the rest of New York's sorry singles? Andi had family, people who loved her. She had a right to be with them, I too. Was I ready for this? No. But I could always leave if I had to, say I'd promised to help Benny ladle lentils at the Vegan Ecumenical Soup Kitchen.

Benny. I needed Benny. Even if it upset Andi.

You're kidding, he said. You don't want me at Thanksgiving, you don't want me in your house at all because you don't want to upset your daughter, then suddenly Ahmad's coming over and you want me at your side?

That's about it, I said.

Hmm, he said. You mean what you said last night?

I did, I said, and blushed.

How about you come over and convince me? I want convincing.

I giggled despite myself. Benny laughed and hung up.

Jeanette didn't need me. Her instant mashed potatoes were reconstituting, she'd only pretended to need my cranberry sauce, which in any case was done. She was in the kitchen now, teaching Andi to top and tail beans. Snap, snap.

This is fun! Andi said, delighted.

I didn't know if Andi knew Ahmad was coming for dinner, I didn't think so. She'd be so happy! I could see her leaping off the couch when Ahmad arrived, the soft expression on his face when he gathered her in his arms, and there it was again, that crazy lump in my throat.

Thanksgiving this year would be a regular Hallmark card.

Almost. I snuck out the door in a long coat, stockings, a garter belt, and not much else.

Benny was in bed, half asleep. I let my coat drop to the floor.

Hallelujah, he said. Come to Poppa!

•

Benny and I arrived at the Den in time for me into slip into a dress, for Jeanette (holding a yam-and-marshmallow casserole) to say, Aren't we looking rosy, for me to wink and smile, for Andi to say, Oh, *he's* back, for me to say, Andi! I won't have you being rude to my friends!, for her to stick out her lip and cross her arms, for me to walk her to her room, and leave her there till she learned some manners, in time for Ahmad, who arrived carrying bottles of wine and wrapped presents in a Bloomingdale bag.

Where's my girl? he asked softly, looking at me, putting down his bags.

I'll get her, I said, and then, as if in afterthought, leaned over to kiss his cheek.

You ready to come out? I said, knocking on Andi's door, then opening it. She was involved in a game, six dolls being instructed by a seventh; she wouldn't look at me.

I have a surprise for you, if you're ready to come out.

She heard Jeanette's voice in the living room, jumped up.

Dotty! she cried. You said she wasn't coming!

No, another surprise. Also a good one.

I'm ready, she said, trying to nudge past me through the door.

Not yet, I said, blocking her way. First you have to promise you'll be polite to our guests.

Yes, she said, still trying to squeeze by.

I'm serious. Look at me, I said, kneeling down, aware that I'd never asked this of her before. You will only *ever* be polite to Benny or any of my friends, do you understand?

Yes, Mom, she said, rolling her eyes.

That's not good enough, I said, unsure what I wanted from her. You're going to be seeing a lot of Benny . . .

It was too late: from the living room, she heard Ahmad laughing.

Ahmad! Andi whispered. Ahmad's come to see me!

Yes, sweetie. Go say hello.

Off she ran.

When I reentered the living room, Ahmad was swinging my

263

daughter around, her legs flying. She wrapped her legs around his torso and held his cheeks with her small brown hands, their foreheads touching, her brown eyes watching his.

Then Ahmad distributed gifts: a Spirograph for Andi, a crystal vase for Jeanette, a box of cigars for the absent Georges. He shrugged at Benny: Sorry, mate, didn't know you'd be here.

For me, a drawing, framed, of young Shira in ecstasy—Botticelli hair flying, arms raised, dancing, as if for a lover, gold-flecked eyes open, looking at the viewer—the very picture I'd imagined him drawing in "Domino," that story he'd hated, the story about Jonah at fourteen.

It was beautiful. Not just because it was beautiful, but because it was from that story. He was trying to tell me something: he was accepting my work, he was accepting me.

56

LET'S MAKE A DEAL

Conversation was subdued: all-time best stuffings, did people really eat tofu turkeys. Then Jeanette got a call from Georges; she shrugged and kissed our cheeks goodbye.

I told Andi it was time for bed. She asked if Ahmad would be there in the morning.

No, lovebug, he won't.

I'm not going to bed, then! she said, clamping her hands to her chair, and you can't make me!

Andi! I said. That's enough! It's past your bedtime!

Ahmad! she insisted. Tell her!

Shira, Ahmad began, then stopped himself. He'd been about to tell me to let her be, but didn't. Our eyes met. He was telling me he wouldn't second-guess me, he wouldn't undermine my authority. He was giving me back my child. Under the table, Benny squeezed my hand.

I extricated my hand and moved toward my daughter. The table was silent, but for her fierce breathing. Her face was pale and strained as she continued to grip her chair; even her jaw was clamped shut.

I knelt down beside her, looked into her eyes. Deep behind their blackness, which was trying to say *no*, she was trying to say *please*. I placed a hand on her small brown cheek, so soft!, another on her shoulder, fragile like a bird's wing.

I hate you! she said. You can't make me go!

265

You must be very sad that Ahmad's not been here.

Andi looked at me, surprised, unsure what to say.

I'm sorry you've been sad. I've been sad, too. Sometimes adults mess up and kids get the worst of it. It's not fair. I'm sorry.

It's your fault! Andi said, as if pleading with me to do something. If it wasn't for you, he'd be here all the time!

I can see how you might think that, but it's not true. Things aren't that simple. It's partly my fault, though, you're right about that. I made a lot of mistakes.

The table was deeply silent now, as if everyone had fallen away to leave me alone with my girl. How could I say the right thing? Behind her rigid face, behind her anger, I could see my own childish hurt: What consolation had I received? There had been none. What might anyone have said that could have made a difference?

I love you, Andi. I love you more than anything. We all love you. No matter what happens, that will never change. Do you understand?

She half nodded. I wasn't sure she understood, but I'd said everything I could.

Almost.

Ahmad loves you, too. As if you were his very own. Even if he doesn't live here, even if he isn't your biological father, he will always be your *real* father.

Andi's eyes darted over to Ahmad, for confirmation or relief from her too-intense mother. He nodded, almost imperceptibly. Satisfied, she looked back at me.

I'll make you a deal, I said.

She nodded enthusiastically, her face relaxing: she was a born deal-maker, she knew that.

You can stay here with us as long as you keep your eyes closed. You can listen to everything we say, you can even talk, but you have to keep your eyes closed. That way, when you're ready to sleep, you can. Deal?

Andi put her fingers on her chin and pursed her lips, the very picture of deliberation.

Maybe the best place for you to sit is on your father's lap.

She didn't bargain. She leapt from her chair and clambered onto

Ahmad's chair. Quickly, his arms surrounded her, her short arms encircled his waist, her face, smiling, pressed against his cashmere sweater. The look he gave me over her shoulder cannot be described: thank you, he seemed to be saying, I'll care for this precious being, this child we love more than anything.

He gave me my daughter, allowing me to give her back again.

•

Soon, Andi was sleeping, her mouth slack against Ahmad's sweater. We put her on the couch, covered her with the guilt quilt. Benny took that opportunity to take his leave.

I saw him to the door, into the hallway.

I'm proud of you, he whispered. I put my finger to his lips.

Thank you, I said.

For what? he asked. I shook my head, stood on my tiptoes to kiss him.

He's good for you, Ahmad said, when I sat back down. I smiled. I may have blushed. I'm going to Pakistan, he continued. I thought you should know.

Wow, I said. May I ask?

I'm going to see my kids. They're still minors, I still have rights, even in my benighted land. I'm going to tell them I love them. They'll decide for themselves if I'm a monster.

What made you decide, after all these years? I asked, and suddenly his answer seemed the most important thing I could hear.

I never told Roger how I felt, and I lost him. Jonah, too. We can't cut off pieces of ourselves hoping to protect ourselves from hurt. My boys may reject me, but I have to know I tried. I leave in December after my last class. I'm terrified!

I can imagine, I said, and I could.

57

LOVE, OUR HARROWING

It was Sunday, the last day of our Thanksgiving weekend, and Ahmad was alone with Andi—the first time since that night. I was at Joe's with a novel, halfheartedly drinking a half-caff. Joe was sitting by the jukebox, the twins on his lap pulling his mustache and squealing. In the background, the warm *shhh* of the cappuccino machine, the lilting sounds of the Old Jewish Couple.

It seemed like years since those sweaty, heady days when I sat at this very window, pondering Romei's *penna*, my place as a footnote at the apex of the postmodern ridge of the Western canon. Years since I'd sat in Slice of Park, surveying my Comfort Zone, elated about New Life. The distance between here and there: I was temping again. Benny wanted to marry. He was traveling next month to see my mother. Ahmad was going to Pakistan to try to reconcile with his sons. He and I had fought—again—and had reconciled—again. Life had changed, again and again, but had I?

Ahmad called. Andi was locked in her room, talking to an imaginary friend. She wouldn't come out. He'd told her he was going to Pakistan, he explained when I arrived back at the Den. He hadn't realized she'd take it so hard.

I could hear her from the front door, shouting at Ovidio, calling him *stupid boy, bad boy!* On Pammy's insistence I'd installed a pretend lock inside Andi's door—only a piece of string looped around a nail; I'd snip it in an emergency, but I wasn't convinced this qualified.

Andi, I called out. It's Mommy.

She became utterly still, like a bird startled, hoping to trust its camouflage markings.

Ahmad says you're upset. You want to talk?

No answer.

She thinks I'm her father, Ahmad whispered.

Well, you are, I whispered back, wondering if we had to go over that again.

No, he whispered, she thinks I'm her *real* father.

She what? I said, pulling Ahmad away from Andi's door. What are you talking about?

She was telling Ovidio, before she got mad at him. She doesn't believe what you said about the guy in India. Her friend, the one who looks like Pippi Longstocking . . .

Martina.

Martina told her that you sent me away because mothers get rid of *real* fathers in order to marry *new* fathers.

Sheila's ex is in jail, I murmured. Insider trading. She remarried.

Might explain why she hates Benny, Ahmad said softly.

How had this happened? I'd been unequivocal when I'd explained about Andi's "real" father. The power of hope: it changes how we hear things, it creates possibility out of nothing. It enabled Romei to write pages I would never read, Ahmad to assume we'd move to Connecticut, Benny to propose. Up to me to disappoint them all?

What do you think I should do? I asked.

You're the mother! Ahmad said. Don't ask me!

You know Andi. I'm asking your advice.

Talk to her, he said. Don't be afraid of her sadness. She's hurt, not broken. Then make her some Ovaltine. I'll be in the living room.

•

269

I noticed my daughter with a Scooter Pie. While you're eating it, I said as she opened the door, we need to talk, and I placed a foot inside her room.

Andi sighed to show her disappointment. Foiled again, she seemed to say.

Come on, I said, sitting on the guilt quilt and patting the spot next to me.

She walked over to me with plodding steps, like a seventy-pound golem, plopped heavily onto the bed: she'd talk, but only under protest.

Where to start?

What do you see up there? I asked.

The ceiling, Andi said, removing the cellophane from her pie. Is this a trick question?

You know what I mean, I said, already feeling I'd made a mess of it. In the corners.

Andi looked up at her metamorphosis mural, the portraits in the far corners.

You and Ahmad, she said reluctantly, and that stupid giraffe. Want a bite? she asked, hoping to distract me with a piece of the pie.

I shook my head.

Why do you think we're up there? I persisted.

I don't know, she said, biting a careful circle around the scalloped edges.

Don't you? I said, unsure what I was looking for. Look at me, sweetie.

Andi looked up and shrugged, miserable. I wasn't making her feel better, this much was clear.

Andi, sweetheart, we're up there because we're your parents and we'll *always* be. Like the stars in the sky, we'll always be there. Do you understand?

Yes, she said, and turned her attention to the center of her pie, eating the remainder in three precise bites. I wasn't convinced.

Ahmad said you told Ovidio that Ahmad was your real father.

Andi said nothing. Her Scooter Pie gone, she had nothing to set between us. I reached over, wiped crumbs from her mouth.

You know Ahmad isn't your *biological* father, your *biological* father lives in India, right?

I know that, Andi said, almost disdainfully. You've told me like a hundred thirty times.

Even if Ahmad isn't your *biological* father, he's your father in all the important ways, all the ways that matter.

She wouldn't look at me, just crossed her arms tight.

He told you he was going to Pakistan?

No, she said.

Andi never lied—she was that desperate to change the subject.

Sweetie, I know he told you.

She nodded.

And this made you upset, I said, putting my arm around her. She wriggled under me. I put my hand in her hair.

Mom! she said, shaking her head to get my hand off her.

Why did it upset you to hear that Ahmad was going to Pakistan?

I don't know. It didn't.

Andi?

Silence.

Did you think he wasn't coming back? I asked, because I knew her fear—that she'd be abandoned, replaced by *other* children in that faraway land which, like India, ate up fathers.

I didn't think anything, she said, standing. Can I go now?

No, sweetie, you can't. You have to sit with me some more.

I watched my daughter hesitate: She was me, at the turning. I could see it. She was at the turning away that said, I'm on my own, it's better for me to be alone, I don't need anyone, life with others is too painful—it couldn't be too late to change that. Could it?

But how? Pretend hurt didn't happen, pretend abandonment wasn't possible? She already knew better. What might have made a difference to me at her age? What if my father had said, *Come here, Shira.* I put my arm around my daughter and said, Lovebug, and kissed the top of her head; this time she didn't resist. I wanted to hold her so tight her heart's fire might be ignited by mine. Convince her that the ice floe was always a choice we made, not a place we needed to stay.

Love is our harrowing, Esther had said, *its sparks, sparks of fire.*

271

What if my father had sat me on his lap and called me his sweetheart and admitted his loss: *Yes, I loved your mother more than anything; she wronged me and I was so hurt, I cut her out of our lives. Maybe I shouldn't have done that. I know you miss her, I miss her too. And you know what, she misses you, I know she does.* Would that have helped? It might have. It might have saved me years with T., my ex-husband, years protecting my heart from love. It might have helped me to know this.

But I knew it now, didn't I? Wasn't that enough? It would have to be. I took the proverbial deep breath, hardly sure what I was about to say.

It's time I told you about your grandmother. I think you're old enough, don't you?

•

I told Andi what I could, that when I was her age, my mother went away and never came back. I was so sad inside, I thought I might die.

Andi's mouth opened and she stared at me.

Sometimes I got angry, so angry it seemed I hated the people I loved most. Do you know what it feels like, Andi, to be so angry and confused?

She continued staring.

Sometimes I thought the only way I could keep living through all the sadness was to pretend it didn't exist, to keep it inside, to never let anyone know how I felt. I tried to hold it back, but it never went away, because as it turns out, you can't make sadness go away. You also can't pretend it's not there. I tried that and it just got stronger, it became a big hard lump in my throat. Do you know what that feels like, to feel so sad and alone?

Maybe, she whispered, sometimes.

I know! I said. It's hard, isn't it?

She nodded, her lower lip trembling. I squeezed her to me and again she didn't resist.

I thought it was bad to cry, but I was wrong. You see, it's alright to cry when you're sad, and you know what, if you love people, some-times you're going to feel sad. Because they go away, or they make mistakes, or they hurt you. Sometimes they don't mean to—they're just not thinking or they're confused because they're sad themselves—do you understand? But that doesn't mean we give up on them, right? Not if we love them. Instead, we act extra, extra brave, and you know what that means? It doesn't mean we do it on our own, it doesn't mean we keep our sadness inside. It means we say, Yes, I'm sad, but I'm going to give that person I love another chance, a chance to explain themselves, to do better.

I don't want Ahmad to go away, my daughter sobbed, suddenly, into my chest. I don't!

I know, my love. I know.

58

THAT AWESOME FLYER

I got Andi another Scooter Pie, and whispered to Ahmad that she was okay, and watched, enamored, as she licked crumbs from her fingers. And thought again about my father, how he'd bound the arteries that led from his heart. My mother may have loved him—maybe she loved him still. But Romei proved himself better than all of us: he'd done what none of us was able to do, he'd exposed his heart for her. Would he win her back? I assumed he would, but maybe not. Maybe she'd never been his to have. The answer lay on the floor beneath my fax machine.

But first I called Benny and offered him the translation for *Gilgul*.

I hadn't been in the study since that night three months before. I'd made Benny remove my computer; it sat awkwardly on a cardboard box on the floor of my room. The air in the study seemed musty—or so I imagined. Pages had indeed accumulated, scattering the floor like leaves. I'd imagined that with time they'd turn black and die, their words effaced, but no, they were bright and clear. And there—shit!—on a page by my foot, my name!

I'd become a character in Romei's drama.

Of course I had, though I hadn't seen it coming. Did I really want to read what he'd written? Meet a ghost of me, the doppelgänger Romei had created to stand in my stead? See myself portrayed as a freak in his funhouse mirror? He'd make me out to be cold, an unforgiving bitch—that's how he saw me, right?

I didn't want to see, but I had to see. I had to look. I couldn't not look.

I could always stop reading if I had to.

I swept the pages into a folder. On the living room couch, I reminded myself where we stood. Last we knew, Dante was stalled, regressing even. Beatrice's death had thrown him for a narrative loop. But he couldn't backtrack forever: he had to move forward, eventually. And he does: he has a vision of Beatrice which gives him a way out of his no-way-out self, the circle line of his self-reflection. Beatrice in glory, again wearing crimson. He repents—performs *t'shuvah*, if you will—and returns to Beatrice, that goddess of the arrow, the straight-and-narrow narrative. Dante's guiding image thenceforth is *pilgrims*, the romei who visit Rome, even his "pilgrim spirit," which ascends to heaven to look at Beatrice—an event he experiences in words too subtle to grasp.

After this, he has one final vision, which he declines to describe, saying only that he resolves at that moment to write no more of Beatrice till he can do so more worthily. Arguably, with *Vita Nuova* he does just that. He ends his journey with exactly what he needed: a pilgrim's sense of purpose and the promise of a new poetic—the one he will use here, a poetic based on narrative, emphasizing the redemptive power of change.

So what redemptive journey did Romei hope to make? What elixir would he bring his ailing wife, if he couldn't bring me? A new poetic? She'd be thrilled with that, I was sure.

I couldn't see myself in the story anywhere, unless it was as an absence: the daughter who was not there, who refused to be there.

When Benny arrived, I was holding Romei's pages tightly to my chest.

He pecked my cheek.

I can fax it here, right? he said of the translation. Do you mind?

His mind was on *Gilgul*, of course, the translation, finishing the issue before he left for Rome. He wanted to get the pages to Romei quickly, so he could include the translation, if Romei agreed, in the next issue, maybe scare up funding to expand the print run.

Of course, I said, clutching my folder. Can you sit for a while?

I'm so beat, you have no idea.

I'm tired too, I thought, but I need you.

And why are you tired? I asked.

Two weddings, he said, shaking his head, and I noticed he was dressed more formally than usual: black jacket, black tie, *tzitzit* swinging under a shiny black vest. Interfaith, he said. A beautiful thing, but the prep! First the Sufi girl and Reconstructionist boy in Central Park, then the Humanistic Jew, whatever that means, and the Christian Scientist . . .

In the library with Colonel Mustard?

The Masonic Temple on Amsterdam.

Poor sweetie! Have you eaten?

He looked at me as if I were crazy.

These *were* Jewish weddings! Look, he said, I brought you a vegan knish! Because I never stop thinking of you.

He produced a knish from his pocket, put it on the table. It was wrapped in a paper napkin decorated with a rainbow, two chirping birds, the names of the Sufi girl, the Reconstructionist boy. He stifled a yawn.

Did you ask if I wanted to do something? he asked.

He's done it to me too! I said, my voice shaking. I spread the pages fanlike on the table.

No shit, Benny said, tugging his beard.

He handed me his hanky, inspecting it first for cleanliness, then held me as I whispered a broken tale of Andi and the fire of love, how it made me think of Romei and had I done the right thing, did he think I'd done the right thing?

Of course you did, my love. Of course you did.

I calmed and he faxed the translated scene to Romei, appending a brief *herewith*, then I fixed us some tea and settled onto the couch to read the next installment of Romei's tale.

•

We don't know how much time has elapsed. Esther, back in Rome, is no longer in physical crisis, or so we assume. In fact, we don't know much about her. All we know is that she won't read the pages Romei wrote for her, the pages imagining her life. Why? We don't know. Romei doesn't explain; perhaps he doesn't know. Her ears are closed.

Romei becomes a crazed writer-animal, desperate for his wife's attention: he leaves pages on her desk, under her dinner plate, amid her socks, inside the books she reads. He sends them special delivery, in burlap-wrapped packages sealed with wax, covered with the stamps and certifications, the *bolli* so loved by Italian officialdom. Fellini extras declaim scenes while Esther, indifferent, waits for her tram, waiters offer her menus with Romei's pages attached. He returns to her desk, her books, finds his pages used for shopping lists, for doodles, the contours of which he searches for clues.

Esther is opaque, a thing-in-herself. We don't know what she says, what she looks like, what she does. She is *nistar*, Romei writes, reduced to her Esther essence.

Nistar?

Hebrew, Benny said, noshing absently on his knish. *Esther*, the word, is related to *nistar*. It means *hidden* or *concealed*.

Like *celan* in Dante's Italian, I said, scooching closer.

No kidding!

Yeah. Does she really call herself Esther, or is that fiction as well?

She really is Esther, Benny said, laughing.

Esther becomes invisible; we *infer* her existence from Romei's actions. Again, the story is all about Romei, crazed, lonely Romei, maybe it always had been.

Strange device, I thought. In that last section Romei "imagined" Esther, and now he's returned to the "real" Esther. As if there were such a thing. Through all of Romei's mirror tricks, all his inversions and fictionalizing, I realized I knew as little about my mother as I had when she first appeared on that park bench. She was still the mystery she had always been.

Shit.

I understand, I said, taking Benny's hand and bringing it to my cheek. Silent Esther, hidden Esther, that's my Esther, the Esther *I* know. The unfathomable Esther who never sought me out, who didn't contact me, who won't ask for me even now.

Shira, Benny said, putting his long arm around my shoulder.

I'm okay, I said, and realized I was. As readers, we wait for Esther to respond, to *do* something, just as I waited my whole life for word from her, but she won't speak, not in Romei's text, not to me, not ever. That's my answer, isn't it?

I don't know, he said.

If I'm right, what does he want from me? To forgive someone who won't ask for forgiveness? How does a person do that?

I took a moment to sink into Benny's chest, to smell the good knish smell of him.

Is that knish all gone? I asked, looking up.

Knish? Benny asked, then looked around as if it still might be there. I squeezed him, kissed his chest, his nose, his sleepy face. He laughed and squeezed me back.

Eventually, Romei gives up. He puts his pages away and sits in Piazza Santa Maria, which to him is as large and empty as a soccer field; the entire city is vacant to him. Her refusal to see him makes him impotent: his penis shrivels, wilts, melts, dissolves—he uses ten too many images to make his point (as if we might not believe him otherwise): his rod is a tent without support, a seagull dead upon the shore, a too-heavy flower doubled over on its stem. Esther no longer fills his *penna*: he cannot write.

Are you sure you make an appearance? Benny asked, yawning.

Very sure, I said, and continued.

Romei goes to New York to promote the English translation of *Baby Talk*. It's 1990.

Ah, says Benny, shifting on the couch, stretching out his long legs, pushing off his Birkenstocks with his toes.

You remember something, I said.

Maybe. Keep going.

Romei stalks me. He becomes a bloodhound for my secrets. He locates my former professors, poses as an Italian poet looking for a translator. Professor Fabrini finds Romei's Romanian accent unlikely, and his professed name—Italo Roma—suspect, and reports him to security, but not before Romei befriends a departmental secretary, who tells him everything he needs to know: my address, publication history (such as it was), his personal opinion that I was none too stable but if Mr. Roma was looking for a translator, he need look no further than Dennis himself, graduate of an advanced course in Italian conversation, author of an unpublished monograph on Carlo Goldoni.

Romei follows me—to work, on a date with a semiotician who whinnies on about signifiers. He claims to have observed me weeping on a park bench. He talks to a neighbor, who, worried for me, says I'm married to a mafia don who'd cut the nuts off a man as soon as look at him. Romei, taking notes but not understanding, asks, Cashews or peanuts?

Good comedy, but I couldn't say I got the point.

All this "information" he presents in the form of a detective report, Esther's version sent over the great sea complete (he says) with eight-by-ten glossies: Shira struggling with groceries, Shira staring at the Hudson. A detective report like the one Janey gets in my story "I Know Who You Are" when she's looking for Elena, the estranged child of her dead husband. If his wife couldn't have her child, she'd have a facsimile. This was the elixir he'd offer her: Shira in a bottle.

He used every form he could think of to catch Esther's attention: a résumé in which I apologize to prospective employers for wasting my life (I work, apparently, in Mobile—i.e., door-to-door—Vacuum Sales, having been fired from a job in Dairy Promotion—i.e., flogging cheese at Zabar's). I was looking for a job dotting my *i*'s and crossing my *t*'s.

A To-Do list (call my mother, finish my translation). Alternative endings to my stories scribbled onto a placemat (Elena forgives father, introduces daughter to daughter's grandmother).

A crossword puzzle, hand-drawn, the clues also referring to my stories. Elena's comfort: *Charly the doll*, Mabel's craving: *Devil Dogs*. A badly drawn cartoon: Shira using a ruler to rap the knuckles of hapless suitors—a clown, a homeless guy, an old man. The caption: *Love hurts*.

A whole postmodernist riff, Benny said.

Maybe, I said, but Romei-the-writer seems at loose ends no less than Romei-the-character; his narrative's reached its edge, his story has broken down.

279

Romei's been called the first postmodernist, Benny said, yawning. He's showing us what he thinks of that.

Maybe, I replied, but I didn't think so: Romei-the-master was showing me Romei-the-character at the end of his rope.

Esther still does not acknowledge him.

Finally, he sits by a clear stream, which is to say, the East River, hoping for inspiration; it arrives in the form of an ad in the *Village Voice*: a reading in Alphabet City, the Purple People Eaters' Writers' Group. Shira, the daughter, will read.

Oh, I said. The reading that made me a star. From *nistar* to star!

Romei told me to go, Benny said.

Because he knew I'd be there.

Apparently. I thought he just wanted to meet me there. But after, he raved about your story. I began to think I'd be a fool if I didn't publish it.

"Confessions": Young Shira in love with the adulterous T. You didn't like it?

It was a hard story to hear out loud. Better on paper.

Good recovery, I said, smiling.

Later, when he told me who you were, he made me promise not to say anything.

So Romei is responsible for our having met. Shit.

And your first publication.

Double shit.

You don't owe him. He had his own agenda.

We wouldn't be sitting here if it weren't for Romei, I said.

We'll invite him to the wedding.

Funny, I said.

You still haven't given me an answer.

I need time.

Right, Benny said.

Don't push me.

You thinking about it? Tell me at least you're weighing the pros and cons.

I am, I said. If he knew my name, that means my mother must have mentioned me, right?

I don't know, Benny said, and if I did . . .

I know: you couldn't say.

He put his arm around me again. I continued.

Romei describes the café where the reading takes place in comical, rhymed verse—*English verse, no less.* His description made me laugh: he included details about the macrobiotic café I'd forgotten: the morose "maitre d'," a six-foot Cambodian who liked to ask diners their astrological sign. The larger-than-life posters of Michio Kushi. The organic beer brewed flat by Trixie's cousin. Described in accurate detail to give authority, I supposed, to what followed. The rest might be fiction, but this scene, we understood, was "real."

First up on the vegetable crate Trixie called her Soap Box: Franky the funky fabulist. He told pointless tales about street people, paralegals, Israeli electronics salesmen, the moral of which always was that only pre-postmodernist hacks looked for morals in lit-er-a-toor. Romei has fun rhyming *Soap* with *trope*, *fable* with *execrable*, *Franky* with *spanky* (as in, *deserves one*).

When Shira climbs onto the Box, with small, hesitant steps, Romei dispenses with doggerel, describes instead a vulnerability that finds expression in tentative gestures, unfinished sentences, a tendency to put hands to face, brown eyes from which gold shines, red dress like a nightgown.

I didn't tell Benny that to describe me, Romei had recycled language he'd used earlier to describe my mother. As if we were one person. Except for the red dress: Esther had worn a sweater set.

Did I wear a dress like a nightgown? I asked.

Shira, it was a decade ago—how could I remember?

Shira, Romei observes, is shorter than her mother but has her mother's eyebrows, perpetually arched, her cheekbones, her knees, her hips, her reticent smile. A catalogue of similarities, also of differences: nose, ankles, breasts—apparently, my mother's were "full," while mine, in Romei's expert opinion, were champagne-glass-size. Our characteristics, like building specs, presented in a column.

What *is* this? I asked.

A Homeric list, Benny said.

He's pulling out all the stops, isn't he?

He's running through all available forms, from light verse to epic, said Benny lazily. I bet you've found others.

At least two kinds of sonnets. An aubade, of sorts.

All twisting the form?

Yes!

There's that Ukrainian villanelle, Benny said. Probably a pastoral, too.

Esther in the park, I said.

Panegyric? he asked, yawning again.

Poems of praise? You could say so! Also twisted.

Actually, Benny said, the whole restaurant scene could be understood as a palinode. A recantation in poetic form of an earlier poem or set of poems.

If he's recanting his earlier work, what's he replacing it with?

Hard to say, Benny said, since he's rejecting all the traditional forms he never used.

Why bother, if only I am to read this?

Maybe he's making a point. About the need to reject assumptions. I'd have to see the whole thing. You'll let me read the earlier sections, won't you?

I nodded and continued. A first-person poem, unrhymed, unmetered, describes Shira on her Soap Box, as she loses her fear, steps closer to the audience. *A bright red sloop in the harbor*, he writes (again in English), I supposed because Shira's red dress stood out in that sea of Indian print. I was quite sure I'd never owned a red dress.

Anne Sexton, Benny said. "For My Lover Returning to His Wife."

I'm reading a story with "confessions" in the title and that makes me a confessional poet? I am *not* confessional!

Benny raised an eyebrow.

A poem about adultery, I suppose?

The end of it. The end of adultery, I mean.

Ah, I said. Romei was telling me he understood "Confessions" to be a literal account of my life. Strange, since I knew I could no longer read his story that way.

"Song for a Red Nightgown," Benny said. I remember now. It's from the same volume as "For My Lover." *Love Poems*. I'll bring it tomorrow.

Terrific, I mumbled. Can't wait. Shit, I said. We have a copy. Ahmad gave it to Roger, hoping it would prove "an accessible introduction to poetry." Roger smiled and filed it among Ahmad's books. Look over there, under *S*.

Do I have to? Benny asked, wrapping both arms around me now, as if settling in for the night.

I can't reach.

You owe me, he said, and ambled to the far bookcase. He didn't need to stand on a sleek Italian chair to reach the top shelf.

You're not going to believe this, he said, after searching the pages.

I'm sure I won't.

Benny was right: Romei knew exactly how to freak me out, he'd put his hands on just the poem to do the job: a *nightgown girl*, an *awesome flyer*, unafraid of begonias and telegrams.

Another flying girl. Unafraid of urgent messages from afar, of truth delivered by extraordinary means. The awesome flying girl, in her nightgown/red dress.

I went to the kitchen to fix us more tea. My hands shook as I picked up my teacup.

We can take a break, Benny said. Continue another day. I could fall asleep any minute.

I need to know. Please don't go.

I might be afraid of the telegram, I thought, but I *would* read it. I hadn't known this about myself, or maybe I'd changed. I would hear what Romei had to say—all of it.

I picked up where I left off. In the audience, Romei listens to his stepdaughter as she reads about a woman's attempt to seek forgiveness through writing: she'll explain through her story how things were so the person she wronged will understand.

Rather a self-serving reduction of "Confessions," don't you think? I asked softly, though he was right: I'd written it for Ahmad, so he could understand about T., and, understanding, forgive the way I'd treated him then. And he had.

Benny didn't open his eyes, just raised that eyebrow again.

The story gives Romei an idea. He will also seek forgiveness through writing: he will explain how things were, so Shira can understand. Illumination comes in the form of a haiku, something to the effect of, *The poem's the thing wherein he'll catch the conscience of the queen.* Except that poetry alone won't do the job: it's too static—he needs the dynamism of narrative, which alone promises new life, or so he's been told.

That's not haiku, Benny murmured, opening his eyes, looking over my shoulder. Too many syllables. Five-seven-five, it should be.

The vowels elide in Italian, I said, glad to return to something I knew. You count syllables in Italian by counting the consonant clusters.

You're so smart, Benny said.

No biggie, I said, proud of myself. Oops! Though actually, he's reversed the order: seven-five-seven. Hourglass shape.

Time's wingéd chariot, Benny said, sitting straight again. Time ticking by.

Jesus, I said. Do you think so?

Benny shrugged and smiled.

Are we supposed to believe he came up with this idea almost ten years ago, to get me to translate a piece about Esther? To use his writing to awaken my conscience? That it was my work that gave him this idea?

He didn't know you were a translator yet. I don't know.

He called me queen. That's weird.

Maybe he was talking about Esther, Benny said. She's the queen who charms the king to save her people. A benign Salomé. You know, the *Book of Esther* and the *Song of Songs* are the only books of the Bible in which the figure of God doesn't appear.

So Shira and Esther have something else in common, I said, trying to be sardonic.

The *Book of Esther* is like a fairy tale, Benny said. You'd like it.

I continued translating. At the end of the reading, Shira stands to the side, scanning the crowd. Romei suspects she does this to mask awkwardness.

He approaches her. (He didn't, you know. I'm sure he didn't, I

said. Wouldn't I have remembered? Benny shrugged. He wasn't famous then, he said, no photos on book jackets, no appearances on
Letterman. You remember something, I said. He did talk to me, didn't
he? I recollect, yes, that he did.)

You are knowing Rome very well, Romei says in English.

She looks at him, with only half her attention.

You are tourist there? he says, knowing this will make her talk.

As a matter of fact, I used to live there, she says. I don't think you
could call me a tourist.

You will visit again soon, I think.

I doubt it. Rome belongs to my past, I may never return.

But is the land of Botticelli, Michelangelo . . . In your story . . .

My story is just a story. If you'll excuse me . . . , I say, and turn
away.

You mention Dante, perhaps you are scholar of Dante?

He hoped flattery would keep my attention. It did.

At one point. I was a graduate student in Italian Studies. I translated *Vita Nuova*, maybe you've heard of it?

Here in the city?

Yes, I say, and excuse myself, to congratulate Paula the tired language poet.

Was I this much of a jerk? I asked.

I wasn't listening.

You were probably hitting on dainty Barbara Baskin!

Barb had composed poems for the audience on the café's drinks
refrigerator, using plastic magnetic letters. It was a performance piece,
an improvisation where the words' color and arrangement were as
important as their sense. Most were about patriarchy. Patriarchy and
menstruation. The longer poems depleted her letter collection, which
gave her performances a certain *frisson*: how would she end with so
few letters, what would she write! Most ended, perforce, with the un-
voweled howl of the oppressed: *rzf glflnx!*

I don't remember Miss Baskin, Benny said.

Redhead. She looked like a bird, all torso, no legs.

Maybe I remember her.

You wanted to photograph her improvised refrigerator poems for

Gilgul. She accused you of trying to petrify her with your objectifying gaze, she called you Medusa.

Maybe I remember her.

Benny was embarrassed, no longer half asleep.

I've changed, you know.

I know.

You believe this, right?

Sure, I said.

I don't believe you believe.

What do you want me to say?

Remember that conversation we had at my house, when I explained about my, uh, patterns with women?

You compulsively revisit a primal scene by trying to destroy fragile girls, but they kick your ass and have the last laugh. You can't get off the bus, you'll always be attracted to this type.

I might have put it more gently.

You aren't contemplating a future with you.

My point is you're not like them. I don't want a fragile girl, I want you.

I'm glad for you, but I'm not sure what you're saying.

I've gotten off the bus, Shira. Being with you is different.

Hmm, I said.

You don't believe me.

Sounds like magic.

When I described my shit to you that night, something happened. You didn't judge me, you just *listened.* I didn't have to defend myself, which meant I heard myself. When Marie asked me to choose between you, I chose you, remember? It sounds New Agey, but in telling you who I was, in saying no to her, I created the possibility of change.

Jesus, Benny! You didn't just say no! You humiliated her and she wrecked your store!

I didn't say I was a saint. But this won't happen with you.

I thought about that time in Benny's kitchen when he'd been a centimeter away from crushing me like a bug. I wasn't convinced. I wanted to be.

You said that to change your pattern you'd have to forgive your father.

That's the weird part.

It's all weird.

The more I turn away from the pattern, the less hold anger has on me. It's the opposite of what I thought.

You thought you'd have to forgive him first, then you could get on with your life.

Something like that. But it's more dialectical. I haven't quite figured it out yet.

Are we talking about Esther again? I asked.

No, Benny said. Believe it or not, we're talking about me.

Sorry.

Why don't you continue?

Sorry. Okay.

It's okay. It's just that I'm having trouble staying awake. I want to hear the rest before I go.

Right, I said. Okay.

I'm going to make myself comfortable on your shoulder, he mumbled. My head, I mean. Not my entire self.

I turned the page, but was just back where I started.

That's it, I said, riffling again through the pages. Oh, wait: there's a footnote.

I pause.

You won't believe this!

I bet I will, Benny said, his eyes drooping.

The bastard gave my story an epigraph!

Read it, Benny said.

Again, O Shulamite, Dance again, That we might watch you dancing!

Chapter seven, verse one. Bloch translation. Apposite.

You don't know that. The citation, I mean.

Benny shrugged.

What do you know about the Shulamite? he asked.

She's the female character in the *Song of Songs*; she dances for her lover. Did Romei write this because the young Shira dances for T. in "Confessions"?

Did you really do that? Benny asked, his eyes opening.

It's fiction, remember? Maybe I did, maybe I didn't. It's not supposed to matter.

The point is, you displayed yourself to him, you signaled your availability, demonstrated your openness to him.

Something like that.

Dancing is a good metaphor for that.

Maybe.

Satisfied, Benny relaxed again against the sofa.

I think I know what he's doing, he said.

He's putting his stamp on my work. Twisting it, making it his own.

Benny thought a moment, burying his hand in his beard.

I don't think that's it. Look, in "Confessions," you compare yourself to Salomé, dancing to get the head of John the Baptist on a platter. Salomé is a cynical figure, love doesn't figure into her story at all. The Shulamite, on the other hand, is innocent. Her love is erotic but pure. And reciprocated. Romei is asking you to re-vision your past, to see yourself not as Salomé but as the Shulamite. Reject the calculating, Salomé part of yourself, identify with that innocent part, the part that loves easily, that feels herself loved. You loved that boy in "Confessions," right?

I shrugged, blinking back something that might have been tears.

Benny continued, He's saying that the thirty-five-year-old woman who wrote "Confessions" was disconnected from her inner Shulamite, if you'll forgive yet more New Age imagery.

That's what the story's about, I said. Loss of innocence.

But the woman who wrote it despised innocence as much as her character did by the end of the story. The author can't accord innocence even to her young, unspoiled self, so she compares her to Salomé. She should have compared herself to the Shulamite.

That's enough, I said.

Benny took my hand, kissed it, but he wasn't finished: There are some, he said, who think Salomé and the Shulamite are the same person, or two sides of the same person: both names derive from *Solomon.*

You want too much from me, I murmured. Both of you.

I don't think so, Benny said, leaning over to kiss me. We want everything, that's not too much. Is that really it, all he wrote?

I nodded and Benny lay back on the couch, extending his legs onto the coffee table. I held Romei's pages close to my heart, feeling in them the end of things.

Had he given up? Had he said all he needed to say? What else *was* there to say? The ball was in my court, freeze-framed, awaiting my shot. I wouldn't hear from him again, I wouldn't hear from my mother. Any decision I made now I'd make on my own.

Almost.

I put my hand again on the bristled cheek of my beloved.

My beloved is mine, he said.

And I am his, I said, kissing his fingers, one by one.

You will always be beautiful to me, he whispered. I put his finger in my mouth, and he moaned.

And you to me, I whispered back, and kissed his arm, his belly, his *tzitzit.*

What would happen if I stayed over tonight? he murmured. I want you. I can't stand this.

He pulled me up to him, coiled his arms around me.

I don't like it either, I said into his chest.

You don't?

I shook my head and stood up, took Benny's hands, gestured for him to stand. Talk to me, I said. Tell me about *Shir haShirim*, and I lifted his T-shirt and kissed his long, slender belly, and when Benny said, *Kiss me with the kisses of your mouth,* I did, and when he invited me to his garden, I came.

59

SHUVI, SHUVI HA-SHULAMIT

What do you think happens next? I asked, stretched over Benny. On the wall of my room, Ahmad's painting of Shira the Shulamite.

I'd say that's up to you, Benny said, smoothing my hair. You know what I want.

I had to laugh.

I was thinking about Romei, I said, his story. What happens next? He ends it, what, nine years ago?

I'm more interested in our story.

Right, I said. Why don't I get us something to drink?

No, he said, restraining me with his arms. I want you here. Please don't go.

Okay. Well. Okay, I said, and rested my head on his chest. Shit! I said. What word did Romei use to describe the red nightgown? Did he say *sanguigno*? He was comparing me to Beatrice, when Dante first sees her, a child in crimson. I have to check!

In the morning, Benny said.

Right, I said. It's not important—thinking that Romei had again described me as innocent, untouched, only now it was the adult Shira he described in this way, the thirty-five-year-old author-of-the-story Shira, despairing Shira, Shira who'd just left her husband and had no idea who she was and what she wanted, who believed in nothing except this quaint idea that she might write—it was *this* Shira he described as innocent, not the girl who'd danced for a boy in her high school chem lab.

How could he have been so sure?

Whatever I was now, I was further than ever from that girl—right? Walking a tightrope between rage and self-revelation, holding at arm's length a wonderful man who might or might not crush me like a grape, unsure how to love my daughter, forever pulling and pushing at my friends as if they were yo-yos. My mother on her death bed, and I with nothing to offer, no comfort, no consolation, my arms closed tight against her like a child, protecting myself from what? A hurt that was finished but still real, still a part of me after nearly forty years?

Do you think there's a kernel of innocence inside us? I whispered.

An inner Shulamite?

I guess.

Shuvi, shuvi ha-Shulamit, Benny said. That's the beginning of the epigraph Romei gave your story. The translation he cites renders this as *Again, O Shulamite, dance again*. But literally it means *Return, return, O Shulamite*. Phrased in the imperative.

Return in the sense . . .

In the sense of *t'shuvah*. Return through repentance.

Is that what you think? Repent and ye shall be saved?

Come back from the place of error, return to your self. That's what I tell my flock.

You think it's there still, inside me.

The flying girl? I can see her.

I don't. I don't see her.

Dance for me, Shulamite, Benny whispered. Let me see you dancing.

You're kidding.

Benny shook his head.

I want to watch you dancing.

I can't. Don't ask me to do that.

Someday. Then you'll know she's still there.

I looked at him. I wouldn't be afraid, he must have known that, I couldn't let myself be afraid. Romei was right: I would always read the telegram. I disengaged myself, stood before my lover, naked. My character Rosaria had agreed to dance for her husband, but his purpose had been shame. Dancing in shame was not the way. I found Benny's eyes in the half-light; he smiled, I closed my eyes, began to move. I swayed to music I remembered from a room that smelled of formaldehyde: Santana, Hendrix, Joan Baez at Woodstock, a guitar riff licking my skin. And before me, T., his eyes filled not with lust but with love, as if I'd misread him, or maybe those were Benny's eyes. I lifted my arms and swirled, and dropped my head back, as the rhythm hitched itself to my hips and gathered in my thighs with the pounding of my heart, the blood rushing through my body, my innocent body, into my arms and breasts . . . Swirling, my arms uplifted, I felt myself rise, wings extended above me, covering me, all of my characters, all of me, Elena, the scared child, Cora, the heartbroken mother, the Shulamite, joyfully wanton, Salomé, bitter and vengeful, Rosaria, ashamed and ill-used, Janey, remorseful and supplicant, Rose, naïve and lost, the wings of an eagle spanning the decades, protecting me, lifting me, all of me. And Benny was there, pulling me toward my center, his fingers tracing my backbone, the web that connects us, his hands on my hips, pulling me toward him. Still dancing, I moved my hips around his, I moved my hips and sang. For some reason, I began to sing.

EPILOGUE

"In that part of our book of memory, before which little can be read, we find, under the heading The New Life Begins, the words I have transcribed here, in this little, this libelous book. *Incipit vita nova.*" So says Dante.

That part before which little can be read—you know that part of my book better than anyone. The part before the beginning, when even you believed in new life.

Through events remarkable and unexpected, I have learned something of that story. I offer it to you here—the beginning, as I understand it; the middle, as I've lived it. The ending remains to be seen—I hope we can write it together.

●

Ahmad went to Pakistan, as promised. When the uncles didn't allow him into their house, he shouted his sons' names—their names, his name, the name of his hotel, the fact that he loved them and would always love them, shouted until an uncle, mortified, punched him in the jaw. One of his sons, Amir, the second oldest, came to his hotel. Afraid, but not afraid enough. Too early to know what will come of this, but Ahmad is different now, he's softer.

He tried to find Shamseh, the girl with the Internet portal, discovered she didn't exist.

The millennium is with us and the world did not end. Millions of pilgrims will go to Rome this year, millions of *romei* seeking

293

indulgence. I owe Romei a great deal—you now know how much. Maybe he deserves indulgence, for his tremendous act of love.

What will the millennium bring? No apocalypse, but change, as they say, is afoot. Benny and I have agreed not to discuss marriage until spring. Don't tell anyone, but when he asks again, I think I'll say yes. No guarantee that he's changed, or that I've changed, no guarantee that we'll be safe with each other, but I want to be near him, I want to be seen forever by those kind hazel eyes. In the meantime, I'm working at the bookstore—I manage it, actually, as Benny works on *Gilgul*. There's been great interest in the translation Benny published last month, as you probably know.

We're still in the Den. Andi's settled into her new life, more resilient than we knew. Hopeful about Amir, Ahmad has made an offer on a house. He plans to bring Andi there on weekends; she's aware she might meet a brother there. I can join them, if I want—there's room, there will always be room. It's going to work out, I truly believe this: our new life.

So what is this new life?

Romei helped me understand. Celan's chasm cannot be crossed, there is no true translation, no absolute fidelity. I still think this. And yet, miraculously, it can be, there is, and there is. We experience the new life in glimmers, I think, in moments when we apprehend the *possibility* of new life. When we choose to love through our innocent selves, and not just our damaged parts. When we love through what hurts us, when we step willingly into *shalhevetyah*, love's great flame, knowing we won't be alone. Or leap into the void, knowing that despite the emptiness that lies between us, we can sometimes find our way, all the way, to each other. Then change, real change, becomes possible.

If you've read this far, you know all there is to know about me, I've opened my heart to you like a flower, I am your flying girl. Your silence mystifies me, I can't pretend it does not. It makes me realize what Romei knew all along, that forgiveness is in the eye of the beholder. Nice if the offender can account for herself—confess, be contrite, make reparations, change. Nice if we can put ourselves in the offender's shoes, as if she were a character in fiction: recognize her humanity, identify with her, empathically imagine our way to forgiveness. But ultimately, forgiveness begins not in the intentions of the offender, but the heart of the offended.

Benny tried to teach me this, but I had to learn it for myself. Some offenses are unforgivable, others will not be confessed: we can't always wait for penance. Sometimes we have no choice but to step into the flame. We know this, you and I, because we know how it is to close our heart around a hurt. I remember you, Mother, I remember that you once loved my father, I remember that once you loved me.

I've opened my heart to you, you know all there is to know about me. This is my offering, you have me, I am yours. It's not the same as forgiveness, but I have leapt into the chasm, I have walked into the flame; I hope to meet you halfway.

Our flight, Alitalia 515, arrives on Thursday, 7 a.m.

ACKNOWLEDGMENTS

Translations from the Italian are my own; in translating *La Vita Nuova*, I occasionally referred to Mark Musa's translation (Oxford University Press, 1992) and, more often, to that of Barbara Reynolds (Penguin Books, 1969). My reading of *La Vita Nuova* was shaped by those translations as well as by Robert Pogue Harrison's *The Body of Beatrice* (The Johns Hopkins University Press, 1988). Dorothy Sayers' introduction to *Purgatory* (Penguin Books, 1955) is responsible for my understanding of Dante's three-part 'technology' for repentance (which is itself derived, Sayers tells us, from St. Thomas Aquinas' *Summa*).

In writing about Romei's *penna*, I relied on Osip Mandelstam's "Conversation about Dante" (reprinted in *The Poets' Dante: Twentieth-Century Responses*, Peter S. Hawkins and Rachel Jacoff, eds. [Farrar, Straus and Giroux, 2001]), which speaks of Dante's bird/flying imagery, the feather, and the feather pen, as well as John Freccero's Introduction to Robert Pinsky's translation of the *Inferno* (Farrar, Straus and Giroux, 1994), which associates *penne*, wings, and birds with both poetic inspiration and carnal love. Shira's Nabokov quotation concludes his essay "'Onegin' in English," which can be found in *The Translation Studies Reader* (Lawrence Venuti, ed. [Routledge, 2000]); her understanding of the translative act (as bringing the translator back to the original moments of a poet's creation) is derived in part from that of Paul Valéry, as presented in his essay "Variations on the *Eclogues*," as well as that of Yves Bonnefoy, as discussed in his essay "Translating Poetry" (both reprinted in *Theories of Translation*, Rainer Schulte and John Biguenet, eds. [University of Chicago Press, 1992]).

All translations from the Latin are taken from Reynolds. The translation of the Celan line (from "Soviel Gestirne," from the collection *Die Niemandsrose*) is mine, though I referred to Michael Hamburger's translation in *Paul Celan: Poems* (Persea Books, 1980). I relied on several translations of the *Song of Songs* when translating various lines and when imagining Esther and Benny's co-translation. Among these are the King James Version but also those of Marvin H. Pope (Doubleday, 1977), Marcia Falk (HarperCollins, 1993), and most notably, Ariel Bloch and Chana Bloch (University of California Press, 1995). The sources of Romei's English translations of the charming chiasmus and the Shulamite epigraph from the *Song of Songs* are noted in the text. My reading of the *Song* was strongly influenced by the Bloch Introduction and Commentary and the beautiful Robert Alter Afterword to that edition, as well as Marcia Falk's Translator's Note.

In writing this book, I was the recipient of extraordinary generosity. I give thanks, in alphabetical order, to the following residencies, conferences, and grant-giving institutions, which allowed me blessed time and space in which to write: Atlantic Center for the Arts, Bread Loaf Writers' Conference, Hawthornden International Retreat for Writers, the Leeway Foundation, the MacDowell Colony (where this book was born), Millay Colony for the Arts, Ragdale Foundation, Sewanee Writers' Conference, Ucross Foundation, Fundación Valparaíso, the Vermont Studio Center, Virginia Center for the Creative Arts, and the Corporation of Yaddo. Many friends read portions of the book; special thanks to Philip McFarland, Robin Black, Patricia Chao, and Elizabeth Cantor for reading the whole and offering definitive assistance. Thanks also to Jim Crace for helping me understand just who Shira was and to Lynn Freed, Margot Livesey, and Erin McGraw, who offered terrific advice about the book's first chapters. Shira herself was born as a result of a seminar on the *Song of Songs* led by Reb Zalman Schachter-Shalomi, z"l; thanks to the former Elat Chayyim Jewish Retreat Center for making such learning possible.

Many of Shira's stories about her own life and her friends can be found in the world. I refer the reader to these fine publications, and thank their editors, whose support to emerging writers is so appreciated: "Love Drugstore," *Kenyon Review* (Vol. 33, No. 3, 2011);

"Confessions of a Cerebral Lover," *Fence* (Vol. 12, No. 2, 2009–10); "Tibet, New York," *New England Review* (Vol. 29, No. 4, 2008); "Zanzibar, Bereft," *Ninth Letter* (Vol. 3, No. 1, Fall/Winter 2006); and "Picnic After the Flood," *One Story* (No. 80, 2006). For Shira's stories about Elena, Mabel, Cora, Janey, and Rosaria, see "Priscilla Learns a Lesson," *Redivider* (Vol. 5, No. 2, 2008); "Slave for a Day," *New England Review* (Vol. 24, No. 4, 2004); "Hello, I'm Cora," *New England Review* (Vol. 23, No. 3, Summer 2002); "I Know Who You Are," *Greensboro Review* (No. 71, Spring 2002); "Rosaria 1988," *New England Review* (Vol. 20, No. 4, Fall 1999). And, finally, for her Celan story, see "Rose No One," *Chelsea* (No. 72, 2002).

ABOUT THE AUTHOR

RACHEL CANTOR was raised in Rome and Connecticut. She is the author of the acclaimed novel *A Highly Unlikely Scenario*, and her short stories have appeared in *The Paris Review*, *One Story*, *Ninth Letter*, and *The Kenyon Review*, among other publications. She lives in Brooklyn, New York.